SPECIAL MESSAGE

THE ULVERSCROFT FOUNDATION
(registered UK charity number 264873)
was established in 1972 to provide funds for research, diagnosis and treatment of eye diseases. Examples of major projects funded by the Ulverscroft Foundation are:-

- The Children's Eye Unit at Moorfields Eye Hospital, London
- The Ulverscroft Children's Eye Unit at Great Ormond Street Hospital for Sick Children
- Funding research into eye diseases and treatment at the Department of Ophthalmology, University of Leicester
- The Ulverscroft Vision Research Group, Institute of Child Health
- Twin operating theatres at the Western Ophthalmic Hospital, London
- The Chair of Ophthalmology at the Royal Australian College of Ophthalmologists

You can help further the work of the Foundation by making a donation or leaving a legacy. Every contribution is gratefully received. If you would like to help support the Foundation or require further information, please contact:

THE ULVERSCROFT FOUNDATION
The Green, Bradgate Road, Anstey
Leicester LE7 7FU, England
Tel: (0116) 236 4325

website: www.foundation.ulverscroft.com

PIETR THE LATVIAN &
THE LATE MONSIEUR GALLET

Who is Pietr the Latvian? Is he a gentleman thief? A Russian drinking absinthe in a grimy bar? A married Norwegian sea captain? A twisted corpse in a train bathroom? Or is he all of these men? Inspector Jules Maigret tracks a mysterious adversary along a trail of bodies . . . The circumstances surrounding a murdered man's death all seem fake: the name the deceased was travelling under, his presumed profession — and, more worryingly, his family's reaction. Maigret must tease out the strands of truth from the tangle before him in order to construct an accurate portrait of the late Monsieur Gallet . . .

Books by Georges Simenon
Published in Ulverscroft Collections:

THE HANGED MAN OF SAINT-PHOLIEN &
THE CARTER OF LA PROVIDENCE

GEORGES SIMENON

PIETR
THE LATVIAN
&
THE LATE
MONSIEUR GALLET

Complete and Unabridged

ULVERSCROFT
Leicester

Pietr the Latvian first published in serial, as *Pietr-le-Letton*, in *Ric et Rac* in 1930

This translation first published in Great Britain in 2013

The Late Monsieur Gallet first published in French as *M. Gallet décédé* by Fayard in 1931

This translation first published in Great Britain in 2013

This Ulverscroft Edition published 2019
by arrangement with
Penguin Random House UK
London

A catalogue record for this book is available
from the British Library.

ISBN 978–1–4448–4297–5

Published by
F. A. Thorpe (Publishing)
Anstey, Leicestershire

Set by Words & Graphics Ltd.
Anstey, Leicestershire
Printed and bound in Great Britain by
T. J. International Ltd., Padstow, Cornwall

This book is printed on acid-free paper

Contents

Pietr the Latvian

Translated by DAVID BELLOS

1

Apparent age 32, height 169 . . .

ICPC to PJ Paris Xvzust Krakow vimontra m ghks
triv psot uv Pietr-le-Letton Bremen vs tyz btolem.

Detective Chief Inspector Maigret of the Flying
Squad raised his eyes. It seemed to him that the
cast-iron stove in the middle of his office with its
chimney tube rising to the ceiling wasn't roaring
properly. He pushed the telegram away, rose
ponderously to his feet, adjusted the flue and
thrust three shovels of coal into the firebox.

Then he stood with his back to the stove, filled
his pipe and adjusted his stud collar, which was
irritating his neck even though it wasn't set very
high.

He glanced at his watch. Four p.m. His jacket
was hanging on a hook on the back of the door.

Slowly he returned to his desk, mouthing a
translation as he went:

International Criminal Police Commission
to Police Judiciaire in Paris: Krakow police
report sighting Pietr the Latvian en route to
Bremen.

The International Criminal Police Commission,
or ICPC, is based in Vienna. Broadly speaking, it

3

oversees the struggle against organized crime in Europe, with a particular responsibility for liaison between the various national police forces on the Continent.

Maigret pulled up another telegram that was similarly written in IPC, the secret international police code used for communication between all the world's police forces. He translated at sight:

Polizei-Präsidium Bremen to PJ Paris: Pietr the Latvian reported en route Amsterdam and Brussels.

Another telegram from the Nederlandsche Centrale in Zake Internationale Misdadigers, the Dutch police HQ, reported:

At 11 a.m. Pietr the Latvian boarded Étoile du Nord, compartment G. 263, car 5, destination Paris.

The final message in IPC had been sent from Brussels and said:

Confirm Pietr the Latvian on board Étoile du Nord via Brussels 2 a.m. in compartment reported by Amsterdam.

Behind Maigret's desk there was a huge map pinned to the wall. The inspector was a broad and heavy man. He stood staring at the map with his hands in his pockets and his pipe sticking out the side of his mouth.

His eyes travelled from the dot representing

Krakow to the other dot showing the port of Bremen and from there to Amsterdam and Paris.

He checked the time once again. Four-twenty. The Étoile du Nord should now be hurtling along at sixty miles an hour between Saint-Quentin and Compiègne.

It wouldn't stop at the border. It wouldn't be slowing down.

In car 5, compartment G. 263, Pietr the Latvian was presumably spending his time reading or looking at the scencry.

Maigret went over to a door that opened onto a closet, washed his hands in an enamel basin, ran a comb through thick dark-brown hair flecked with only a few silver strands around the temple, and did his best to straighten out his tie — he'd never learned how to do a proper knot.

It was November and it was getting dark. Through the window he could see a branch of the Seine, Place Saint-Michel, and a floating wash-house, all in a blue shroud speckled by gas lamps lighting up one after the other.

He opened a drawer and glanced at a dispatch from the International Identification Bureau in Copenhagen.

Paris PJ Pietr-le-Letton 32 169 01512 0224 0255 02732 03116 03233 03243 03325 03415 03522 04115 04144 04147 05221 . . .

This time he made an effort to speak the translation aloud and even went over it several times, like a schoolchild reciting a lesson:

5

Description Pietr the Latvian: apparent age 32 years, height 169 cm, sinus top straight line, bottom flat, extension large max, special feature septum not visible, ear unmarked rim, lobe large, max cross and dimension small max, protuberant antitragus, vex edge lower fold, edge shape straight line edge feature separate lines, orthognathous upper, long face, biconcave, eyebrows thin fair light, lower lip jutting max thick lower droop, light.

This 'word-picture' of Pietr was as clear as a photograph to Inspector Maigret. The principal features were the first to emerge: the man was short, slim, young and fair-haired, with sparse blond eyebrows, greenish eyes and a long neck.

Maigret now also knew the shape of his ear in the minutest detail. This would enable him to make a positive identification in a milling crowd even if the suspect was in disguise.

He took his jacket off the hook and slipped his arms into it, then put on a heavy black overcoat and a bowler hat.

One last glance at the stove, which seemed on the verge of exploding.

At the end of the corridor, on the stair landing that was used as a waiting room, he reminded Jean:

'You won't forget to keep my stove going, will you?'

The wind swirling up the stairs took him by surprise, and he had to shelter from the draught in a corner to get his pipe to light.

Wind and rain blew in squalls over the platforms of Gare du Nord despite the monumental glass canopy overhead. Several panes had blown out and lay in shards on the railway tracks. The lighting wasn't working properly. People huddled up inside their clothes.

Outside one of the ticket windows an alarming travel notice had been posted:

Channel forecast: gale-force winds.

One woman, whose son was to catch the Folkestone boat train, looked upset; her eyes were red. She kept on telling the boy what he should do, right up to the last minute. In his embarrassment he had no choice but to promise not to go out on deck.

Maigret stood near platform II where people were awaiting the arrival of the Étoile du Nord. All the leading hotels, as well as Thomas Cook, had their agents standing by.

He stood still. Other people were agitated. A young woman clad in mink yet wearing only sheer silk stockings walked up and down, stamping her heels.

He just stood there: a hulk of a man, with shoulders so broad as to cast a wide shadow. When people bumped into him he stayed as firm as a brick wall.

The yellow speck of the train's headlamp appeared in the distance. Then came the usual hubbub, with porters shouting and passengers tramping and jostling their way towards the station exit.

A couple of hundred passengers paraded past Maigret before he picked out in the crowd a short man wearing a broad-checked green travelling cape of a distinctly Nordic cut and colour.

The man wasn't in a hurry. He had three porters behind him. Bowing and scraping, an agent from one of the grand hotels on the Champs-Élysées cleared the way in front of him.

Apparent age 32, height 169 . . . sinus top . . .

Maigret kept calm. He looked hard at the man's ear. That was all he needed.

The man in green passed close by. One of his porters bumped Maigret with one of the suitcases.

At exactly the same moment a railway employee began to run, shouting out something to his colleague standing at the station end of the platform, next to the barrier.

The chain was drawn closed. Protests erupted.

The man in the travelling cape was already out of the station.

Maigret puffed away at his pipe in quick short bursts. He went up to the official who had closed the barrier.

'Police! What's happened?'

'A crime . . . They've just found . . . '

'Carriage 5? . . . '

'I think so . . . '

The station went about its regular business; only platform 11 looked abnormal. There were fifty passengers still waiting to get out, but their

8

path was blocked. They were getting excited.

'Let them go . . . ' Maigret said.

'But . . . '

'Let them go . . . '

He watched the last cluster move away. The station loud-speaker announced the departure of a local train. Somebody was running somewhere. Beside one of the carriages of the Étoile du Nord there was a small group waiting for something. Three of them, in railway company livery.

★   ★   ★

The stationmaster got to them first. He was a large man and had a worried look on his face. Then a hospital stretcher was wheeled through the main hall, past clumps of people who looked at it uneasily, especially those about to depart.

Maigret walked up the side of the train with his usual heavy tread, smoking as he went. Carriage 1, carriage 2 . . . He came to carriage 5.

That's where the group was standing at the door. The stretcher came to a halt. The stationmaster tried to listen to the three men, who were all speaking at the same time.

'Police! Where is he?'

Maigret's presence provided obvious relief. He propelled his placid mass towards the centre of the frantic group. The other men instantly became his satellites.

'In the toilet . . . '

Maigret hauled himself up onto the train and saw that the toilet door on his right was open. On the floor, in a heap, was a body, bent double

9

in a strangely contorted posture.

The conductor was giving orders from the platform.

'Shunt the carriage to the yard . . . Hang on! . . . Track 62 . . . Let the railway police know . . . '

At first he could only see the back of the man's neck. But when he tipped his cap off its oblique angle, he could see the man's left ear. Maigret mumbled to himself: *lobe large, max cross and dimension small max, protuberant antitragus . . .*

There were a few drops of blood on the linoleum. Maigret looked around. The railway staff were standing on the platform or on the running board. The stationmaster was still talking.

So Maigret clenched his pipe between his teeth even harder and turned the man's head over.

If he hadn't seen the traveller in the green cloak leave the station, if he hadn't seen him taken to a car by an interpreter from the Majestic, he could have had doubts.

It was the same physiognomy. The same fair toothbrush moustache under a sharply defined nose. The same sparse blond eyebrows. The same grey-green eyes.

In other words: Pietr the Latvian!

Maigret could hardly turn around in the tiny washroom, where the tap was still running and a jet of steam was seeping from some poorly sealed joint.

He was standing right next to the corpse. He pulled the man's upper body upright and saw on his chest, on his jacket and shirt, the burn-marks made by gunshot from point-blank range.

It was a big blackish stain tinged with the dark red of coagulating blood.

★ ★ ★

One detail struck the inspector. He happened to notice one of the man's feet. It was twisted on its side, as was the whole body, which must have been squashed into a corner so as to allow the door to close.

The shoe was black and happened to be of a very cheap and common kind. Apparently it had been re-soled. The heel was worn on one side, and a coin-shaped gap had opened up in the middle of the sole.

The local chief of the railway police had now reached the carriage and was calling up from the platform. He was a self-confident man wearing a uniform with epaulettes.

'So what is it, then? Murder? Suicide? Don't touch anything until the law gets here, OK? Be careful! I'm the one who's in charge. OK?'

Maigret had a tough time disentangling his own feet from the dead man's legs to extricate himself from the toilet. With swift, professional movements he patted the man's pockets. Clean as a whistle. Nothing in them at all.

He got out of the carriage. His pipe had gone out, his hat was askew and he had a bloodstain on his cuff.

'Well, if it isn't Maigret! ... What do you make of it, then?'

'Not much. Go have a look yourself . . . '

'It's suicide, right?'

'If you say so . . . Did you call the prosecutor's office?'

'As soon as I heard . . . '

The loudspeaker crackled with some message or other. A few people had noticed there was something unusual going on and stood in the distance, watching the empty train and the group of people standing next to the running board of carriage 5.

Maigret strode off without saying a word. He left the station and hailed a cab.

'Hôtel Majestic! . . . '

The storm had got even worse. Gusts swept down the streets and made pedestrians totter about like drunks. A roof tile smashed onto the pavement. Buses, and more buses.

The Champs-Élysées was almost entirely deserted. Drops of rain had begun to fall. The porter at the Majestic dashed out to the taxi with a huge red umbrella.

'Police! . . . Has someone from the Étoile du Nord just checked in?'

That prompted the porter to fold his umbrella.

'Yes, sir, that true.'

'Green cape . . . Fair moustache . . . '

'That right. Sir go reception.'

People were scrambling to shelter from the rain. Maigret got inside the hotel just in time to avoid drops as big as walnuts and cold as ice.

Despite this, the receptionists and interpreters behind the polished wood counter were as elegant and efficient as ever.

'Police . . . A guest in a green cape . . . Small fair mousta — '

'Room 17, sir. His bags are on their way up right now . . . '

2

Mixing with Millionaires

Inevitably Maigret was a hostile presence in the Majestic. He constituted a kind of foreign body that the hotel's atmosphere could not assimilate.

Not that he looked like a cartoon policeman. He didn't have a moustache and he didn't wear heavy boots. His clothes were well cut and made of fairly light worsted. He shaved every day and looked after his hands.

But his frame was proletarian. He was a big, bony man. Iron muscles shaped his jacket sleeves and quickly wore through new trousers.

He had a way of imposing himself just by standing there. His assertive presence had often irked many of his own colleagues.

It was something more than self-confidence but less than pride. He would turn up and stand like a rock with his feet wide apart. On that rock all would shatter, whether Maigret moved forward or stayed exactly where he was.

His pipe was nailed to his jawbone. He wasn't going to remove it just because he was in the lobby of the Majestic.

Could it be that Maigret simply preferred to be common and self-assertive?

You just couldn't miss the man wearing a big black velvet-collared overcoat in that brightly lit

14

lobby, where excitable society ladies scattered trails of perfume, tinkling laughter and loud whispers amidst the unctuous compliments of impeccable flunkeys.

He paid no attention. He wasn't part of the flow. He was impervious to the sound of jazz floating up from the dance-floor in the basement.

The inspector started to go up one of the stairs. A liftboy called out and asked if he wanted to take the lift, but Maigret didn't even turn round.

At the first landing someone asked him:

'Are you looking for . . . ?'

It was as is if the sound waves hadn't reached him. He glanced at the corridors with their red carpets stretching out so far that they almost made you sick. He went on up.

On the second floor he read the numbers on the bronze plaques. The door of no. 17 was open. Valets with striped waistcoats were bringing in the luggage.

The traveller had taken off his cloak and looked very slender and elegant in his pinstripe suit. He was smoking a papirosa and giving instructions at the same time.

No. 17 wasn't a room, but a whole suite: lounge, study, bedroom and bathroom. The doors opened onto two intersecting corridors, and at the corner, like a bench placed by a crossroads, there was a huge, curved sofa.

That's where Maigret sat himself down, right opposite the open door. He stretched out his legs and unbuttoned his overcoat.

Pietr saw him and, showing neither surprise

15

nor disquiet, he carried on giving instructions. When the valets had finished placing his trunks and cases on stands, he came to the door, held it open for an instant to inspect the detective, then closed it himself.

Maigret sat there for as long as it took to smoke three pipes, and to dismiss two room-service waiters and one chambermaid who came up to inquire what he was waiting for.

On the stroke of eight Pietr the Latvian came out of his room, looking even slimmer and smarter than before, in a classically tailored dinner jacket that must have come from Savile Row.

He was hatless. His short, ash-blond hair was already thinning. His hairline was set far back and his forehead not especially high; you could glimpse a streak of pink scalp along the parting.

He had long, pale hands. On the fourth finger of his left hand he wore a chunky platinum signet ring set with a yellow diamond.

He was smoking again — another papirosa. He walked right up to Maigret, stopped for a moment, looked at him as if he felt like saying something, then walked on towards the lift as if lost in thought.

★ ★ ★

Ten minutes later he took his seat in the dining room at the table of Mr and Mrs Mortimer-Levingston. The latter was the centre of attention: she had pearls worth a cool million on her neck.

The previous day her husband had come to

the rescue of one of France's biggest automobile manufacturers, with the result that he was now its majority shareholder.

The three of them were chatting merrily. Pietr talked a lot, but discreetly, with his head leaning forwards. He was completely at ease, natural and casual, despite being able to see the detective's dark outline through the glazed partition.

Inspector Maigret asked reception to show him the guest list. He wasn't surprised to see that Pietr had signed in under the name of Oswald Oppenheim, ship-owner, from Bremen.

It was a foregone conclusion that he had a genuine passport and full identity papers in that name, just as he no doubt did in several others.

It was equally obvious that he'd met the Mortimer-Levingstons previously, whether in Berlin, Warsaw, London or New York.

Was the sole purpose of his presence in Paris to rendezvous with them and to get away with another one of the colossal scams that were his trademark?

Maigret had the Latvian's file card in his jacket pocket. It said:

Extremely clever and dangerous. Nationality uncertain, from Baltic area. Reckoned to be either Latvian or Estonian. Fluent in Russian, French, English and German. High level of education. Thought to be capo of major international ring mainly involved in fraud. The ring has been spotted successively in Paris, Amsterdam (Van Heuvel case), Berne (United Shipowners affair),

Warsaw (Lipmann case) and in various other European cities where identification of its methods and procedures was less clear.

Pietr the Latvian's associates seem to be mainly British and American. One who has been seen most often with him and who was identified when he presented a forged cheque for cash at the Federal Bank in Berne was killed during arrest. His alias was Major Howard of the American Legion, but it has been established that he was actually a former New York bootlegger known in the USA as Fat Fred.

Pietr the Latvian has been arrested twice. First, in Wiesbaden, for swindling a Munich trader out of half a million marks; second, in Madrid, for a similar offence involving a leading figure at the Spanish royal court.

On both occasions he used the same ploy. He met his victims and presumably told them that the stolen sums were safely hidden and that having him arrested would not reveal where they were. Both times the complaint was withdrawn, and the plaintiffs were probably paid off.

Since then has never been caught red-handed.

Is probably in cahoots with the Maronnetti gang (counterfeit money and forged documents) and the Cologne gang (the 'wall-busters').

There was another rumour doing the rounds of European police departments: Pietr, as the ring-leader and money-launderer of one or more gangs, was said to be sitting on several million that had been split up under different names in different banks and even invested in legitimate industries.

The man smiled subtly at the story Mrs Mortimer-Levingston was telling, while with his ivory hand he plucked luscious grapes from the bunch on his plate.

★   ★   ★

'Excuse me, sir. Could I please have a word with you?'

Maigret was speaking to Mortimer-Levingston in the lobby of the Majestic after Pietr and Mortimer's wife had both gone back up to their rooms.

Mortimer didn't have the athletic look of a Yank. He was more of the Mediterranean type.

He was tall and thin. His very small head was topped with black hair parted down the middle.

He looked permanently tired. His eyelids were weary and blue. In any case he led an exhausting life, somehow managing to turn up in Deauville, Miami, Venice, Paris, Cannes and Berlin before getting back to his yacht and then dashing off to do a deal in some European capital or to referee a major boxing match in New York or California.

He looked Maigret up and down in lordly fashion.

'And you are . . . ?'

'Detective Chief Inspector Maigret of the Flying Squad . . . '

Mortimer barely frowned and stood there leaning forwards as if he had decided to grant just one second of his time.

'Are you aware you have just dined with Pietr the Latvian?'

'Is that all you have to say?'

Maigret didn't budge an inch. It was pretty much what he'd expected.

He put his pipe back in his mouth — he'd allowed himself to remove it in order to speak to the millionaire — and muttered:

'That's all.'

He looked pleased with himself. Levingston moved off icily and got into the lift.

It was just after 9.30. The symphony orchestra that had been playing during dinner yielded the stage to a jazz band. People were coming in from outside.

Maigret hadn't eaten. He was standing calmly and patiently in the middle of the lobby. The manager repeatedly gave him worried and disapproving looks from a distance. Even the lowliest members of staff scowled as they passed by, when they didn't manage to jostle him.

The Majestic could not stomach him. Maigret persisted in being a big black unmoving stain amidst the gilding, the chandeliers, the comings and goings of silk evening gowns, fur coats and perfumed, sparkling silhouettes.

Mrs Levingston was the first to come back down in the lift. She had changed, and now wore a lamé cape lined with ermine that left her shoulders bare.

She seemed astonished not to find anyone

waiting for her and began to walk up and down, drumming the floor with her gold-lacquered high heels.

She suddenly stopped at the polished wooden counter where the receptionists and interpreters stood and said a few words. One of the staff pushed a red button and picked up a handset.

He looked surprised and called a bellboy, who rushed to the lift.

Mrs Mortimer-Levingston was visibly anxious. Through the glass door you could see the sleek shape of an American-made limousine standing at the kerb.

The bellboy reappeared, spoke to the member of staff, who in his turn said something to Mrs Mortimer. She protested. She must have been saying:

'But that's impossible!'

Maigret then went up the staircase, stopped outside suite 17, knocked on the door. As he'd expected after the circus he'd just watched, there was no answer.

He opened the door and found the lounge deserted. Pietr's dinner jacket was lying casually on the bed in the bedroom. One trunk was open. A pair of patent-leather shoes had been left at opposite ends of the carpet.

The manager came in and grunted:

'You're already here, are you?'

'So? . . . Vanished, has he? Levingston as well! Is that right?'

'Now there's no need to go overboard. Neither of them is in his room, but we'll probably find them somewhere else in the hotel.'

'How many exits are there?'

'Three. The main entrance on the Champs-Élysées . . . Then there's the entrance in the covered mall, and the service entrance on Rue de Ponthieu . . . '

'Is there a security guard? Call him . . . '

The telephone worked. The manager was in a temper. He took it out on an operator who couldn't understand him. He kept his gaze fixed on Maigret, and it was not kind.

'What does all this mean?' he asked as he waited for the guard to come up from the glass-walled box where he was on duty beside the service entrance.

'Nothing, or almost, as you said . . . '

'I hope there's not been a . . . a . . . '

The word *crime*, dreaded like the plague by hoteliers the world over from the humblest lodging-house landlord to the manager of a luxury resort, just would not pass his lips.

'We'll find out.'

Mrs Mortimer-Levingston appeared.

'Well? . . . ' she inquired.

The manager bowed and muttered something. A figure appeared at the far end of the corridor — an old man with a straggly beard and ill-cut clothes at odds with the luxurious appearance of the hotel. He was obviously meant to stay in the back, otherwise he too would have been given a fine uniform and been sent to the barber every day.

'Did you see anyone go out?'

'When?'

'In the last few minutes . . . '

'A guy from the kitchen, I think . . . I wasn't paying attention . . . A guy with a cap . . . '

'Was he short? Fair?' Maigret interrupted.

'Yes . . . I think so . . . I wasn't watching . . . He was quick . . . '

'Nobody else?'

'I dunno . . . I went round the corner to buy the paper . . . '

Mrs Mortimer-Levingston began to lose her temper.

'Well now! Is that how you conduct a manhunt?' she said to Maigret. 'I've just been told you're a policeman . . . My husband might have been killed . . . What are you waiting for?'

The look that then fell upon her was Maigret through and through! Completely calm! Completely unruffled! It was as if he'd just noticed the buzzing of a bee. As if what he had before him was something quite ordinary.

She was not accustomed to being looked at in that way. She bit her lip, blushed crimson beneath her make-up and stamped her heel with impatience.

He was still staring at her.

Because he was pushing her to the limit, or perhaps because she didn't know what else to do, Mrs Mortimer-Levingston threw a fit.

3

The Strand of Hair

It was nearly midnight when Maigret got back to his office on Quai des Orfèvres. The storm was at its peak. The trees on the riverbank were rattling back and forth and the wash-house barge was tossing about in the waves.

The building was almost empty. At least Jean was still at his post in the lobby at the entrance to a corridor of empty offices.

Voices could be heard coming from the duty room. Then, further down, there was light streaking out from beneath a door — a detective or an inspector working on some case. One of the official cars in the courtyard below was running its engine.

'Is Torrence back?' Maigret asked.

'He's just come in.'

'My stove?'

'It was so hot in your office I had to open the window. There was condensation running down your wall!'

'Get me some beers and sandwiches. None of that soft white bread, mind you.'

He pushed a door and called out:

'Torrence!'

Detective Torrence followed his chief to his office. Before he'd left Gare du Nord Maigret

24

had called Torrence on the telephone and told him to keep going on the case on his own.

Inspector Maigret was forty-five and his junior was barely thirty years old. Even so, there was something solid and bulky about Torrence that made him an almost full-scale model of his boss.

They'd conducted many cases together without ever saying an unnecessary word.

Maigret took off his overcoat and his jacket and loosened his tie. He stood for a while with his back to the stove to let the heat seep in. Then he asked:

'So?'

'The Prosecution Service had an emergency meeting. Forensics took photographs but couldn't find any fingerprints — except the dead man's, of course. They don't match any we have on record.'

'If I remember correctly, don't they have a file on our friend from the Baltic?'

'Just the 'word-picture'. No fingerprints, no anthropometric data.'

'So we can't be sure that the dead man is someone other than Pietr.'

'But there's no guarantee that it *is* him, either!'

Maigret had taken out his pipe and a pouch that had only a sprinkling of brown dust left in it. Mechanically Torrence handed him an opened packet of shag.

There was a pause. Tobacco crackled in Maigret's pipe. Then came a sound of footsteps and tinkling glassware on the other side of the door, which Torrence opened.

The waiter from Brasserie Dauphine brought in six glasses of beer and four thick-stuffed

25

sandwiches on a tray, which he laid on the table.

'Are you sure that'll be enough?' he asked, seeing that Maigret had company.

'That's fine.'

Maigret started drinking and munching without putting his pipe out, though he did push a glass over to his assistant's side of the desk.

'Well?'

'I questioned all the staff who were on the train. There's definite proof that someone was on board without a ticket. Could be the victim, could be the culprit! We're assuming he got on at Brussels, on the track side. It's easier to hide in a Pullman car than in any other because each carriage has a lot of luggage space. Pietr had tea in the restaurant car between Brussels and the French border and spent his time flicking through a pile of French and English newspapers, including the financial dailies. He went to the toilet between Maubeuge and Saint-Quentin. The head waiter remembers that because as he went past him Pietr said, 'Take a whisky to my seat'.'

'And he went back to his seat later on?'

'Fifteen minutes later, he was back at his regular place with a whisky in front of him. But the head waiter didn't see Pietr again, since he didn't go back by way of the restaurant car.'

'Did anybody try to use the toilet after him?'

'Sure! A lady traveller tried to get in, but the lock was jammed. It wasn't until the train got to Paris that a staff member managed to force it open. The mechanism had been clogged with iron filings.'

'Up to that point, had anybody set eyes on the second Pietr?'

'Absolutely not. He would have been very noticeable. He was wearing shoddy clothes and would have stood out a mile on a de luxe express.'

'What about the bullet?'

'Shot at point-blank range. Automatic revolver, 6 mm. The shot caused such burning of the skin that according to the doctor the victim would have died from the heat shock alone.'

'Any sign of a struggle?'

'None at all. The pockets were empty.'

'I know that . . . '

'Sorry! However, I did find this in a small button-down pocket on the inside of his waistcoat.'

Torrence then extracted from his wallet a folded piece of transparent paper inside which you could see a strand of brown hair.

'Hand it over . . . '

Maigret hadn't stopped eating and drinking all the while.

'A woman's hair? Or a child's?'

'Forensics says it's a woman's hair. I left him a few strands that he's promised to examine closely.'

'And the autopsy?'

'All done by 10 a.m. Probable age: thirty-two. Height 1 m 68 cm. No hereditary abnormalities. One of his kidneys was in poor shape, which could mean he was a boozer. Stomach contained tea and other digested matter that couldn't be identified straight away. They'll work on the analysis tomorrow. Now the examination is over the body is being kept on ice at the morgue.'

Maigret wiped his mouth, stationed himself in his favourite position in front of the stove and held out his hand, which Torrence mechanically supplied with a packet of tobacco.

'For my part,' Maigret said eventually, 'I saw Pietr, or whoever has taken over his role, check in at Hôtel Majestic and have dinner with the Mortimer-Levingstons, which seems to have been arranged in advance.'

'The millionaires?'

'Yes, that's right. After the meal, Pietr went back to his suite. I warned the American. Mortimer then went to his room. They were obviously planning to go out as a three-some, since Mrs Mortimer came down straight after, in full evening gear. Ten minutes later, both men had vanished. Our Latvian had switched his evening wear for less swanky clothes. He'd put on a cap, and the guard just assumed he was a kitchen worker. But Levingston left as he was, in formal attire.'

Torrence said nothing. In the long pause that ensued, you could hear the fire roaring in the stove and the window panes rattling in the storm.

Torrence finally broke the silence.

'Luggage?' he asked.

'Done. Nothing there! Just clothes and underwear . . . The usual accoutrements of a first-class traveller. Not a scrap of paper. The Mortimer woman is certain that her husband has been murdered.'

★　★　★

28

Somewhere a bell rang. Maigret opened the drawer in his desk where that afternoon he'd put all the telegrams about Pietr the Latvian.

Then he looked at the map. He drew a line with his finger from Krakow to Bremen, then to Amsterdam, Brussels and Paris.

Somewhere near Saint-Quentin, a brief halt: a man died.

In Paris, the line came to a full stop. Two men vanish from the middle of the Champs-Élysées.

All that's left are suitcases in a suite and Mrs Mortimer-Levingston, whose mind is as empty as Pietr's travelling chest.

The gurgle from Maigret's pipe was getting so annoying that the inspector took a swatch of chicken feathers from another drawer, cleaned the shaft, then opened the stove door and flung the soiled feathers in the fire.

Four of the beer glasses were empty but for sticky froth marks on the rim. Somebody came out of one of the offices on the corridor, locked his door and went away.

'Who's a lucky man!' Torrence observed. 'That's Lucas. Tonight he got a tip-off from some moneyed brat and arrested a pair of drug dealers.'

Maigret was poking the fire, and when he stood up his face was crimson. In routine fashion he picked up the translucent paper, extracted the strand of hair and turned it over in the light. Then he went back to the map and studied the invisible track of Pietr's journey. It made a sweeping arc of almost 180 degrees.

If he had started out from Krakow, then why

had he gone all the way north to Bremen before swerving back down to Paris?

He was still holding the slip of paper. He muttered:

'There must have been a picture inside this once.'

In fact, the tissue was a glassine envelope, a slipcover of the kind photographers use to protect customers' orders. But it was an obsolete size known as 'album format' that could only now be found in provincial backwaters. The photo that this cover must have protected would have been about half the size of a standard postcard, printed on off-white glacé paper on cardboard backing.

'Is anyone still there at the lab?' Maigret suddenly asked.

'I guess so. They must still be processing the photos of the Étoile du Nord affair.'

There was only one full glass left on the table. Maigret gulped it down and put on his jacket.

'You'll come along? . . . Those kinds of portrait photos usually have the name and address of the photographer printed or embossed on them . . . '

Torrence got the point. They set off through a labyrinth of passageways and stairs up into the attic floors of the Law Courts and finally found the forensics lab.

An expert took the slipcover, ran it through his fingers, almost sniffed at it. Then he sat at an arc lamp and wheeled over a carriage-mounted multiplying glass.

The principle is straightforward: blank paper that has been in protracted contact with another sheet that has been printed or written on eventually acquires an imprint of the letters on that other sheet. The imprint cannot be seen by the naked eye, but photography can reveal it.

The fact that there was a stove in the lab meant that Maigret was destined to end up there. He stood watch for the best part of an hour, smoking pipe after pipe, while Torrence trailed the photographer as he came and went.

At long last the darkroom door opened. A voice cried out:

'We've got it!'

'Yes?'

'The photo credit is: *Léon Moutet, Art Photography, Quai des Belges, Fécamp.*'

Only a real expert could decipher the plate. Torrence, for instance, could only see a blur.

'Do you want to see the post-mortem photos?' the expert asked cheerfully. 'They're first-rate! But it was a tight fit inside that railway toilet! Would you believe it, we had to hang the camera from the ceiling . . . '

'Have you got an outside line?' Maigret asked, gesturing towards the phone.

'Yes . . . the switchboard shuts down at nine, so before she goes off the operator connects me to the outside.'

Maigret called the Majestic and spoke to one of the desk interpreters.

'Has Mr Mortimer-Levingston come back in?'

'I'll find out for you, sir. To whom do I have the honour of . . . '

'Police!'

'No, sir, he's not back.'

'What about Mr Oswald Oppenheim?'

31

'Not back either, sir.'

'What is Mrs Mortimer up to?'

A pause.

'I asked you what Mrs Mortimer is doing.'

'She is . . . I think she is in the bar . . . '

'Do you mean she's drunk?'

'She has had a few cocktails, sir. She said she would not go up to her suite until her husband comes back . . . Do you . . . ?'

'What's that?'

'Hello? . . . This is the manager speaking,' another voice broke in. 'Any progress? Do you think this will get into the papers? . . . '

Cruelly, Maigret hung up. To please the photographer he took a look at the first proof photos laid out in the drying trays, still gleaming wet. While doing that he was talking to Torrence.

'You're going to settle in at the Majestic, old pal. The main thing is to take no notice whatsoever of the manager.'

'What about you, *patron?*'

'I'm going back to the office. There's a train to Fécamp at 5.30, It's not worth going home and waking up Mme Maigret. Hang on . . . The Dauphine should still be open. On your way, order me up a beer . . . '

'Just one . . . ?' Torrence inquired, with a deadpan expression on his face.

'As you like, old pal! The waiter's smart enough to know it means three or four. Have him throw in a few sandwiches as well.'

They traipsed down an unending spiral staircase in single file.

The black-gowned photographer was left on

his own to admire the prints he'd just made. He still had to number them.

The two detectives parted company in the freezing courtyard.

'If you leave the Majestic for any reason, make sure one of our men holds the fort,' Maigret instructed. 'I'll telephone the front desk if I need to get in touch . . . '

He went back to his office and stoked the fire so vigorously he could have snapped the grate.

4

The *Seeteufel*'s First Mate

The station at La Bréauté, on the main line to Le Havre, where Maigret had to change trains at 7.30 a.m., gave him a foretaste of Fécamp.

The ill-lit station buffet had grimy walls and a counter offering only a few mouldy pieces of cake alongside a miserable fruit stack made of three bananas and five oranges.

The foul weather had even more impact here than in Paris. Rain was coming down in buckets. Crossing from one track to the other meant wading through knee-deep mud.

The branch-line train was a rickety affair made up of carriages on their way to scrap. In the pale half-light of dawn you could hardly make out the fuzzy shapes of farmhouses through the pelting rain.

Fécamp! The air was laden with the smell of herring and cod. Mountains of casks. Ships' masts peering over the locomotive. Somewhere a siren blared.

'Quai des Belges?'

Straight ahead. All he had to do was walk through slimy puddles gleaming with fish scales and rotting innards.

The photographer was also a shopkeeper and a newspaper vendor. He stocked oilskins, sailcloth pea-jackets and hempen rope alongside New Year's greeting cards.

A weakling with very pale skin: as soon as he heard the word 'police' he called his wife to the rescue.

'Can you tell me what photo was in this slipcover?'

It dragged on. Maigret had to squeeze words out of him one by one and do his thinking for him.

In the first place, the technician hadn't used that format for eight years, ever since he'd acquired new equipment to do postcard-sized portraits.

Who might have had his or her photograph taken eight or more years ago? Monsieur Moutet took a whole fifteen minutes to remember that he'd got an album with archive copies of all the portraits done in his establishment.

His wife went to get it. Sailors came and went. Kids came in to buy a penny's worth of sweets. Outside, ships' tackle scraped on the dock. You could hear the waves shifting shingle along the breakwater.

Maigret thumbed through the archive album, then specified what he was looking for:

'A young woman with extremely fine brown hair . . . '

That did it.

'Mademoiselle Swaan!' the photographer exclaimed. He turned up the snapshot straight away. It was the only time he'd had a decent subject to photograph.

She was a pretty woman. She looked twenty. The photo fitted the slipcover exactly.

'Who is she?'

'She's still living in Fécamp. But now she's got a clifftop villa five minutes from the Casino . . . '

'Is she married?'

'She wasn't then. She was the cashier at the Railway Hotel.'

'Opposite the station, I suppose?'

'Yes, you must have seen it on your way here. She was an orphan from some small place around here . . . Les Loges . . . Do you know where I mean? . . . Anyway, that's how she got to meet a traveller staying at the hotel . . . They got married . . . At the moment she's living in the villa with her two children and a maid . . . '

'Mr Swaan doesn't live in Fécamp?'

There was a pause. The photographer and his wife exchanged glances. The woman answered:

'Since you're from the police, I suppose we'd better tell you everything. Anyway you'd find it all out in the end, but . . . They're only rumours, but . . . Mr Swaan almost never stays in Fécamp. When he does come he stops for a few days at the most . . . Sometimes it's just a flying visit . . . He first came not long after the war . . . The Grand Banks were being reorganized, after five years' interruption. He wanted to look into it properly, so he said, and to make investments in businesses that were being started up again. He claimed to be Norwegian . . . His first name is Olaf . . . The herring fishermen who sometimes go as far as Norway say there are plenty of people over there who have that name . . . Nonetheless, people said he was really a German spy. That's why, when he got married, his wife was kept at arm's length. Then we discovered he really was a sailor and was first mate on a German merchantman, and that was why he didn't show up very often . . . Eventually people stopped bothering about him, but we're still wary . . . '

'You said they had children?'

'Two . . . A little girl of three and a baby a few months old . . . '

Maigret took the photograph out of the album and got directions to the villa. It was a bit too early to turn up. He waited in a harbour café for two hours, listening to fishermen talking about the herring catch, which was at its height. Five trawlers were tied up at the quay. Fish was being unloaded by the barrelful. Despite the wind and rain, the air stank.

To get to the villa he walked along the deserted breakwater and around the shuttered Casino still plastered with last summer's posters. At last he got to a steep climb that began at the foot of the cliff. As he plodded up he got occasional glimpses of iron railings in front of villas. The one he was looking for turned out to be a comfortable-looking red-brick structure, neither large nor small. He guessed that the garden with its white-gravel paths was well tended in season. The windows must have had a good view into the far distance.

★ ★ ★

Maigret rang the bell. A great Dane came to sniff at him through the railings, and its lack of bark made it seem all the more ferocious. At the second ring, a maid appeared. First she took the dog back to his kennel, and then asked:

'What is it about?'

She spoke with the local accent.

'I would like to see Mr Swaan, please.'

She seemed hesitant.

'I don't know if sir is in . . . I'll go and ask.'

She hadn't opened the gate. Rain was still pouring down, and Maigret was soaked through. He watched the maid go up the steps and vanish inside the house. Then a curtain shifted at a window. A few moments later the maid reappeared.

'Sir will not be back for several weeks. He is in Bremen . . . '

'In that case I would like to have a word with Madame Swaan . . . '

The maid hesitated again, but ended up opening the gate.

'Madame isn't dressed. You will have to wait . . . '

The dripping detective was shown into a neat lounge with white curtains and a waxed floor. The furniture was brand new, but just the same as you would find in any lower-middle-class home. They were good-quality pieces, in a style that would have been called modern around 1900.

Light oak. Flowers in an 'artistic' stone vase in the middle of the table. Crochet-work place-mats. On the other hand, there was a magnificent sculpted silver samovar on a side-table. It must have been worth more than the rest of the room's contents put together.

Maigret heard noises coming from the first floor. A baby could be heard crying through one of the ground-floor walls; someone else was mumbling something in a soft and even voice, as if to comfort it. At last, the sound of slippered feet gliding along the corridor. The door opened. Maigret found himself facing a young woman who had dressed in a hurry so as to meet him.

She was of medium height, more plump than slim, with a pretty and serious face that betrayed a pang of anxiety. She smiled nonetheless and said:

'Why didn't you take a seat?'

Rivulets of rainwater flowed from Maigret's overcoat, trousers and shoes into little puddles on the polished floor. In that state he could not have sat down on the light-green velvet of the armchairs in the lounge.

'Madame Swaan, I presume? . . . '

'Yes, monsieur . . . '

She looked at him quizzically.

'I'm sorry to disturb you like this . . . It's just a formality . . . I'm with the Immigration Service . . . We're conducting a survey . . . '

She said nothing. She didn't seem any more or less anxious than before.

'I understand Mr Swaan is a Swede. Is that correct?'

'Oh no, he's Norwegian . . . But for the French I guess it's the same thing . . . To begin with, I myself . . . '

'He is a ship's officer?'

'He's first mate on the *Seeteufel*, out of Bremen . . . '

'As I thought . . . So he is in the employ of a German company?'

She blushed.

'The ship-owner is German, yes . . . At least, on paper . . . '

'Meaning? . . . '

'I don't think I need to keep it from you . . . You must be aware that the merchant fleet has been in crisis since the war . . . Even here you can find ocean-going captains who've been unable to find commissions and who have to take positions as first or even second mates . . . Others have joined the Newfoundland or the North Sea fishing fleets.'

She spoke quite fast, but in a gentle and even tone.

'My husband didn't want to take on a commission in the Pacific, where there's more work, because he wouldn't have been able to come back to Europe more than once every two years . . . Shortly after we got married, some Americans bought the *Seeteufel* in the name of a German shipping firm . . . Olaf first came to Fécamp looking specifically for more schooners to buy . . . Now you must see . . . The aim was to run booze to the USA . . . Substantial firms were set up with American money . . . They have offices in France, Holland, or Germany . . . The truth is that my husband works for one of these companies. The *Seeteufel* sails what's called *Rum Alley*. It doesn't really have anything to do with Germany.'

'Is he at sea at the moment?' Maigret asked, keeping his eyes on that pretty face, which struck him as an honest and even at times a touching one.

'I don't think so. You must realize that the sailings aren't as regular as those of a liner. But I always try to keep abreast of the *Seeteufel*'s position. At the moment he ought to be in Bremen, or very nearly there.'

'Have you ever been to Norway?'

'Never! I've actually never left Normandy, so to speak. Just a couple of times, for short stays in Paris.'

'With your husband?'

'Yes . . . On our honeymoon, as well.'

'He's got fair hair, hasn't he?'

'Yes . . . Why do you ask?'

'And a thin, close-cropped blond moustache?'

'Yes . . . I can show you a picture of him if you like.'

She opened a door and went out. Maigret could hear her moving about in the bedroom next door.

She was out for longer than made sense, and the noises of doors opening and closing and of comings and goings around the house were just as illogical.

At last she came back, looking somewhat perplexed and apologetic.

'Please excuse me . . . ' she said. 'I can't manage to put my hand on that photo . . . A house with children is always upside down . . . '

'One more question . . . To how many people did you give a copy of this photograph of yourself?'

Maigret showed her the archive print he'd

41

been given by the photographer. Madame Swaan went bright red and stuttered:

'I don't understand . . . '

'Your husband presumably has one?'

'Yes . . . We were engaged when . . . '

'Does any other man have a print?'

She was on the verge of tears. The quiver of her lips gave away her distress.

'No, nobody.'

'Thank you, madame. That will be all.'

As he was leaving a little girl slipped into the hallway. Maigret had no need to memorize her features. She was the spitting image of Pietr the Latvian!

'Olga! . . . ' her mother scolded, as she hustled her back through a half-open door.

Maigret was back outside in the rain and the wind.

'Goodbye, madame . . . '

He caught a final glimpse of her through the closing door. He was aware that he had left her at a loss, after bursting in on her in the warmth of her own home. He picked up a trace in her eyes of something uncertain but undoubtedly akin to anxiety as she shut her front door.

5

The Russian Drunkard

You don't boast about these kinds of things, they would raise a laugh if they were mentioned out loud, but all the same, they call for a kind of heroism.

Maigret hadn't slept. From 5.30 to 8 a.m. he'd been shaken about in draughty railway carriages. Ever since he'd changed trains at La Bréauté he'd been soaked through. Now his shoes squelched out dirty water at every step and his bowler was a shapeless mess. His overcoat and trousers were sopping wet.

The wind was slapping him with more rain. The alleyway was deserted. It was no more than a steep path between garden walls. The middle of it had turned into a raging torrent.

He stood still for quite a while. Even his pipe had got wet in his pocket. There was no way of hiding near the villa. All he could do was stick as close as possible to a wall and wait.

Anyone coming by would catch sight of him and look round. He might have to stay there for hours on end. There was no definite proof that there was a man in the house. And even if he were there, why should he come out?

Grumpy as he was, Maigret filled his wet pipe with tobacco all the same, and wedged himself as best he could into a cranny in the wall . . .

This was no place for a detective chief inspector of the Police Judiciaire. At most it was a job for a new recruit. Between the age of twenty-two and thirty he'd stood this sort of watch a hundred times over.

He had a terrible time getting a match to light. The emery board on the side of the box was coming off in strips. If one of the sticks hadn't finally ignited, maybe even Maigret would have given up and gone home.

He couldn't see anything from where he was standing except a low wall and the green-painted railing of the villa. He had brambles at his ankles and a draught all down his neck.

Fécamp was laid out beneath him, but he could not see the town. He could only hear the roar of the sea and now and again a siren or the sound of a car.

After half an hour on watch he saw a woman with a shopping basket, who looked like a cook, making her way up the steep slope. She only saw Maigret when she passed close by him. His huge, unmoving shape standing next to the wall in a wind-swept alley so scared her that she started to run.

Perhaps she worked for one of the villas at the top of the rise? A few minutes later a man appeared at the bend and stared at Maigret from afar. Then a woman joined him, and both went back inside.

It was a ridiculous situation. The inspector knew there wasn't one chance in ten that his surveillance would be of any use.

Yet he stuck it out — just because of a vague feeling that didn't even deserve to be called an intuition. In fact it was a pet theory of his that he'd never worked out in full and remained vague in his mind, but which he dubbed for his own use *the theory of the crack in the wall*.

Inside every wrong-doer and crook there lives a human being. In addition, of course, there is an opponent in a game, and it's the player that the police are inclined to see. As a rule, that's what they go after.

Some crime or offence is committed. The match starts on the basis of more or less objective facts. It's a problem with one or more unknowns that a rational mind tries to solve.

Maigret worked like any other policeman. Like everyone else, he used the amazing tools that men like Bertillon, Reiss and Locard have given the police — anthropometry, the principle of the trace, and so forth — and that have turned detection into forensic science. But what he sought, what he waited and watched out for, was the *crack in the wall*. In other words, the instant when the human being comes out from behind the opponent.

At the Majestic he'd seen the player. But here, he had a premonition of something else. The tidy, quiet villa wasn't one of the props that Pietr used to play his hand. Especially the wife and the children he'd seen and heard: they belonged to a different physical and moral order.

That's why he was waiting, albeit in a foul mood, for he was too fond of his big cast-iron stove and his office with glasses of frothy beer on the table not to be miserable in such awful weather.

He'd started his watch a little after 10.30. At half past noon he heard footsteps scrunching the gravel and swift, practised movements opening the gate, which brought a figure to within three metres of the inspector. The lie of the land made it impossible for Maigret to retreat. So he stood his ground unwaveringly, or, to be more precise, inertly, standing on two legs that could be seen in the round through the sopping wet trousers that clung to them.

The man leaving the villa was wearing a poor-quality belted trenchcoat, with its worn-out collar upturned. He was also wearing a grey cap. The get-up made him look very young. He went down the hill with his hands in his pockets, all hunched up and shivering because of the contrast in temperature.

He was obliged to pass within a metre of the Detective Chief Inspector. He chose that moment to slow down, take a packet of cigarettes out of his pocket and light up. It was as if he'd positively tried to get his face into the light so as to allow the detective to study it in detail!

Maigret let him go on a few paces, then set off on his tail, with a frown on his face. His pipe had gone out. His whole being exuded a sense of displeasure as well as an ardent desire to understand.

The man in the trenchcoat looked like the Latvian and yet did not resemble him! Same height: about 1 m 68cm. At a pinch he could be the same age, though in the outfit he was wearing he looked closer to twenty-six than thirty-two. There was nothing to determine that this man was not the original of the 'word-picture' that Maigret knew by heart and also had on a piece of paper in his pocket.

And yet . . . it was not the same man! For one thing, his eyes had a vaguer, more sentimental expression. They were a lighter shade of grey, as if the rain had scrubbed them. Nor did he have a blond toothbrush moustache. But that wasn't the only thing that made him different.

Maigret was struck by other details. His outfit was nothing like that of an officer of the merchant fleet. It didn't even fit the villa, given the comfortable middle-class style of living that it implied.

His shoes were worn and the heels had been redone. Because of the mud, the man hitched up his trouser legs, showing faded grey cotton socks that had been clumsily darned.

There were lots of stains on the trenchcoat. Overall, the man fitted a type that Maigret knew well: the migrant low-lifer, predominantly of Eastern European origin, who slept in squalid lodging houses and sometimes in railway stations. A type not often seen outside Paris, but accustomed to travelling in third-class carriages when not riding the footboards or hopping freight trains.

He got proof of his insight a few minutes later. Fécamp doesn't have any genuine low dives, but behind the harbour there are two or three squalid bars favoured by dockhands and seamen.

Ten metres before these places there's a regular café kept clean and bright. The man in the trenchcoat walked right past it and straight into the least prepossessing of the bars, where he put his elbow on the counter in a way that Maigret saw right through.

It was the straightforwardly vulgar body-language of a guttersnipe. Even if he'd tried, Maigret couldn't have imitated it. The inspector followed the man into the bar. He'd ordered an absinthe substitute and was just standing there, wordless, with a blank stare on his face. He didn't register Maigret's presence, though the inspector was now right next to him.

Through a gap in the man's jacket Maigret could see that his linen was dirty. That's not something that can be simulated, either! His shirt and collar — now not much more than a ribbon — had been worn for days, maybe for weeks on end. They'd been slept in — God knows where! They'd been sweated in and rained on.

The man's suit was not unstylish, but it bore the same signs and told the same miserable story of a vagrant life.

'Same again!'

The glass was empty, and the barman refilled it, serving Maigret a measure of spirits at the same time.

'So you're back in these parts again? . . . '

The man didn't answer. He downed his drink in one gulp and gestured for a refill straight away.

'Anything to eat? . . . I've got some pickled herring . . . '

Maigret had sidled up to a small stove, and stood in front of it to warm his back, now as shiny as an umbrella.

'Come to think of it . . . I had a man in here last week from your part of the world . . . Russian he was, from Archangelsk . . . Sailing a Swedish three-master that had to put in to port because of the bad weather . . . Hardly had time to drink his fill, I can tell you! . . . Had a devil of a job on his hands . . . Torn sails, snapped yards, you name it . . . '

The man, now on his fourth imitation absinthe, was drinking steadily. The barman filled his glass every time it was empty, glancing at Maigret with a conniving wink.

'As for Captain Swaan, I ain't seen him since you was here last.'

Maigret shuddered. The man in the trenchcoat who'd now downed his fifth neat ersatz absinthe staggered towards the stove, bumped into the detective and held out his hands towards the warmth.

'I'll have a herring, all the same . . . ' he said.

He had a quite strong accent — a Russian accent, as far as the detective could judge.

There they were, next to each other, shoulder to shoulder, so to speak. The man wiped his face with his hand several times, and his eyes grew ever more murky.

'Where's my glass? . . . ' he inquired testily.

It had to be put in his hand. As he drank he stared at Maigret and pouted with disgust.

There was no mistaking that expression! As if to assert his opinion all the more clearly, he threw his glass to the ground, leaned on the back of a chair and muttered something in a foreign tongue.

The barman, somewhat concerned, found a way of getting close to Maigret and whispering quietly in a way that was nonetheless audible to the Russian:

'Don't take any notice of him. He's always like that . . . '

The man gave a drunkard's strangled laugh. He slumped into the chair, put his head in both his hands and stayed like that until a plate of herring was pushed over the table between his elbows. The barman shook his shoulder.

'Eat up! . . . It'll do you good . . . '

The man laughed again. It was more like a bitter cough. He turned round so he could see Maigret and stare at him aggressively, then he pushed the plate of herring off the table.

'More drink! . . . '

The barman raised his arms and grunted as if it was an excuse:

'Russians, I ask you!'

Then he put his finger to his head and turned it, as if he was tightening a loose screw.

★   ★   ★

Maigret had pushed his bowler to the back of his head. His clothes were steaming, giving off a grey haze. He was only up to his second glass of spirits.

'I'll have some herring!' he said.

He was still eating it with a slice of bread when

50

the Russian got up on unsteady legs, looked around as if he didn't know what to do and grinned for the third time when he set eyes on Maigret.

Then he slumped down at the bar, took a glass from the shelf and a bottle from the enamel sink where it was being kept cool in water. He helped himself without watching how much he was taking and smacked his tongue as he drank.

Eventually he took a 100 franc note out of his pocket.

'Is that enough, you swine?' he asked the waiter.

He threw the banknote up in the air. The barman had to fish it out of the sink.

The Russian struggled with the door handle, which wouldn't open. There was almost a fight because the barman tried to help his customer, who kept elbowing him away.

At long last the trenchcoat faded away into the mist and rain along the harbour-side, going towards the station.

'That's an odd 'un,' the barman sighed, intending to be heard by Maigret, who was paying his bill.

'Is he often in?'

'Now and again . . . Once he spent the whole night here, on the bench where you're sitting . . . He's a real Russian! . . . Some Russian sailors who were here in Fécamp at the same time as he was told me so . . . Apparently he's quite educated . . . Did you look at his hands? . . . '

'Don't you think he's got the same looks as

Captain Swaan? . . . '

'Oh! So you know him . . . Well, of course he does! But not so much as you'd mistake one for the other . . . All the same . . . For ages I thought it was his brother.'

★　★　★

The beige silhouette vanished round a corner. Maigret started to walk faster. He caught up with the Russian just as he was going into the third-class waiting room at the station. The man slumped onto a bench and once again put his head in his hands.

An hour later they were in the same railway compartment with a cattle trader from Yvetot who launched into shaggy-dog stories in Norman dialect. Now and again he nudged Maigret to draw his attention to the other passenger.

The Russian slipped down little by little and ended up in a crumpled heap on the bench. His face was pale, his chin was on his chest, and his half-open mouth stank of cheap spirits.

6

Au Roi de Sicile

The Russian woke up at La Bréauté and stayed awake from then on. It has to be said that the express from Le Havre to Paris was completely packed. Maigret and his travelling companion had to stand in the corridor, stuck near a door, watching random scenery fly by as the darkness swallowed it bit by bit.

The man in the trenchcoat seemed entirely unflustered at having a detective by his side. On arrival at Gare Saint-Lazare, he didn't try to use the milling crowd to throw Maigret off his tail. On the contrary: he went down the great staircase in leisurely fashion, realized that his packet of cigarettes was wet through, bought another one at a station stall and was on the verge of going into a bar. Then he changed his mind and began to loiter along the pavement. He made a sorry sight: a man so absent from the world and in such low spirits that he was no longer capable of reacting to anything.

★   ★   ★

It's a long way from Gare Saint-Lazare to Hôtel de Ville, there's the whole city centre to get through. Between six and seven in the evening, pedestrians flood the pavements in ocean waves, and traffic pulses along the streets like blood pumping down an artery.

With his mud- and grease-stained coat belted at the waist and his recycled heels, the narrow-shouldered pauper waded on through the bright lights and the bustle. People elbowed and bumped into him, but he never stopped or looked over his shoulder.

He took the shortest route, by way of Rue du 4-Septembre and then through Les Halles, which proved he'd gone this way before.

He reached the ghetto of Paris, that's to say, the area around Rue des Rosiers, in the Marais. He sidled past shop fronts with signs in Yiddish, kosher butchers and window displays of *matzot*. At one corner, giving on to a passageway so dark and deep it looked like a tunnel, a woman tried to take him by the arm, but let go without his saying a word. Presumably he had made a strong impression on her.

At last he ended up in Rue du Roi-de-Sicile, a winding street giving on to dead-end alleys, narrow lanes and overpopulated courtyards — a half-Jewish, half-Polish colony. Two hundred metres along, he dived into a hotel entrance.

★　★　★

The hotel's name, Au Roi de Sicile, was written out on ceramic tiles. Underneath the nameplate were notices in Yiddish, Polish, maybe also Russian and other suchlike languages that Maigret didn't know.

There was a building site next door where the remains of a house that had needed buttressing to keep it standing were still visible. It was still raining, but in this rat-trap there was no wind.

Maigret heard a window closing with a sharp clack on the third floor of the hotel. No less resolutely than the Russian, he went inside.

There was no door in the entrance hall, just a staircase . . . At the mezzanine level there was a kind of glass box where a Jewish family was having dinner.

Inspector Maigret knocked, but instead of opening the door the concierge raised a hatch, like at a ticket counter. A rancid smell wafted from it. The man was wearing a skullcap. His overweight wife carried on with her meal.

'What is it?'

'Police! Give me the name of the tenant who just came in.'

The man grunted something in his own language, then went to a drawer and brought out a grimy ledger that he shoved through the hatch without a word.

At the same instant Maigret sensed he was being watched from the unlit stairwell. He turned round quickly and saw an eye shining from about ten stairs above.

'Room number?'

'Thirty-two . . . '

He thumbed through the ledger and read:

Fyodor Yurevich, age 28, born Vilna, labourer, and Anna Gorskin, age 25, born Odessa, no occupation.

The Jew had gone back to the table to continue eating his meal like a man without a worry. Maigret drummed on the window. The hotel-keeper stood up slowly and reluctantly.

'How long has he been staying here?'

'About three years.'

'What about Anna Gorskin?'

'She's been here longer than he has . . . Maybe four and a half years . . . '

'What do they live on?'

'You've read the book . . . He's a labourer.'

'Don't try that on me!' Maigret riposted in a voice that sufficed to change the hotelier's attitude.

'It's not for me to stick my nose in where it's not wanted, is it?' he now said in an oilier tone. 'He pays up on time. He comes and he goes and it's not my job to follow him around . . . '

'Does anybody come to see him?'

'Sometimes . . . I've got over sixty tenants in here and I can't keep an eye on all of them at once . . . As long as they're doing no harm! . . . Anyway, as you're from the police you should know all about this establishment . . . I make proper returns . . . Officer Vermouillet can confirm that . . . He's the one who comes every week . . . '

Maigret turned around on an impulse and called out:

'Anna Gorskin, come down now!'

There was a ruffling noise in the stairway, then the sound of footsteps, and finally a woman stepped out into a patch of light.

She looked older than the ledger's claim of twenty-five. That was probably hereditary. Like many Jewish women of her age, she had put on weight, but she was still quite good-looking. She had remarkable eyes: very dark pupils set in amazingly white and shining corneas. But the rest of her was so sloppy as to spoil that first impression. Her black, greasy and uncombed hair fell in thick bunches onto her neck. She was wearing a worn-out dressing gown, loosely tied and allowing a glimpse of her underwear. Her stockings were rolled down above her thick knees.

'What were you doing in the stairwell?'

'I live here, don't I? . . . '

Maigret sensed straight away what kind of a woman he was dealing with. Excitable, irreverent, hammer and tongs. At the drop of a hat she could throw a fit, rouse the entire building, give an ear-splitting scream and probably accuse him of outlandish offences. Did she perhaps know she was unassailable? In any case, she looked at her enemy with defiance.

'You'd be better advised to go look after your man . . . '

'None of your business . . . '

The hotelier stayed behind his window, rocking his head from left to right, from right to left, with a morose and reproving look on his face; but there was laughter in his eyes.

'When did Fyodor leave?'

'Yesterday evening . . . At eleven . . . '

She was lying! Plain as day! But there was no

point coming at her head-on — unless he wanted to pin back her arms and march her down to the station.

'Where does he work?'

'Wherever he chooses . . . '

You could see her breasts heave under her ill-fitting dressing gown. There was a hostile, haughty sneer on her face.

'What've the police got against Fyodor, anyway?'

Maigret decided to say rather quietly:

'Get upstairs . . . '

'I'll go when I feel like it! You ain't got no right to order me about.'

What was the point of answering back and risking creating an ugly incident that would only hold things up? Maigret shut the ledger and handed it back to the hotel-keeper.

'All above board and hunky-dory, right?' the latter said, after gesturing at the young woman to keep quiet. But she stood her ground with her fists on her hips, one side of her lit by the light from the hotelier's office, the other in darkness.

Maigret looked at her again. She met his gaze straight on and felt the need to mutter:

'You don't scare me one bit . . . '

He just shrugged and then made his way down a staircase so narrow his shoulders touched both of its squalid walls.

★ ★ ★

In the corridor he ran into two bare-necked Poles who turned away as soon as they saw him. The street was wet, making the cobblestones glint. In every corner, in the smallest pools of shadow, in the back alleys and passageways you could sense a swarm of humiliated and rebellious humanity. Shadowy figures flitted past. Shop-keepers sold products whose very names were unknown in France.

Less than 100 metres away was Rue de Rivoli and Rue Saint-Antoine — broad, well-lit streets with trams, market stalls and the city police . . . Maigret caught a passing street urchin with a cauliflower ear by the shoulder:

'Go fetch me a policeman from Place Saint-Paul . . . '

But the lad just looked at him with fear in his eyes, then answered in some incomprehensible tongue. He didn't know a word of French!

The inspector then spied a beggar.

'Here's a five franc coin . . . Take this note to the cop at Place Saint-Paul.'

The tramp understood. Ten minutes later a uniformed sergeant turned up.

'Call the Police Judiciaire and tell them to send me an officer straight away . . . Dufour, if he's free . . . '

Maigret cooled his heels for at least another half-hour. People went into the hotel. Others came out. But the light stayed on at the third-floor window, second from the left.

Anna Gorskin appeared at the doorway. She'd put on a greenish overcoat over her dressing gown. She was hatless and despite the rain she was wearing red satin sandals. She splashed her way across the street. Maigret kept out of sight, in the shadows.

She went into a store and came out a few minutes later laden with a host of small white packets, plus two bottles. She vanished back into the hotel.

★ ★ ★

At long last Inspector Dufour showed up. He was thirty-five and spoke three languages quite fluently, which made him a precious asset. But he had a habit of making the simplest things sound complicated. He could turn a common burglary or a banal snatch-and-grab case into a dramatic mystery, tying himself up in knots of his own making. But as he was also uncommonly persistent, he was highly suitable for a well-defined job like staking out or tailing a suspect.

Maigret gave him a description of Fyodor Yurevich and his girlfriend.

'I'll send you a back-up. If one of those two comes out, stay on their tail. But one of you has to stay behind to man the stake-out . . . Got that?'

'Are we still on the Étoile du Nord case? . . . It's a mafia hit, right?'

Maigret went off without answering. He got to his office at Quai des Orfèvres fifteen minutes later, dispatched an officer to back up Dufour, leaned over his stove and swore at Jean for not stoking it up to a red-hot glow. He hung his sopping greatcoat on the back of the door. It had gone so stiff that the shape of his shoulders could still be made out in it.

'Did my wife call?'

'This morning . . . She was told you were out on a case . . . '

She was used to that. He knew that if he went home she would just give him a kiss, stir the pot on the stove and serve him a delicious plate of stew. The most she would dare — but only when he'd sat down to eat — would be to put her chin on her hand and ask:

'Everything OK? . . . '

The meal would always be ready for him, whether he turned up at noon or at five.

'Torrence?' he asked Jean.

'He called at 7 a.m.'

'From the Majestic?'

'I don't know. He asked if you'd left.'

'What else?'

'He called again at ten past five this afternoon. He asked for you to be told he was waiting for you.'

Maigret had only had a herring to eat since the morning. He stayed upright in front of his stove for a while. It was beginning to roar, for Maigret had an unrivalled knack for getting even the least combustible coal to catch. Then he plodded his way to the cupboard, where there was an enamel sink, a towel, a mirror and a suitcase. He dragged the case into the middle of his office, undressed and put on clean underwear and dry clothes. He rubbed his unshaven chin.

'It'll have to do . . . '

He looked lovingly at the fire, which was now burning grandly, placed two chairs next to it and carefully laid out his wet clothes on them. There was one sandwich left over from the previous night on his desk, and he wolfed it down, still standing, ready to depart. Only there wasn't any beer. He was more than a little parched.

'If anything at all comes in for me, I'm at the Majestic,' he said to Jean. 'Get them to call me.'

And at long last he slumped into the back seat of a taxi.

7

The Third Interval

Torrence wasn't to be found in the lobby, but in a first-floor room in front of a top-notch dinner. He explained with a broad wink:

'It's all the manager's fault! . . . He practically went down on bended knee to get me to accept this room and the gourmet meals he sends up . . . '

He was speaking in a whisper. He pointed to a door.

'The Mortimers are next door . . . '

'Mortimer came back?'

'Around six this morning. In a foul mood. Wet, dirty, with chalk or lime all over his clothes . . . '

'What did he say?'

'Nothing . . . He tried to get back to his room without being noticed. But they told him his wife had waited up for him in the bar. And she had! . . . She'd ended up befriending a Brazilian couple . . . They had to keep the bar open all night just for them . . . She was atrociously drunk . . . '

'And then?'

'He went as white as a ghost. His mouth went all twisted. He said a curt hello to the Brazilians, then took his wife by the armpits and dragged her off without another word . . . I reckon she slept it off until four this afternoon . . . There wasn't a sound from their suite until then . . . Then I heard whispering . . . Mortimer rang the front desk to have the newspapers brought up . . . '

'Nothing about the case in the papers, I hope?'

'Not a word. They've respected the embargo. Just a two-liner saying that a corpse had been found on the Étoile du Nord and that the police were treating it as suicide.'

'Next?'

'Room service brought them up some lemon juice. Mortimer took a stroll around the lobby, went straight past me two or three times, looking worried. He sent coded wires to his New York bank and to his secretary, who's been in London these past few days . . . '

'That's it?'

'At the moment they're just finishing dinner. Oysters, cold chicken, salad. The hotel keeps me abreast of everything. The manager is so delighted to have me shut away up here that he'll sweat blood to do me any favour I ask. That's why he came up just now to tell me that the Mortimers have got tickets to see *The Epic* at the Gymnase Theatre tonight. A four-acter by someone or other . . . '

'Pietr's suite?'

'Quiet as the grave! Nobody has been in it. I locked the door and put a blob of wax on the keyhole, so nobody can get in without my knowing . . . '

Maigret had picked up a chicken leg and was chewing at it quite shamelessly while looking round for a stove that wasn't there. In the end he sat on the radiator and asked:

'Isn't there anything to drink?'

Torrence poured him a glass of a superb Macon blanc, which his chief drank thirstily. Then there was a scratching at the door and a valet entered in a conspiratorial manner.

'The manager requests me to inform you that Mr and Mrs Mortimer's car has been brought to the front.'

Maigret glanced at the table still laden with food with the same sorrow he had expressed in his eyes on leaving the stove in his office.

'I'll go,' he said regretfully. 'You stay here.'

He tidied himself up in front of the mirror, wiping his mouth and his chin. A moment later he was in a taxi waiting for the Mortimer-Levingstons to get into their limousine.

* * *

They weren't long in coming. Mortimer was wearing a black overcoat that hid his dinner jacket; she was swaddled in furs, as on the previous night.

She must have still been tired, because her husband was discreetly propping her up with one hand. The limousine set off without a whisper.

Maigret hadn't known that this was an opening night at the Gymnase, and he was almost refused entry. City police formed a guard of honour beneath the canopy. In spite of the rain passers-by stopped to watch the guests alight from their cars. Inspector Maigret had to

65

ask to see the manager and wait his turn in corridors, where he stuck out as the only person not wearing formal attire. The manager was at his wits' end, waving his arms about.

'There's nothing I'd like better than to oblige! But you're the twentieth person to ask me for a 'spare seat'! There aren't any spare seats! There aren't any seats! ... And you're not even properly dressed! ... '

He was being assailed from all quarters.

'Can't you see? Put yourself in my shoes ... '

In the end Maigret had to stay standing up next to a door with the usherettes and the programme-sellers.

The Mortimer-Levingstons had a box. There were six people in it, of whom one was a princess and another a government minister. People came and went. Hands were kissed, smiles exchanged.

The curtain rose on a sunlit garden. Shushes, murmurs, footsteps. Finally the actor's voice could be heard, wobbly at first but then more confident, creating an atmosphere.

Latecomers were still taking their seats. More shushing. Somewhere a woman giggled.

Mortimer was more lord of the manor than ever. Evening dress suited him to a tee. The white shirt-front brought out the ivory hue of his skin.

Did he see Maigret? Did he not? An usherette brought the inspector a stool to sit on, but he had to share it with a portly lady in black silk, the mother of one of the actresses.

First interval, second interval. Comings and goings in the boxes. Artificial enthusiasm.

Greetings exchanged between the parterre and the circle. The foyer, the corridors and even the front steps buzzed like a hive in high summer. Names were dropped in a whisper — names of maharajahs, ministers, statesmen and artists.

Mortimer left his box on three occasions, reappearing in a stage-box and then in the pit, and finally to have a chat with a former prime minister, whose hearty laugh could be heard twenty rows away.

End of Act Three. Flowers on the stage. A skinny actress was given an ovation. Seats flapping up made a racket and shuffling feet sounded like the swell of the sea. When Maigret turned to look up at the Americans' box, Mortimer-Levingston had vanished.

★   ★   ★

Now for the fourth and last act. That was when anybody who had an excuse got into the wings and the actors' and actresses' dressing-rooms. Others besieged the cloakrooms. There was much fussing over cars and taxis.

Maigret lost at least ten minutes looking around inside the theatre. Then, without hat or coat, he had to quiz the doorman and the policemen on duty outside to find out what he needed to know.

He learned eventually that the Mortimers' olive-green limousine had just driven off. He was shown where it had been parked, outside a bar often frequented by traders in cloakroom receipts. The car had gone towards Porte

Saint-Martin. The American plutocrat hadn't retrieved his overcoat.

Outside, clumps of theatre-goers huddled wherever they could get out of the rain.

Maigret smoked a pipe with his hands in his pockets and a grumpy look on his face. The bell rang. People flocked inside. Even the municipal police went in to watch the last act.

The Grands Boulevards looked as scruffy as they always did at 11 p.m. The shafts of rain lit by the streetlamps were thinning out. The audience spewed out of a cinema which then switched off its lighting, brought in its billboards, and shut its doors. People stood in line at a bus stop, beneath a green-striped lamp-post. When the bus came there was an argument, because there were no number-tags left in the ticket machine. A policeman got involved. Long after the bus had left he remained in contentious discussion with an indignant fat man.

At last a limousine came to a gliding halt on the tarmac. The door opened even before it was at a standstill. Mortimer-Levingston, in tails but without a hat, bounded up the stairs and went into the warm and brightly lit lobby. Maigret took a look at the chauffeur. He was 100 per cent American: he had a hard face with a jutting chin, and he sat stock still in his seat as if he'd been turned to stone by his uniform.

The inspector opened one of the padded doors barely an inch or two. Mortimer was standing at the back of his box. A sarcastic actor was speaking his lines in staccato. Curtain. Flowers. Thunderous applause.

People rushing for the exits. More shushing. The lead actor uttered the name of the author and went to fetch him from a box to bring him centre stage. Mortimer kissed some hands and shook others, gave a 100 franc tip to the usherette who brought him their coats. His wife was pale-faced, with blue rings under her eyes. When they had got back into their car there was a moment of indecision.

The couple were having an argument. Mrs Levingston was agitated. Her husband lit a cigarette and put out his lighter with an angry swipe of his hand. Eventually, he said something to the chauffeur through the intercom tube, and the car set off, with Maigret in a taxi following behind.

★   ★   ★

It was half past midnight. Rue La Fayette. The white colonnade of La Trinite was sheathed in scaffolding. Rue de Clichy.

The limousine stopped in Rue Fontaine, outside Pickwick's Bar. A concierge in a blue and gold uniform. Coat check. A red curtain lifted and a snatch of tango emerged.

Maigret went in behind the couple and sat at a table near the door, which must have always stayed empty because it caught every draught.

The Mortimers had been seated near to the jazz band. The American read the menu and chose what he would have for supper. A professional dancer bowed to his wife. She went on the floor. Levingston watched her with remarkable intensity. She exchanged a few remarks with her dancing partner but never once turned towards the corner where Maigret was sitting.

Most people here were in formal attire, but there were also a few foreigners in lounge suits. Maigret waved away a hostess who tried to sit at his table. A bottle of champagne was put in front of him, automatically. There were streamers all about. Puffer balls flew through the air. One landed on Maigret's nose, and he glowered at the old lady who'd aimed it at him.

Mrs Mortimer had gone back to her table. The dancer wandered around the floor for a moment then went towards the exit and lit a cigarette. Suddenly he lifted the red plush curtain and vanished. It took three minutes for Maigret to think of going to see what was happening outside.

The dancer had gone.

The rest of the night dragged on drearily. The Mortimers ate copiously — caviar and truffles *au champagne*, then lobster *à l'américaine*, followed by cheese.

Mrs Mortimer didn't go back to the dance-floor.

Maigret didn't like champagne, but he sipped at it to slake his thirst. He made the mistake of nibbling the roasted almonds on the table, and that made him even thirstier.

He checked the time on his wristwatch: 2 a.m.

People began leaving the nightspot. Nobody took the slightest notice of a dancer performing her routine. A drunk foreigner with three women at his table was making more noise than all the other customers put together. The professional dancer, who had stayed outside for only fifteen minutes, had taken some other ladies round the dance-floor. But it was all over. Weariness had set in.

Mrs Mortimer looked worn out; her eyelids were dark blue.

Her husband signalled to an attendant. Fur coat, overcoat and top hat were brought.

Maigret sensed that the dancer, who was talking to the sax player, was watching him nervously.

He summoned the manager, who kept him waiting. He lost a few minutes.

When he finally got outside, the Americans' limousine was just going round the corner into Rue Notre-Dame-de-Lorette. There were half a dozen taxis waiting at the rank opposite. Maigret began crossing the road.

A gunshot rang out. Maigret put his hand to his chest, looked around, could not see anything, but heard the footsteps of someone running away down Rue Pigalle.

He staggered on for a few metres, propelled by his own inertia. The concierge ran up to him and held him upright. People came out of Pickwick's Bar to see what was going on. Among them Maigret noticed the tense figure of the professional dancer.

8

Maigret Gets Serious

Taxi drivers who 'do nights' in Montmartre don't need things spelled out to them and often get the point without a word being said.

When the shot was fired, one of the waiting drivers at the rank opposite Pickwick's Bar was about to open the passenger door for Maigret, not knowing who he was. But maybe he guessed from the way the inspector held himself that he was about to give a ride to a cop.

Customers at a small bar on the opposite side of the street came running. Soon there would be a whole crowd gathered round the wounded man. In the blink of an eye the driver lent a hand to the doorman who was propping up Maigret, without a clue what else to do. In less than half a minute the taxi was on its way with the inspector in the back.

The car drove on for ten minutes or so and came to a halt in an empty street. The driver got out the front, opened the passenger door, and saw his customer sitting in an almost normal posture, with one hand under his jacket.

'I can see it's no big deal, like I thought. Where can I take you?'

Still, Maigret looked quite upset, mainly because it was a flesh wound. His chest had been torn; the bullet had grazed a rib and exited near his shoulder blade.

'Quai des Orfèvres . . . '

The driver muttered something that couldn't be made out. En route, the inspector changed his mind.

'Take me to Hôtel Majestic . . . Drop me off at the service entrance on Rue de Ponthieu . . . '

He screwed up his handkerchief into a ball and stuffed it over his wound. He noted that the bleeding had stopped.

As he progressed towards the heart of Paris he appeared to be in less pain, but increasingly worried.

★   ★   ★

The taxi-driver tried to help him out. Maigret brushed him off and crossed the pavement with a steady gait. In a narrow entranceway he found the watchman drowsing behind his counter.

'Anything happen?'

'What do you mean?'

It was cold. Maigret went back out to pay the driver, who grunted once again because all he was getting for his great exploit was a measly 100 franc tip.

In the state he was in, Maigret was an impressive sight. He was still pressing his handkerchief to his chest wound, under his jacket. He held one shoulder higher than the other, but all the same he was being careful to save his strength. He was slightly light-headed. Now and again he felt as if he was floating on air, and he had to make an effort to get a grip on himself so as to see clearly and move normally.

He climbed an iron stairway that led to the upper floors, opened a door, found he was in a corridor, got lost in the labyrinth and came upon another stairway identical to the first, except that it had a different number on it.

He was going round in circles in the hotel's back passages. Luckily he came across a chef in a white toque, who stared at him in fright.

'Take me to the first floor . . . Room next to the Mortimers' suite.'

In the first place, however, the chef wasn't privy to the names of the hotel guests. In the second place, he was awed by the five blood streaks that Maigret had put on his face when he'd wiped it with his hand. He was struck dumb by this giant of a man lost in a narrow servants' corridor with his coat worn over his shoulders and his hand permanently stuck to his chest, distorting the shape of his waistcoat and jacket.

'Police!'

Maigret was running out of patience.

He felt the threat of a dizzy spell coming on. His wound was burning hot and prickling, as if long needles were going through it.

At long last the chef set off without looking over his shoulder. Soon Maigret felt carpet beneath his feet, and he realized he'd left the service area and was in the hotel proper. He kept an eye on the room numbers. He was on the odd-numbered side.

Eventually he came across a terrified valet.

'The Mortimers' suite?'

'Downstairs . . . But . . . You . . . '

He went down a stairway, and meanwhile, the news spread among the staff that there was a strange wounded man wandering about the hotel like a ghost.

Maigret stopped to rest against a wall for a moment and left a bloodstain on it; three very dark red drops also fell on the carpet.

At last he caught sight of the Mortimers' suite and, beside it, the door of the room where Torrence was to be found. He got to the door, walking slightly crabwise, pushed it open . . .

'Torrence! . . . '

The lights were on. The table was still laden with food and drink. Maigret's thick eyebrows puckered. He could not see his partner. On the other hand he could smell something in the air that reminded him of a hospital.

He took a few more wobbly steps. And suddenly came to a stop by a settee.

A black-leather-shod foot was sticking out from under it.

★   ★   ★

He had to try three times over. As soon as he took his hand off his wound, blood spurted out of it at an alarming rate. Finally he took the towel that was lying on the table and wedged it under his waistcoat, which he fastened as tight as he could. The smell in the room made him nauseous.

He lifted one end of the settee with weak arms and swung it round on two of its legs. It was

75

what he expected: Torrence, all crumpled up, with his shoulder twisted round as if he'd had his bones broken to make him fit into a small space.

There was a bandage over the lower part of his face, but it wasn't knotted. Maigret got down on his knees.

Every gesture was measured and even slow — no doubt because of the state he was in. His hand hovered over Torrence's chest before daring to feel for his heart. When it reached its target, Maigret froze. He didn't stir but stayed kneeling on the carpet and stared at his partner.

Torrence was dead! Involuntarily Maigret twisted his lips and clenched his fist. His eyes clouded over and he uttered a terrible oath in the shut and silent room.

It could have sounded merely grotesque. But it did not! It was fearsome! Tragic! Terrifying!

Maigret's face had hardened. He didn't cry. That must be something he was unable to do. But his expression was full of such anger and pain as well as astonishment that it came close to looking stunned.

Torrence was thirty years old. For the last five years he had worked pretty much exclusively for Inspector Maigret.

His mouth was wide open, as if he'd made a desperate attempt at getting his last gasp of air.

One floor up, a traveller was taking off his shoes, directly over the dead man's body.

Maigret looked around to seek out the enemy. He was breathing heavily.

Several minutes passed in this manner. Maigret got up only when he sensed some hidden process beginning to work inside him.

He went to the window, opened it and looked out on the empty roadway of the Champs-Élysées. He let the breeze cool his brow then went to pick up the gag he'd ripped off Torrence's mouth.

It was a damask table napkin embroidered with the monogram of the Majestic. It still gave off a faint whiff of chloroform. Maigret stayed upright. His mind was a blank, with just a few shapeless thoughts knocking about inside it and raising painful associations.

Once again, as he had done in the hotel passageway, he leaned his shoulder on the wall, and quite suddenly his features seemed to sink. He had aged; his spirits were low. Was he at that moment in time on the verge of bursting into tears? No, he was too big and substantial. He was made of a tougher cloth.

The settee was squint and touching the table that hadn't been cleared. On one plate chicken bones were mixed up with cigarette butts.

The inspector stretched out an arm towards the telephone. But he didn't pick up the receiver. Instead, he snapped his fingers in anger, turned back towards the corpse and stared at it.

He scowled bitterly and ironically when he thought of all the regulations, formal procedures and precautions he had to observe to please the examining magistrate.

Did any of that matter? It was Torrence, for heaven's sake! Almost the same as if it had been himself, dammit!

Torrence, who was part of the team, who . . .

Despite his apparent calm he unbuttoned his colleague's waistcoat with such feverish energy that he snapped off two of its buttons. That's when he saw something that made his face go quite grey.

On Torrence's shirt, *exactly over the centre of his heart*, there was a small brown mark.

Smaller than a chickpea! There was just one single drop of blood, and it had coagulated into a clot no larger than a pinhead. Maigret's eyes clouded over, and he twisted his face into a grimace of outrage he could not express in words.

It was disgusting, but in terms of crime it was the very apex of skill! He need look no further. He knew what the trick was, because he'd learned about it a few months earlier, in an article in a German crime studies journal.

First the chloroform towel, which overpowers the victim in twenty to thirty seconds. Then the long needle. The murderer can take his time and find just the right place between the ribs to get it straight into the heart, taking a life without any noise or mess.

Exactly the same method had been used in Hamburg six months earlier.

A bullet can miss its targets or just wound a man — Maigret was living proof of that. But a needle plunged into the heart of a man already made inert kills him scientifically, with no margin of error.

★　★　★

Inspector Maigret recalled one detail. That same evening, when the manager had reported that the Mortimers were leaving, he'd been sitting on the radiator, gnawing a chicken leg, and he'd been so overcome with his own comfort that he'd been on the verge of giving himself the hotel stake-out and sending Torrence to tail the millionaire at the theatre. That memory disturbed him. He felt awkward looking at his partner and felt nauseous, though he couldn't tell whether it was because of his wound, his emotions or the chloroform that was still hanging in the air.

It didn't even occur to him to start a proper methodical investigation.

It was Torrence lying there! Torrence, who'd been with him on all his cases these last few years! Torrence, a man who needed just one word, a single sign, to understand whatever he meant to say!

It was Torrence lying there with his mouth wide open as if he were still trying to suck in a bit of oxygen and keep on living! Maigret, who was unable to shed tears, felt sick and upset, with a weight on his shoulders, and nausea in his heart.

He went back to the telephone and spoke so quietly that he had to be asked to repeat his request.

'Police Judiciaire? . . . Yes . . . Hello! . . . Headquarters? . . . Who is that speaking? . . . What? . . . Tarraud? . . . Listen, my lad . . . You're going to run round to the chief's address . . . Yes, his home address . . . Tell him . . . Tell him to join me at the Majestic . . . Straight away . . . Room . . . I don't know the room number, but he'll be shown up . . . What? . . . No, nothing else . . .

'Hello? . . . What's that? . . . No, nothing wrong with me . . . '

He hung up. His colleague had started asking questions, puzzled by the odd sound of Maigret's voice, and also because what he'd asked for was odder still.

He stood there for a while longer, with his arms swinging by his side. He tried not to look at the corner of the room where Torrence lay. He caught sight of himself in a mirror and realized that blood had soaked through the towel. So, with great difficulty, he took off his jacket.

★　★　★

One hour later the Superintendent of Criminal Investigation knocked at the door. Maigret opened it a slit and grunted at the valet who'd brought up the chief to say he was no longer needed. He only opened the door further when the flunkey had vanished. Only then did the super realize that Maigret was bare-chested. The door to the bathroom was wide open, and the floor was a puddle of reddish water.

'Shut the door, sharpish,' Maigret said, with no regard for hierarchy.

On the right side of his chest was an elongated and now swollen flesh wound. His braces were hanging down his legs.

He nodded towards the corner of the room where Torrence was lying and put a finger to his lips.

'Shush! . . . '

The superintendent shuddered. In sudden agitation, he inquired:

'Is he dead?'

Maigret's chin fell to his chest.

'Could you give me a hand, chief?' he mumbled gloomily.

'But . . . you're . . . It's a serious . . . '

'Shush! The bullet came out, that's the main thing. Help me wrap it up tight . . . '

He'd put the basin on the floor and cut the sheet in two.

'The Baltic gang . . . ' he explained. 'They missed me . . . but they didn't miss my poor Torrence . . . '

'Have you disinfected the wound?'

'Yes, I washed it with soap then put some tincture of iodine on it . . . '

'Do you think . . . '

'That's enough for now! . . . With a needle, chief! . . . They anaesthetized him, then killed him with a needle . . . '

Maigret wasn't himself. It was as if he was on the other side of a net curtain that made him look and sound all fuzzy.

'Hand me my shirt . . . '

His voice was blank. His gestures were measured and imprecise. His face was without expression.

'You had to come here . . . Seeing as it's one of our own . . . Not to mention that I didn't want to make waves . . . You can have him taken away later . . . Keep all mention of it out of the papers . . . Chief, you do trust me, don't you?'

All the same there was a catch in Maigret's

voice. It touched the super, who took him by the hand.

'Now tell me, Maigret . . . What's wrong?'

'Nothing . . . I'm quite calm, I swear . . . I don't think I've ever been so calm . . . But now, it's between them and me . . . Do you understand? . . . '

The superintendent helped him get his waistcoat and his jacket on. The dressing changed Maigret's appearance, broadening his waist and making his figure less neat, as if he had rolls of fat.

He looked at himself in the mirror and screwed up his face ironically. He was well aware that he now looked all soft. He'd lost that rock-solid, hard-cased look of a human mountain that he liked his enemies to see.

His face was pale, puffy and streaked with red. He was beginning to get bags under his eyes.

'Thank you, chief. Do you think you can do the necessary, as far as Torrence is concerned?'

'Yes, we can keep it out of the news . . . I'll alert the magistrates . . . I'll go to see the prosecutor in person.'

'Good! I'll get on with the job . . . '

He was tidying his mussed hair as he spoke. Then he walked over to the corpse, stopped in his tracks and asked his colleague:

'I'm allowed to close his eyes, aren't I? . . . I think he would have liked me to do it . . . '

His fingers were shaking. He kept them on the dead man's eyelids for a while, as if he was stroking them. The superintendent became agitated and begged him:

'Maigret! Please . . . '

The inspector got up and cast a last glance around the room.

'Farewell, chief . . . Don't let them tell my wife I've been hurt . . . '

His vast bulk filled the whole doorway for a moment. The Superintendent of Criminal Investigation almost called him back in, because he was a worrying sight.

During the war comrades in arms had said farewell to him just like that, calmly, with the same unreal gentleness, before going over the top.

Those men had never come back!

9

The Hit-man

International gangsters who engage in top-flight scams rarely commit murder. You can take it as a general rule that they never kill — at least, not the people they've chosen to unburden of a million or two. They use more scientific methods of thievery. Most of those gentlemen don't carry guns.

But they do sometimes use elimination to settle scores. Every year, one or two crimes that will never be properly solved take place somewhere. Most often, the victim is unidentifiable, and is buried under a patently false name.

The dead are either snitches, or men who drank too much and blabbed under the influence, or underlings aiming to rise, thus threatening the sitting hierarchy.

In America, the home of specialization, these kinds of execution are never carried out by a gang member. Specialists called hit-men are used. Like official executioners, they have their own teams and rates of remuneration.

The same has sometimes occurred in Europe, notably in the famous case of the Polish Connection (whose leaders all ended up on the scaffold). That set-up carried out several murders on behalf of more highly placed crooks who were keen not to have blood on their own hands.

Maigret knew all that as he went down the stairs towards the front desk of the Majestic.

'When a customer calls down for room service, where does his call get directed?' he asked.

'He gets connected to the room service manager.'

'At night, as well?'

'Sorry! After nine in the evening, night staff deal with it.'

'And where can I find the night staff?'

'In the basement.'

'Take me there.'

Maigret ventured once more into the innards of this hive of luxury designed to cater for a thousand guests. He found an employee sitting at a telephone exchange in a cubby-hole next to the kitchen. He had a register at his desk. It was the quiet time.

'Did Inspector Torrence call down between 9 p.m. and 2 a.m.?'

'Torrence?'

'The officer in the blue room, next door to suite 3 . . . ' the receptionist explained in the language of the house.

The reasoning was elementary. Torrence had been attacked in the room by someone who had necessarily entered it. The murderer must have got behind his victim in order to put the chloroform gag over his face. And Torrence hadn't suspected a thing.

Only a hotel valet could have got away with it.

He had either been called up by the policeman or else he'd come in unprompted, to clear the table.

Keeping quite calm, Maigret put the question another way round:

'Which member of staff knocked off early last night?'

The operator was taken aback by the question.

'How did you know? Sheer coincidence . . . Pepito got a call telling him his brother was sick . . . '

'What time?'

'Around ten . . . '

'Where was he, at that point?'

'Upstairs.'

'On which telephone did he take the call?'

They called the main exchange. The operator confirmed that he'd not put any call through to Pepito.

Things were moving fast! But Maigret remained placid and glum.

'His card? . . . You must have an employee card . . . '

'Not a proper one . . . We don't keep files on what we call room staff; there's too much turnover.'

They had to go to the hotel office, which was unmanned at that hour. Nonetheless Maigret had them open up the employee records, where he found what he was looking for:

Pepito Moretto, Hôtel Beauséjour, 3, Rue des Batignolles. Appointed on . . .

'Get me Hôtel Beausejour on the telephone . . . '

Meanwhile Maigret interrogated another employee and learned that Pepito Moretto had been recommended by an Italian maître d'hôtel and had joined the staff of the Majestic three days before the Mortimer-Levingstons' arrival. No complaints about his work. He'd begun in the dining room, but then transferred to room service at his own request.

Hôtel Beauséjour came on the line.

'Hello! . . . Can you get Pepito Moretto to come to the phone? . . . Hello! . . . What was that? . . . His luggage too? . . . Three a.m.? . . . Thank you! . . . Hello? . . . One more thing . . . Did he get any mail at the hotel? . . . No letters at all? . . . Thank you! . . . That's all.'

Maigret hung up, remaining as unnaturally calm as he ever was.

'What's the time?' he asked.

'Five ten . . . '

'Call me a cab.'

He gave the driver the address of Pickwick's Bar.

'You know it closes at 4 a.m.?'

'Doesn't matter.'

★ ★ ★

The car came to a stop outside the nightclub. It was shuttered, but a streak of light could be seen coming from under the door. Maigret was aware that in most late-night venues the staff — often forty strong — usually has a meal before going home.

87

They eat in the same room that the customers have just vacated even while the streamers are being tidied away and the cleaners get to work.

Despite that, he didn't ring the bell at Pickwick's. He turned his back on the club, and his eye alighted on a café-tobacconist's at the corner of Rue Fontaine, the sort of place where nightclub staff often gather during intervals or after work.

The bar was still open. When Maigret walked in there were three men with their elbows on the counter, sipping coffee with something stronger in it, talking business.

'Is Pepito not in tonight?'

'He left quite a while ago,' the barman replied.

Maigret noticed that one of the customers who had perhaps recognized him was gesturing at the barman to keep his mouth shut.

'We had an appointment at two . . . ' he said.

'He was here . . . '

'I know! . . . I told the dancer from over the road to bring a message to him.'

'You mean José . . . ?'

'Correct. He was supposed to tell Pepito I couldn't make it.'

'José did come over, actually . . . I think they had a chat . . . '

The customer who'd gestured to the barman was now drumming his fingers on the counter. He was pale with fury, because the few sentences that had just been said in the café were all that was needed to explain what had happened.

Around ten or a little before, Pepito had murdered Torrence at the Majestic. He must

88

have had detailed instructions, because he knocked off work straight away, on the excuse that he'd had a phone call from his brother, and came straight to the bar at the corner of Rue Fontaine. Then he waited.

At some point the dancer who'd just been named as José came over the road and passed Pepito a message that a child could guess: shoot Maigret as soon as he steps outside Pickwick's Bar.

In other words, with two crimes in a few hours, the only two people who posed a threat to the Baltic gang would be got rid of!

Pepito fired his gun and fled. His role was over. He hadn't been seen. So he could go and get his bags from Hôtel Beausejour . . .

Maigret paid for his drink, went out, looked back over his shoulder and saw the three customers vigorously upbraiding the barman.

He knocked at the door of Pickwick's Bar, and a cleaner opened it for him.

As he'd thought, the employees were having a late supper at tables that had been put end-to-end to make a refectory. Chicken leftovers, pieces of partridge, hors d'œuvres — everything that the customers hadn't eaten. Thirty pairs of eyes turned towards the inspector.

'Has José been gone long?'

'Sure! . . . Straight after . . . '

But the head waiter, recognizing Maigret, whom he'd served, stuck his elbow in the ribs of the man who was talking.

Maigret wasn't fooled.

'Give me his address! And it had better be the right one, OK? Or else you'll be sorry . . . '

'I don't have it . . . Only the boss has . . . '

'Where is he?'

'On his estate, at La Varenne.'

'Give me the books.'

'But . . . '

'Shut up!'

They pretended to look in the drawers of a small office desk behind the podium. Maigret shoved his way into the group that was fiddling about and found the staff register straight away.

José Latourie, 71, Rue Lepic

He exited in the same ponderous manner as he'd come in, while the still-worried waiters went back to their meal.

It was no distance to Rue Lepic. But no. 71 is a long way up the hillside street, and Maigret had to stop twice to get his puff back.

At last he got to the door of a lodging house of the same general kind as Hôtel Beauséjour, though more sordid still. He rang, and the front door opened automatically.

He knocked at a glass window, and the night porter eventually got out of bed for him.

'José Latourie?'

'Still out. His key's here . . . '

'Hand it over! Police! . . . '

'But . . . '

'At the double! . . . '

The fact is, nobody could stand in Maigret's way that night. Yet he wasn't his usual stern and rigid self. Maybe people could sense something even worse?

'Which floor?'

'Fourth!'

The long and narrow room had a stuffy smell. The bed hadn't been made. Like most other people in the same line of trade, José must have slept until four in the afternoon, and hotels don't make up beds later than that.

An old pair of pyjamas that had worn through at the collar and elbows was flung across the sheets. On the floor lay a pair of moccasins with worn soles and broken uppers that must have been used as bedroom slippers. There was a travelling bag in imitation leather, but all it had in it were old newspapers and a patched-up pair of black trousers.

Over the sink was a bar of soap, a pot of skin cream, aspirin tablets and a tube of barbitone. Maigret picked up a ball of scrap paper from the floor and smoothed it out with care. He only needed one sniff to know that it had contained heroin.

★　★　★

Fifteen minutes later Inspector Maigret had gone through the room from top to bottom, but then he noticed a slit in the upholstery of the only armchair in the room. He slipped his finger inside the stuffing and pulled out, one by one, eleven one-gram packs of the same drug.

He put them in his wallet and went back down the stairs. He hailed a city policeman at Place

91

Blanche and gave him instructions. The copper went to stand sentry next to no. 71.

Maigret thought back on the black-haired young man: an uneasy gigolo with unsteady eyes who'd bumped into his table out of agitation when he'd come back from his appointment with Moretto.

Once he'd done the job he hadn't dared go back home, as he would rather lose the few rags that he had and those eleven sachets, which must have had a street price of at least 1,000 francs. He'd be nabbed sooner or later, because he didn't have the nerve. He must have been scared stiff.

Pepito was a cooler kind of customer. Maybe he was in a railway station waiting for the first train out. Maybe he'd gone to ground in the suburbs. Or maybe he'd just moved to a different doss-house in another part of Paris.

Maigret hailed a cab and was on the point of asking for the Majestic when he reckoned they wouldn't have finished the job yet. That's to say, Torrence would still be there.

'Quai des Orfèvres . . . '

As he walked past Jean, Maigret realized that the doorman already knew, and he averted his eyes like a guilty man.

He didn't tend to his stove. He didn't take off his jacket or collar.

He sat at his desk, leaning on his elbows, stock still, for two hours. It was already light when he took notice of a screed that must have been put on his pad at some point during the night.

For the eyes of Detective Chief Inspector Maigret. Urgent.

Around 23.30 man in tails entered Hôtel du Roi de Sicile. Stayed ten minutes. Left in a limousine. The Russian did not exit.

Maigret took it in his stride. And then more news started flooding in. First there was a call from the Courcelles police station, in the seventeenth arrondissement:

'A man by the name of José Latourie, a professional dancer, has been found dead by the railings of Parc Monceau. Three knife wounds. His wallet was not taken. The time and circumstances of the crime have not been established.'

But Maigret knew what they were! He could see Pepito Moretto tailing the young man when he came out of Pickwick's and then, reckoning he was too upset and therefore likely to give the game away, Moretto took his life without even bothering to remove the man's wallet or ID — as a taunt, perhaps. As if to say, 'You think you can use this guy as a lead to get back to us? Be my guest! You can have him!'

Eight thirty. The manager of the Majestic was on the line:

'Hello? . . . Inspector Maigret? . . . It's unbelievable, incredible . . . A few minutes ago no. 17 rang! . . . No. 17! . . . Do you remember? . . . The man who . . . '

'Yes, he's called Oswald Oppenheim . . . Well?'

'I sent up a valet . . . Oppenheim was in bed, cool as a cucumber. He wanted his breakfast.'

10

The Return of Oswald Oppenheim

Maigret hadn't moved a muscle for two hours. When he wanted to get up he could barely lift his arm and he had to ring Jean to come and help him put on his overcoat.

'Get me a cab . . . '

A few minutes later he was in the surgery of Dr Lecourbe in Rue Monsieur-le-Prince. There were six people in the waiting room, but he was taken through the living quarters and, as soon as the doctor was free, he was shown into the consulting room.

It took an hour. His body was stiffer. The bags under his eyes were so deep that Maigret looked different, as if he'd got make-up on.

'Rue du Roi-de-Sicile! I'll tell you where to stop . . . '

From far off he caught sight of his two officers walking up and down opposite the lodging house. He got out of the car and went over to them.

'Still inside?'

'Yes . . . There's been one of us on duty at all times . . . '

'Who left the building?'

'A little old man all bent double, then two youngsters, then a woman of about thirty . . . '

94

'Did the old man have a beard?'

'Yes . . . '

He went off without saying another word, climbed the narrow staircase and went past the concierge's office. A moment later he was shaking the door of room 32. A woman's voice responded in a language he couldn't identify. The door gave way, and he set eyes on a half-naked Anna Gorskin getting out of bed.

'Where's your boyfriend?' he asked.

He spoke in staccato, like a man in a hurry, and didn't bother to look over the premises.

Anna Gorskin shouted:

'Get out of here! . . . You've no right . . . '

But he stayed unmoved, and picked up off the floor a trenchcoat he knew well. He seemed to be looking for something else. He noticed Fyodor Yurevich's dirty grey trousers at the foot of the bed.

On the other hand there were no men's socks to be found in the room.

The Jewish woman glowered ferociously at the inspector as she put on her dressing gown.

'You think that just because we're foreign . . . '

Maigret didn't give her time to throw a tantrum. He went out quietly and closed the door, which she opened again before he had gone down one flight. She stood on the landing just breathing heavily, not saying a word. She leaned over the railing, staring at him, and then, unable to contain her imperious need to do *something*, she spat on him.

Her spittle fell with a dull thud a metre away.

Inspector Dufour asked:

'Well? . . . '

'Keep a watch on the woman . . . At any rate, she can't disguise herself as an old man.'

'You mean that . . . '

No! He didn't mean anything! He wasn't up to having an argument. He got back in the taxi.

'To the Majestic . . . '

The junior detective was downcast as he watched Maigret leave.

'Do your best!' Maigret called out to him. He didn't want to take it out on the young man. It wasn't his fault if he'd been taken for a ride. After all, hadn't Maigret himself let Torrence get killed?

★ ★ ★

The manager was waiting for him at the door, which was a new departure for him.

'At last! . . . You see . . . I don't know what do to do any more . . . They came to fetch your . . . your friend . . . They reassured me it would not be in the papers . . . But the *other one* is here! He's here! . . . '

'Nobody saw him come in?'

'Nobody! . . . That's what . . . Listen! . . . Like I told you on the telephone, he rang . . . When the valet went in, he ordered a coffee . . . He was in bed . . . '

'What about Mortimer? . . . '

'Do you think they're connected? . . . That's impossible! He's a well-known figure . . . He's had ministers and bankers call on him right herc! . . . '

'What's Oppenheim up to now? . . . '

'He's just had a bath . . . I think he's getting dressed . . . '

'And Mortimer?'

'The Mortimers haven't rung yet . . . They're still asleep . . . '

'Give me a description of Pepito Moretto . . . '

'Certainly . . . What I've heard . . . Actually, I never set eyes on him myself . . . I mean, noticed him . . . We have so many employees! . . . But I did some research . . . Short, dark skin, black hair, broad shoulders, could go for days without saying a word . . . '

Maigret copied it all down on a scrap of paper that he put in an envelope that he then addressed to the super. That ought to be enough, combined with the fingerprints that must have been found in the room where Torrence died.

'Have this taken to Quai des Orfèvres . . . '

'Certainly, sir . . . '

The manager was more pliant now because he sensed that events could easily get out of hand, to disastrous effect.

'What are you going to do, inspector?'

But Maigret had already moved off and was standing all clumsy and awkward in the middle of the lobby. He looked like a tourist in a historic church trying to work out without the help of a guide what there was to inspect.

★   ★   ★

There was a ray of sunshine shedding golden light on the entire lobby of the Majestic. At nine in the morning it was almost deserted. Just a few travellers at separate tables having breakfast while reading the papers.

In the end Maigret slumped into a wicker chair next to the fountain, which for one reason or another wasn't working that morning. The goldfish in the ceramic pond had decided to stop swimming about, and the only thing moving were fish-jaws going up and down, chewing water.

They reminded the inspector of Torrence's open mouth. That must have made a strong impression on him, because he wriggled about for a long time before finding a comfortable position.

A sprinkling of flunkeys passed by from time to time. Maigret did not take his eyes off them, because he knew that a bullet could fly at any moment.

The game he was in had got near to show-down.

The fact that Maigret had unmasked the identity of Oppenheim, alias Pietr the Latvian, was no big deal. In itself it didn't put the detective at risk.

The Latvian was hardly in hiding. On the contrary, he was flaunting himself in front of his trackers, as he was confident they had nothing on him.

The proof of that was the flurry of telegrams that had tracked him step by step from Krakow to Bremen, from Bremen to Amsterdam, and from Amsterdam to Brussels and Paris.

But then came the corpse on the Étoile du

Nord! Most of all, there was Maigret's discovery of the unexpected relations between the East European and Mortimer-Levingston.

And that was a major discovery!

Pietr was a self-avowed crook who was happy to taunt international police forces: 'Just try to catch me red-handed!'

Mortimer was, in the eyes of the whole world, an honest and upright man!

There were just two people who might have guessed the connection between them.

That very evening, Torrence was murdered! And Maigret came under fire from a revolver in Rue Fontaine!

A third, bewildered person, who probably knew next to nothing but might serve as a lead to further investigation, had also been eliminated: José Latourie, a professional dancer.

So Mortimer and the Latvian, presumably reassured by the three disposals, had gone back to their allotted places. There they were upstairs, in their luxury suites, giving orders on the telephone to a whole team of domestics of a five-star hotel, taking baths, eating meals, getting dressed.

Maigret was waiting for them on his own. He wasn't comfortable in his wicker chair: one side of his chest was stiff and throbbing, and he could barely use his right arm, because it was wracked by persistent pain.

He could have arrested them there and then. But he knew that wouldn't be any use. At most he might get someone to testify against Pietr the Latvian, alias Fyodor Yurevich, alias Oswald

Oppenheim, and who must have had many other identities as well, including that of Olaf Swaan.

But what had he got against the American millionaire Mortimer-Levingston? Within an hour of arrest, the US Embassy would lodge a protest! The French banks and companies and financial institutions on whose boards he sat would wheel in political support.

What evidence did he have? What clues? The fact that he'd vanished for a few hours when Pietr was also absent?

That he'd had supper at Pickwick's Bar and that his wife had danced with José Latourie?

That a police sergeant had seen him go into a scruffy lodging house at the sign of the Roi de Sicile?

It would all be torn to shreds! Apologies would have to be made and, to satisfy the Americans, there would have to be a scapegoat. Maigret would be sacked, at least for show.

But Torrence was dead!

He must have been carried across the hall at the crack of dawn on a stretcher. Or else the manager had warded off the possibility of an early riser seeing such an unpleasant spectacle by having the corpse taken out by the service entrance!

That was very likely! Narrow corridors, spiral staircases . . . the stretcher would have bumped into the railings . . .

Behind the mahogany counter the telephones rang. Comings and goings. Hurried commands. The manager came up to him:

'Mrs Mortimer-Levingston is leaving . . . They've

just rung from upstairs to have her trunk brought down . . . The car is waiting . . . '

Maigret smiled faintly.

'Which train?'

'She's flying to Berlin from Le Bourget airfield . . . '

He'd barely finished his sentence when she appeared, dressed in a light-grey travelling cape, carrying a crocodile-skin handbag. She was moving quickly but when she got to the revolving door she couldn't resist turning round.

Maigret made a great effort to stand up so as to be certain she would see him. He was sure she had bitten her lip. Then she left even more hurriedly, waving her hands about and giving orders to her chauffeur.

The manager was wanted elsewhere. The inspector was all on his own beside the fountain, which suddenly began to spout. It must have been on a time-clock.

It was 10 a.m.

Maigret smiled inwardly, sat down weightily but with great care, because the slightest movement pulled on his wound, which was hurting him more and more.

'You get rid of the weakest links . . . '

That's what it was! First José Latourie, reckoned to be unreliable, had been got rid of with three stabs; and now Mrs Mortimer, who was also quite emotional. They were packing her off to Berlin! And doing her a favour.

★   ★   ★

The tough guys were staying behind: Pietr, who was taking ages to get dressed; Mortimer-Levingston, who had probably not lost an ounce of his aristocratic grandeur; and Pepito Moretto, the team's hit-man.

Connected by invisible threads, all three were gearing themselves up.

The enemy was in their midst, in a wicker armchair, sitting quite still with his legs stretched out in the middle of the lobby as the hotel began to get busier. Haze from the tinkling fountain misted his face.

The lift came down and stopped.

The first to emerge was Pietr, wearing a beautifully tailored cinnamon-coloured suit and smoking a Henry Clay cigar.

He was master of the house. That was what he paid for. Casually, confidently, he sauntered round the hall, stopped here and there, looked into the showcases that prestige shops set up in the lobbies of grand hotels, glanced at the board displaying the latest foreign currency rates and finally took up position less than three metres away from Maigret to stare at the artificial-looking goldfish in the pond. He flicked cigar ash into the water and then sailed off to the library.

11

Arrivals and Departures

Pietr glanced through a few newspapers, paying particular attention to the *Revaler Bote*, from Tallinn. There was only one out-of-date issue at the Majestic. It had probably been left behind by another guest.

He lit another cigar at a few minutes to eleven, went across the lobby and sent a bellhop to fetch his hat.

Thanks to the sun falling on one side of the Champs-Élysées, it was quite mild.

Pietr went out without his coat, with just a grey homburg on his head, and walked slowly up to the Arc de Triomphe like a man out for a breath of fresh air.

Maigret kept fairly close behind, making no effort to remain unseen. As the dressing on his wound made moving about uncomfortable, he did not appreciate the walk.

★ ★ ★

At the corner of Rue de Berry he heard a whistle that wasn't very loud and took no notice of it. Then another whistle. So he turned round and saw Inspector Dufour performing a mystifying dumb show so as to let him know he had something to tell him.

Dufour was in Rue de Berry, pretending to be fascinated by a pharmacist's window display, so his gesticulations appeared to be addressed to a waxwork female head, one of whose cheeks was covered with a meticulous simulation of eczema.

'Come over here . . . Come on! Quickly . . . '

Dufour was offended and indignant. He'd been prowling around the Majestic for an hour, using every trick of the trade — and now his chief was ordering him to break cover all at once!

'What's happened?'

'The Jewish woman . . . '

'She went out?'

'She's here . . . And since you made me cross over, she can see us, right now . . . '

Maigret looked around.

'Where from?'

'From Le Select . . . She's sitting inside . . . Look! The curtain's moving . . . '

'Carry on watching her . . . '

'Openly?'

'Have a drink at the table next to hers, if you like.'

At this point in the game there was no point playing hide-and-seek. Maigret walked on and caught up with Pietr in a couple of hundred metres. He hadn't tried to take advantage of Maigret's conversation with Dufour to slip away.

And why should he slip away? The match was being played on a new pitch. The two sides could see each other. Pretty much all the cards were on the table now.

Pietr walked up and down the Champs-Élysées

twice over, from Étoile to the Rond-Point and back again, and by then Maigret had grasped his character, entirely.

He had a slender, tense figure that was fundamentally more thoroughbred than Mortimer's, but his breeding was of a kind particular to Northern peoples.

Maigret was already familiar with the type. He'd met others of the same ilk in the Latin Quarter during his days as a medical student (though he never completed the course), and they had baffled the Southerner that he was.

He had a particular recollection of one such, a skinny, blond Pole whose hair was already thinning at the age of twenty-two. He was the son of a cleaning lady, and for seven years he came to lectures at the Sorbonne without any socks, living on one egg with a slice of bread a day. He couldn't afford to buy the print versions of the lectures so he had to study in public libraries. He got to know nothing of Paris, of women, or of French ways. But scarcely had he got his degree than he was appointed a senior professor in Warsaw. Five years later Maigret saw him on a return visit to Paris, as a member of a delegation of foreign scientists. He was as skinny and icy as ever, but he went to a dinner at the presidential palace.

Maigret had met others, too. Not all of them were quite so special. But they were all amazingly keen to learn a huge range of different things. And learn they did!

To learn for the sake of learning! Like that Belgian professor who knew all the languages of the Far East — more than forty of them — without ever having set foot in Asia or being at all interested in the peoples whose languages he dissected, to amuse himself.

Ferocious will-power of the same kind could be seen in the grey-green eyes of Pietr the Latvian. But as soon as you thought you could pigeon-hole him in the category of intellectuals, you noticed other features that didn't fit at all.

In a sense you could feel the shadow of Fyodor Yurevich, the Russian vagrant in the trenchcoat, hovering over the neat figure of the guest at the Majestic.

It was a moral certainty that they were one and the same man; their identity was about to become a patent fact as well.

The evening he got to Paris, Pietr went missing. Next morning Maigret caught up with him in Fécamp in the shape of Fyodor Yurevich.

Fyodor returned to Rue du Roi-de-Sicile. A few hours later, Mortimer dropped in on him at his lodging. Several people then came out of the building, including a bearded old man.

Next morning Pietr was back in his place at Hôtel Majestic.

What was astounding was that, apart from a fairly striking physical resemblance, these two incarnations had absolutely nothing in common.

Fyodor Yurevich was a genuine Slavic vagrant, a sentimental and manic *déclassé*. Everything fitted perfectly. He didn't make the slightest error even when he leaned on the counter in the drinking hole in Fécamp.

On the other hand there wasn't a thread out of

place in the character of the East European intellectual, breathing refinement from head to toe. The way he asked the bellhop for a light, the way he wore his top-quality English homburg, his casual stroll in the sun along the Champs-Élysées and the way he looked at window-displays — it was all quite perfect.

It was so perfect it had to go deeper than play-acting. Maigret had acted parts himself. Although the police use disguise and deep cover less often than people imagine, they still have to do it from time to time. But Maigret in make-up was still Maigret in some aspect of his being — in a glance, or a tic. When he'd dressed up as a cattle-dealer, for example (he had done that once, and got away with it), he was *acting the role* of a cattle-dealer. But he hadn't *become* a cattle-dealer. The persona he'd put on remained external to him.

Pietr-Fyodor was both Pietr and Fyodor *from inside*.

The inspector's view could be summed up this way: he was both one thing and the other not only in dress but in essence.

He'd been living two quite different lives in alternation for many years, that was clear, and maybe all his life long.

These were just the random thoughts that struck Maigret as he walked slowly through the sweet-smelling light air.

All of a sudden, though, the character of Pietr the Latvian cracked wide open.

★　★　★

107

What brought this about was significant in itself. He had paused opposite Fouquet's and was about to cross the street, manifestly intending to have an aperitif at the bar of that high-class establishment.

But then he changed his mind. He carried on along the same side of the avenue, then suddenly began to hurry before darting down Rue Washington.

There was a café nearby of the sort you find nestled in all the really plush areas of the city, to cater for taxi-drivers and domestic staff.

Pietr went in, and Maigret followed him, opening the door just as the Latvian was ordering an ersatz absinthe.

He was standing at the horseshoe counter. From time to time a waiter in a blue apron gave it a desultory wipe with a dirty dishcloth. There was a knot of dust-covered building workers to the Latvian's left, and, on his right, a gas company cashier.

The leader of the Baltic gang clashed with the surroundings in every detail of his impeccably tasteful and stylish attire.

His blond toothbrush moustache and his thin, almost transparent eyebrows caught the light. He stared at Maigret, not straight on, but in the mirror at the back of the bar.

That's when the inspector noticed a quiver in Pietr's lips and an almost imperceptible contraction of his nostrils.

Pietr must have been watching himself in the mirror too. He started drinking slowly, but soon he gulped down what was left in his glass in one

108

go and waved a finger to say:

'Same again!'

Maigret had ordered a vermouth. He looked even taller and wider than ever in the confined space of the bar. He didn't take his eyes off the Latvian.

He was having something like double vision. Just as had happened to him in the hotel lobby, he could see one image superimposed on another: behind the current scene, he had a vision of the squalid bar in Fécamp. Pietr was going double. Maigret could see him in his cinnamon suit and in his worn-out raincoat at the same time.

'I'm telling you I'd rather do that than get beaten up!' one of the builders exclaimed, banging his glass down on the counter.

Pietr was now on his third glass of green liquid. Maigret could smell the aniseed in it. Because the gas company cashier had moved away, he was now shoulder to shoulder with his target, at touching distance.

Maigret was two heads taller than Pietr. They were both facing the mirror, and gazed at each other in that pewter-tinted screen.

The Latvian's face began to decompose, starting with his eyes. He snapped his white dry-skinned fingers, then wiped his forehead with his hand. A struggle then slowly began on his face. In the mirror Maigret saw now the guest of the Majestic, now the face of Anna Gorskin's tormented lover.

But the second visage didn't emerge in full. It kept getting pushed back by immense muscular effort. Only the eyes of Pietr's Russian self stayed stable.

He was hanging on to the edge of the counter with his left hand. His body was swaying.

*　*　*

Maigret tried out an experiment. In his pocket he still had the photograph of Madame Swaan that he'd extracted from the archive album of the photographer in Fécamp.

'How much do I owe you?' he asked the barman.

'Two francs twenty . . . '

He pretended to look for the money in his wallet and managed to drop the snapshot into a puddle of spilt drink between the counter's raised edges. He paid no attention to it, and held out a five franc note. But he looked hard at the mirror.

The waiter picked the photograph up and started wiping it clean, apologetically.

Pietr was squeezing the glass in his hand. His face was rigid and his eyes were hard.

Then suddenly there was an unexpected noise, a soft but sharp crack that made the barman at the cash register turn round with a start.

Pietr opened his fist. Shards of broken glass tinkled on to the counter.

He'd gradually crushed it. He was bleeding from a small cut on his index finger. He threw down a 100 franc note and left the bar without looking at Maigret.

Now he was striding straight towards the

110

Majestic, showing no sign of drunkenness. His gait was just as neat and his posture just the same as when he had left it. Maigret stuck obstinately to his heels. As he got within sight of the hotel he recognized a car pulling away. It belonged to the forensics lab and must have been taking away the cameras and other equipment used for fingerprint detection.

This encounter stopped him in his tracks. His confidence sagged: he felt unmoored, without a post to lean on.

He passed by Le Select. Through the window Inspector Dufour waved his arm in what was supposed to be a confidential gesture but could be understood by anyone with eyes as an invitation to look at the table where the Jewish woman was sitting.

Maigret went up to the front desk at the Majestic:

'Mortimer?'

'He's just been driven to the American Embassy, where he's having lunch . . . '

Pietr was on his way to his seat in the empty dining room.

'Will you be lunching with us, sir?' the manager asked Maigret.

'Lay me a setting opposite that man, thank you.'

The hotelier found that hard to swallow.

'Opposite? . . . ' he sputtered. 'I can't do that! The room is empty and . . . '

'I said, opposite.'

The manager would not give up and ran after the detective.

'Listen! It will surely cause a to-do . . . I can put you at a table where you'll be able to see him just as well.'

'I said, at his table.'

It was then, pacing about the lobby, that he realized he was weary. Weary with an insidious lassitude that affected him all over, and his whole self besides, body and soul.

He slumped into the wicker chair he had sat in that morning. A couple consisting of a lady ripe in years and an overdressed young man stood up straight away. From behind her lorgnette the woman said in a voice that was meant to be overheard:

'These five-stars aren't what they used to be . . . Did you see that . . . '

'That' was Maigret. And he didn't even smile back.

12

A Woman with a Gun

'Hello! . . . Err . . . Um . . . Is that you?'

'Maigret speaking,' the inspector sighed. He'd recognized Dufour's voice.

'Shush! . . . I'll keep it short, chief . . . Went toilet . . . Handbag on table . . . Looked . . . Gun inside!'

'Is she still at Le Select?'

'She's eating . . . '

Dufour must have looked like a cartoon conspirator in the telephone booth, waving his arms about in mysterious and terrified ways. Maigret hung up without a word as he didn't have the heart to respond. Little foibles which usually made him smile now made him feel almost physically sick.

The manager had resigned himself to laying a place for Maigret opposite the Latvian, who'd asked the waiter:

'In whose honour . . . ?'

'I can't say, sir. I do as I'm told . . . '

So he let it drop. An English family group of five burst into the dining room and warmed up the atmosphere a bit.

Maigret deposited his overcoat and hat in the cloakroom, walked across the dining room and halted for a moment before sitting down. He even made as if to say hello.

113

But Pietr didn't seem to notice him. The four or five glasses of spirits he'd drunk seemed to have been forgotten. He conducted himself with icily impeccable manners.

He gave not the slightest hint of nerves. With his gaze on a far horizon, he looked more like an engineer trying to solve some technical problem in his head.

He drank modestly, though he'd selected one of the best burgundies of the last two decades.

He ate a light meal: omelette *aux fines herbes*, veal cutlet in crème fraîche.

In the intervals between the dishes he sat patiently with his two hands flat on the table, paying no attention to what was going on around him.

The dining room was beginning to fill up.

'Your moustache is coming unstuck', Maigret said suddenly.

Pietr didn't react. After a while he just stroked his lips with two fingers. Maigret was right, though it was hardly noticeable.

Maigret's imperturbability was legendary among his colleagues, but even so he was having trouble holding himself back.

He was going to have an even tougher time of it that afternoon.

Obviously he did not expect Pietr to do anything to put himself in jeopardy, given the close surveillance. All the same, he'd surely taken one step towards disaster in the morning. Wasn't it reasonable to hope he would be pushed all the way down by the unremitting presence of a man acting like a blank wall, shutting him off from the light?

Pietr had coffee in the lobby and then asked

for his lightweight overcoat to be brought down. He strolled down the Champs-Élysées and a little after two went into a local cinema.

He didn't come out until six. He'd not spoken to anyone, not written anything, nor made a move that was in any way suspicious.

Sitting comfortably in his seat he'd concentrated on following the twists and turns of an infantile plot.

If he'd looked over his shoulder as he then sauntered towards Place de l'Opera to have his aperitif he'd have realized that the figure behind him was made of tough, persistent stuff. But he might also have sensed that the inspector was beginning to doubt his own judgement.

That was indeed the case. In the darkness of the cinema, doing his best not to watch the images flickering on the screen, Maigret kept on thinking about what would happen if he were to make an arrest on the spot.

But he knew very well what would happen! No convincing material evidence on his side. On the other side, a heavy web of influence weighing on the examining magistrate, the prosecutor, going right up to the foreign minister and the minister of justice!

He was slightly hunched as he walked. His wound was hurting, and his right arm was getting even stiffer. The doctor had said firmly:

'If the pain starts to get worse, come back here straight away! It'll mean you've got an infection in the wound . . . '

So what? Did he have time to bother about that?

'Did you see that?' a guest at the Majestic had said that morning.

Heavens above, yes! 'That' was a cop trying to stop leading criminals from doing any more harm, a cop set on avenging a colleague who'd been murdered in that very same five-star hotel!

'That' didn't have a tailor in London, he didn't have time to get manicured every morning, and his wife had been cooking meals for him for three days in a row without knowing what was going on.

'That' was a senior detective earning 2,200 francs a month who, when he'd solved a case and put criminals behind bars, had to sit down with paper and pencil and itemize his expenses, clip his receipts and documentation to the claim, and then go and argue it out with accounts!

Maigret had no car of his own, no millions, not even a big team. If he commandeered a city policeman or two, he still had to justify the use he made of them.

Pietr, who was sitting a metre away from him, paid for a drink with a 50 franc note and didn't bother to pick up the change. It was either a habit or a trick. Then, presumably to irritate the inspector, he went into a shirt-maker's and spent half an hour picking twelve ties and three dressing gowns. He left his calling card on the counter while a smartly dressed salesman scurried after him.

The lesion was definitely becoming inflamed. Sometimes he had intense shooting pains in the whole of his shoulder and he felt like vomiting, as if he had a stomach infection as well.

116

Rue de la Paix, Place Vendôme, Faubourg Saint-Honoré! Pietr was gadding about . . .

Back to the Majestic at last . . . The bellhops rushed to help him with the revolving door.

'Chief . . . '

'You again?'

Officer Dufour emerged tentatively from the shadows with a worried look in his eyes.

'Listen . . . She's vanished . . . '

'What are you talking about?'

'I did my best, I promise! She left Le Select. A minute later she went into a couturier's at no. 52. I waited an hour and then interrogated the doorman. She hadn't been seen in the first-floor showroom. She'd simply walked straight through, because the building has a second exit on Rue de Berry.'

'That's enough!'

'What should I do?'

'Take a break!'

Dufour looked Maigret in the eye, then turned his gaze sharply aside.

'I swear to you that . . . '

To his amazement, Maigret patted him on the shoulder.

'You're a good lad, Dufour! Don't let it get you down . . . '

Then he went inside the Majestic, saw the manager making a face and smiled back.

'Oppenheim?'

'He's just gone up to his room.'

Maigret saw a lift that was free.

'Second floor . . . '

He filled his pipe and suddenly realized with

another smile that was somewhat more ironical than the first that for the last several hours he'd forgotten to have a smoke.

★ ★ ★

He went to the door of no. 17 and didn't waver. He knocked. A voice told him to come in. He did so, closing the door behind him.

Despite the radiators a log fire had been lit in the lounge, for decoration. The Latvian was leaning on the mantelpiece and pushing a piece of paper towards the flames with his toe, to get it to light.

At a glance Maigret saw that he was not as cool as before, but he had enough self-control not to show how much that pleased him.

He picked up a dainty gilded chair with his huge hand, carried it to within a metre of the fire, set it down on its slender legs and sat astride it.

Maybe it was because he had his pipe back between his teeth. Or maybe because his whole being was rebounding from the hours of depression, or rather, of uncertainty, that he'd just been through.

In any case, the fact is he was now tougher and weightier than ever. He was Maigret twice over, so to speak. Carved from a single piece of old oak, or, better still, from very dense stone.

He propped his elbows on the back of the chair. You could feel that if he was driven to an extremity he could grab his target by the scruff of his neck with his two broad hands and bang

118

his head against the wall.

'Mortimer is back,' he said.

The Latvian watched the paper burn, then slowly looked up.

'I'm not aware . . . '

It did not escape Maigret's eye that Pietr's fists were clenched. It also did not escape him that there was a suitcase next to the bedroom door that had not been in the suite before. It was a common suitcase that cost 100 francs at most, and it clashed with the surroundings.

'What's inside that?'

No answer. Just a nervous twitch. Then a question:

'Are you going to arrest me?'

He was anxious, to be sure, but there was also a sense of relief in his voice.

'Not yet . . . '

Maigret got up and pushed the suitcase across the floor with his foot, and then bent down to open it.

It contained a brand-new grey off-the-peg suit, with its tags still on it.

The inspector picked up the telephone.

'Hello! . . . Is Mortimer back? . . . No? . . . No callers for no. 17? Hello! . . . Yes . . . A parcel from a shirt-makers on the Grands Boulevards? . . . No need to bring it up . . . '

He put the phone down and carried on interrogating aggressively:

'Where is Anna Gorskin?'

At last he felt he was making progress!

'Look around . . . '

'You mean she's not in this suite . . . But she

119

was here . . . She brought this suitcase, and a letter . . . '

The Latvian gave a quick stab at the charred paper to make it collapse. Now it was just a pile of ash.

Maigret was fully aware that this was no time for careless words. He was on the right track, but the slightest slip would give his advantage away.

Out of sheer habit he got up and went to the fire so abruptly that Pietr flinched and made as if to put up his arms in self-defence, then blushed with embarrassment. Maigret was only going to stand with his back to the fire! He took short, strong puffs at his pipe.

Silence ensued for such a long time and with so much unspoken that it strained nerves to breaking point.

The Latvian was on a tightrope and still putting on a show of balance. In response to Maigret's pipe he lit a cigar.

★ ★ ★

Maigret started to pace up and down and nearly broke the telephone table when he leaned on it. The Latvian didn't see that he'd pressed the call button without picking up the receiver. The result was instantaneous. The bell rang. It was reception.

'Hello! . . . You called?'

'Hello! . . . Yes . . . What was that?'

'Hello! . . . This is reception . . . '

Cool as a cucumber, Maigret went on:

'Hello! . . . Yes . . . Mortimer! . . . Thank you!

120

. . . I'll drop in on him soon . . . '

'Hello! Hello! . . . '

He'd scarcely put the earpiece back on its hook when the telephone rang again. The manager was cross:

'What's going on? . . . I don't get it . . . '

'Dammit! . . . ' Maigret thundered.

He stared heavily at the Latvian, who had gone even paler and who, for at least a second, wanted to make a dash for the door.

'No big deal,' Maigret told him. 'Mortimer-Levingston's just come in. I'd asked them to let me know . . . '

He could see sweat beading on Pietr's brow.

'We were discussing the suitcase and the letter that came with it . . . Anna Gorskin . . . '

'Anna's not involved . . . '

'Excuse me . . . I thought . . . Isn't the letter from her?'

'Listen . . . '

Pietr was shaking. Quite visibly shaking. And he was in a strangely nervous state. He had twitches all over his face and spasms in his body.

'Listen to me . . . '

'I'm listening,' Maigret finally conceded, still standing with his back to the fire.

He'd slipped his good hand into his gun pocket. It would take him no more than a second to aim. He was smiling, but behind the smile you could sense concentration taken to an utmost extreme.

'Well then? I said I was listening . . . '

But Pietr grabbed a bottle of whisky, muttering through clenched teeth:

'What the hell . . . '

Then he poured himself a tumbler and drank it straight off, looking at Maigret with the eyes of Fyodor Yurevich and a dribble of drink glinting on his chin.

13

The Two Pietrs

Maigret had never seen a man get drunk at such lightning speed. It's true he had also never seen anyone fill a tumbler to the brim with whisky, knock it back, refill it, knock the second glass back, then do the same a third time before shaking the bottle over his mouth to get the last few drops of 104 degrees proof spirit down his throat.

The effect was impressive. Pietr went crimson and the next minute he was as white as a sheet, with blotches of red on his cheeks. His lips lost their colour. He steadied himself on the low table, staggered about, then said with the detachment of a true drunk:

'This is what you wanted, isn't it? . . . '

He laughed uncertainly, expressing a whole range of things: fear, irony, bitterness and maybe despair. He tried to hold on to a chair but knocked it over, then wiped his damp brow.

'You do realize that you'd never have managed by yourself . . . Sheer luck . . . '

Maigret didn't move. He was so disturbed by the scene that he nearly put an end to it by having the man drink or inhale an antidote.

What he was watching was the same transformation he'd seen that morning, but on a scale ten times, a hundred times greater.

A few minutes earlier he'd been dealing with a man in control of himself, with a sharp mind backed up by uncommon willpower . . . A society man, a man of learning, of the utmost elegance.

Now there was just this bag of nerves tugged this way and that as if by a crazy puppeteer, with eyes like tempests set in a wan and twisted face.

And he was laughing! But despite his laughter and his pointless excitement, he had his ear open and was bending over as if he expected to hear something coming up from underneath.

Underneath was the Mortimers' suite.

'We had a first-rate set-up!' His voice was now hoarse. 'You'd never have got to the bottom of it. It was sheer chance, I'm telling you, or rather, several coincidences in a row!'

He bumped into the wall and leaned on it at an oblique angle, screwing up his face because his artificial intoxication — alcohol poisoning, to be more precise — must have given him a dreadful headache.

'Come on, then . . . While there's still time, try and work out which Pietr I am! Quite an actor, aren't I?'

He was sad and disgusting, comical and repulsive at the same time. His level of intoxication was increasing by the second.

'It's odd they're not here yet! But they will be! . . . And then . . . Come on, guess! . . . which Pietr will I be? . . . '

His mood changed abruptly and he put his head in his hands. You could see on his face that he was in pain.

'You'll never understand . . . The story of the two Pietrs . . . It's like the story of Cain and Abel . . . I suppose you're a Catholic . . . In our country we're Protestant and know the Bible by heart . . . But it's no good . . . I'm sure Cain was a good-natured boy, a trusting guy . . . Whereas that Abel . . . '

There was someone in the corridor. The door opened.

It even took Maigret aback, and he had to clench his pipe harder between his teeth.

For the person who had just come in was Mortimer, in a fur coat, looking as hale and ruddy as a man who has just come from a gourmet dinner.

He gave off a faint smell of liqueur and cigar.

His expression altered as soon as he got into the lounge. Colour drained from his face. Maigret noticed he was asymmetrical in a way that was difficult to place but which gave him a murky look.

You could sense he'd just come in from outside. There was still some cooler air in the folds of his clothes.

There were two sides to the scene. Maigret couldn't watch both simultaneously.

He paid more attention to the Latvian as he tried to clear his mind once his initial fright had passed. But it was already too late. The man had taken too large a dose. He knew it himself, even as he desperately applied all his willpower to the task.

His face was twisted. He could probably see people and things only through a distorting haze.

When he let go of the table he tripped, came within a whisker of falling over but miraculously recovered his balance.

'My dear Mor . . . ' he began.

His eyes crossed Maigret's and he spoke in a different voice:

'Too bad, eh! Too . . . '

The door slammed. Rapid footsteps going away. Mortimer had beaten a retreat. At that point Pietr fell into an armchair.

Maigret was at the door in a trice. Before setting off, he stopped to listen.

But the many different noises in the hotel made it impossible to identify the sound of Mortimer's footsteps.

'I'm telling you, this is what you wanted . . . ' Pietr stuttered, and then with slurred tongue carried on speaking in a language Maigret didn't know.

The inspector locked the door behind him and went along the corridor until he got to a staircase. He ran down.

He got to the first-floor landing just in time to bump into a woman who was running away. He smelt gun-powder.

He grabbed the woman by her clothes with his left hand. With his right hand he hit her wrist hard, and a revolver fell to the floor. The gun went off, and the bullet shattered the glass pane in the lift.

The woman struggled. She was exceptionally strong. Maigret had no means to restrain her other than twisting her wrist, and she fell to her knees, hissing:

'Let go! . . . '

The hotel began to stir. An unaccustomed sound of excitement arose along all the corridors and filtered out all the exits.

The first person to appear was a chambermaid dressed in black and white. She raised her arms and fled in fright.

'Don't move!' Maigret ordered — not to the maid, but to his prisoner.

But both women froze. The chambermaid screamed:

'Mercy! . . . I haven't done anything . . . '

Then things turned quite chaotic. People started pouring in from every direction. The manager was waving his arms about in the middle of the crowd. Further down there were women in evening dress making a terrible din.

Maigret decided to bend over and put handcuffs on his prisoner, who was none other than Anna Gorskin. She fought back, and in the struggle her dress got torn, making her bosom visible, as it often was. A fine figure of a woman she was too, with her sparkling eyes and her twisted mouth.

'Mortimer's suite . . . ' Maigret shouted to the manager.

But the poor man didn't know if he was coming or going. Maigret was on his own in the middle of a panicky crowd of people who kept bumping into each other, with womenfolk screaming, weeping and falling over.

The American's suite was only a few metres away. The inspector didn't need to open the door, it was swinging on its hinges. He saw a body on the floor, bleeding but still moving. Then he ran back up to the next floor, banged on the door he'd locked himself, got no response, and then forced it open.

Pietr's suite was empty!

The suitcase was still on the floor where he had left it, with the off-the-peg suit laid over it.

An icy blast came from the open window. It gave on to a courtyard no wider than a chimney. Down below you could make out the dark rectangular shapes of three doors.

* * *

Maigret went back down with heavy tread. The crowd had calmed down somewhat. One of the guests was a doctor. But the women — like the men, moreover! — weren't too bothered about Mortimer, to whom the doctor was attending. All eyes were on the Jewish woman slumped in the corridor with handcuffs on her wrists, snarling insults and threats at her audience. Her hat had slipped off and bunches of glossy hair fell over her face.

A desk interpreter came out of the lift with the broken glass, accompanied by a city policeman.

'Get them all out of here,' Maigret ordered. People protested behind his back. He looked big enough to fill the whole width of the corridor. Grumpily, obstinately, he went over to Mortimer's body.

'Well? . . . '

The doctor was a German with not much French, and he launched into a long explanation in a medley of two languages.

The millionaire's lower jaw had literally vanished. There was just a wide, red-black mess in its place. Despite this, his mouth was still moving, though it wasn't quite a mouth any more, and from it came a babbling sound, with a lot of blood.

Nobody could understand what it meant, neither Maigret nor the doctor who was, it turned out later, a professor at the University of Bonn; nor could the two or three other persons standing nearest.

Cigar ash was sprinkled over the fur coat. One of Mortimer's hands was wide open.

'Is he dead?' Maigret asked.

The doctor shook his head, and both men fell silent.

The noise in the corridor was abating. The policeman was moving the insistent rubberneckers down the corridor one pace at a time.

Mortimer's lips closed and then opened again. The doctor kept still for a few seconds. Then he rose and, as if relieved of a great weight, declared:

'Dead, *ja* . . . It was hard . . . '

Someone had stepped on the fur coat, which bore a clear imprint of the sole of a shoe.

The policeman, with his silver epaulettes, appeared in the open doorway and didn't say anything at first.

'What should I . . . '

'Get them all out of here, every single one . . . ' Maigret commanded.

'The woman is screaming . . . '

'Let her scream . . . '

He went to stand in front of the fireplace. But there was no fire in this hearth.

14

The Ugala Club

Every race has its own smell, and other races hate it. Despite opening the window and puffing relentlessly at his pipe, Inspector Maigret could not get rid of the background odour that made him uncomfortable.

Maybe the whole of Hôtel du Roi de Sicile was impregnated with the smell. Perhaps it was the entire street. The first whiff hits you when the hotel-keeper with the skullcap opens his window, and the further you go up the stairs, the stronger it gets.

In Anna Gorskin's room, it was overpowering. That's partly because there was food all over the place. The *saucisson* was full of garlic but it had gone soft and turned an unprepossessing shade of pink. There were also some fried fish lying on a plate in a vinegary sauce.

Stubs from Russian cigarettes. Half a dozen cups with tea-dregs in them. Sheets and underwear that felt still damp. The tang of a bedroom that has never been aired.

He'd come across a small grey canvas bag inside the mattress that he'd taken apart. A few photos as well as a university diploma dropped out of it.

One of photographs displayed a steep cobbled

street of gabled houses of the kind you see in Holland, but painted a bright white to show off the neat black outlines of windows, doors and cornices.

On the house in the foreground was an inscription in ornate lettering reminiscent of Gothic and Cyrillic script at the same time

6
Rütsep
Max Johannson
Tailor

It was a huge building. There was a beam sticking out from the roof with a pulley on the end used to winch up wheat for storage in the loft. From street level, six steps with an iron railing led up to the main door.

On those steps a family group was gathered round a dull, grey little man of about forty — that must be the tailor — trying to look solemn and superior.

His wife, in a satin dress so tight it might burst, was sitting on a carved chair. She was smiling cheerfully at the photographer, though she'd pursed her lips to make herself look a little more distinguished.

The parents were placed behind two children holding hands. They were both boys, aged around six or eight, in short trousers, black long socks, in white embroidered sailor collar shirts with decorations on the cuffs.

Same age! Same height! A striking likeness between them, and with the tailor.

132

But you couldn't fail to notice the difference in their characters. One had a decisive expression on his face and was looking at the camera aggressively, with some kind of a challenge. The other was stealing a glance at his brother. It was a look of trust and admiration.

The photographer's name was embossed on the image: *K. Akel, Pskov.*

The second black-and-white photograph was bigger and more significant. Three refectory tables could be seen lengthwise, laden with bottles and plates, and, at their head, a display-piece made of six flags, a shield with a design that couldn't be made out, two crossed swords and a hunting horn. The diners were students between seventeen and twenty years of age, wearing caps with narrow silver-edged visors and velvet tops which must have been that acid shade of green which is the Germans' favourite colour, and their northern neighbours' too.

They all had short hair and most of their faces were fine-featured. Some of them were smiling unaffectedly at the camera lens. Others were toasting it with an odd kind of beerstein made of turned wood. Some had shut their eyes against the magnesium flare.

Clearly visible in the middle of the table was a slate with the legend:

Ugala Club
Tartu

Students have clubs of that kind in universities all over the world. One young man, however, was

133

separate from the others. He was standing in front of the display without his cap. His shaved head made his face stand out. Unlike most of the others, in lounge suits, this young man was wearing a dinner jacket — a little awkwardly, as it was still too big for his shoulders. Over his white waistcoat he wore a wide sash, as if he'd been made Knight Commander of something. It was the sash of office of the captain of the club.

Curiously, although most of those present looked at the photographer, the really shy ones had turned instinctively towards their leader. Looking at him with the greatest intensity from his side was his double, who had to twist his neck almost out of joint in order to keep his eyes on his brother.

The student with the sash and the one who was gazing at him were unquestionably the same as the lads in front of the house in Pskov, that's to say the sons of tailor Johannson.

The diploma was written in antique-looking script on parchment, in Latin. The text was larded with archaic formulas that appointed one Hans Johannson, a student of philosophy, as a Fellow of the Ugala Club. It was signed at the bottom by the *Grand Master of the Club, Pietr Johannson*.

★   ★   ★

In the same canvas bag there was another package tied up with string, also containing photographs as well as letters written in Russian. The photographs were by a professional in

134

Vilna. One of them portrayed a plump and stern-looking middle-aged Jewish lady bedecked with as many jewels as a Catholic reliquary.

A family resemblance with Anna Gorskin was obvious at first glance. There was a photo of her too, aged around sixteen, in an ermine toque.

The correspondence was on paper printed with the tri-lingual letterhead of

Ephraim Gorskin
Wholesale Furrier
Royal Siberian Furs a Specialty
Branches in Vilna and Warsaw

Maigret was unable to translate the handwritten part. But he did at least notice that one heavily underlined phrase recurred several times over.

He slipped these papers into his pocket and conscientiously went over the room one last time. It had been occupied by the same person for such a long time that it had ceased to be just a hotel room. Every object and every detail down to the stains on the wallpaper and the linen told the full story of Anna Gorskin.

There was hair everywhere: thick, oily strands, like Asian hair.

Hundreds of cigarette butts. Tins of dry biscuits; broken biscuits on the floor. A pot of dried ginger. A big preserving jar containing the remains of a goose confit, with a Polish label. Caviar.

Vodka, whisky, and a small vessel, which Maigret sniffed, holding some left-over opium in compressed sheets.

Half an hour later he was at Quai des Orfèvres, listening to a translation of the letters, and he hung on to sentences such as:

' . . . Your mother's legs are swelling more and more . . . '

' . . . Your mother is asking if you still get swollen ankles when you walk a lot, because she thinks you have the same ailment as she does . . . '

' . . . We seem to be safe now, though the Vilna question hasn't been settled. We're caught between the Lithuanians and the Poles . . . But both sides hate the Jews . . . '

' . . . Could you check up on M. Levasseur, 65, Rue d'Hauteville, who has ordered some skins but has not provided any credit guarantee? . . . '

' . . . When you've got your degree, you must get married, and then the both of you must take over the business. Your mother isn't any use . . . '

' . . . Your mother won't get out of her chair all day long . . . She's becoming impossible to manage . . . You ought to come home . . . '

' . . . The Goldstein boy, who got back two weeks ago, says you're not enrolled at the University of Paris. I told him he was wrong and . . . '

' . . . Your mother's had her legs tapped and she . . . '

' . . . You've been seen in Paris in unsuitable company, I want to know what is going on . . . '

' . . . I've had more unpleasant information about you. As soon as business permits, I shall

136

come and see for myself . . . '

' . . . If it wasn't for your mother, who does not want to be left alone and who according to the doctor will not recover, I would be coming to get you right now. I order you to come home . . . '

' . . . I'm sending you five hundred zloty for the fare . . . '

' . . . If you are not home within a month I will curse you . . . '

Then more on the mother's legs. Then what a Jewish student on a home visit to Vilna told them about her bachelor life in Paris.

' . . . Unless you come home straight away I want nothing more to do with you . . . '

Then the final letter:

' . . . How have you managed for a whole year since I stopped sending you any money? Your mother is very upset. She says it is all my fault . . . '

Detective Chief Inspector Maigret did not smile once. He put the papers in his drawer and locked it, drafted a few telegrams and then went down to the police cells.

Anna Gorskin had spent the night in the common room. But Maigret had at last ordered them to put her in a private cell, and he went and peered at her through the grating in the door. Anna was sitting on the stool. She didn't jump but slowly turned her face towards the hatch, looked straight at Maigret and sneered at him.

He went into the cell and stood there looking at Anna for quite a while. He realized that there was no point trying to be clever or asking those oblique questions that sometimes prompt an inadvertent admission of guilt.

He just grunted:

'Anything to confess?'

'I admit nothing!'

'Do you still deny killing Mortimer?'

'I admit nothing!'

'Do you deny having bought grey clothes for your accomplice?'

'I admit nothing!'

'Do you deny having them taken up to his room at the Majestic together with a letter in which you declared you were going to kill Mortimer and also made an appointment to meet outside the hotel?'

'I admit nothing!'

'What were you doing at the Majestic?'

'I was looking for Madame Goldstein.'

'There's nobody of that name at the hotel.'

'I was unaware of that . . .'

'So why were you running away with a gun in your hand when I came across you?'

'In the first floor corridor I saw a man fire at someone and then drop his gun on the floor. I picked it up off the floor in case he decided to fire it at me. I was running to raise the alarm . . .'

'Had you ever set eyes on Mortimer?'

'No . . .'

'But he went to your lodgings in Rue du Roi-de-Sicile.'

'There are sixty tenants in the building.'

'Do you know Pietr the Latvian, or Oswald Oppenheim?'

'No . . . '

'That does not hold water . . . '

'*I don't give a damn!*'

'We'll find the salesman who brought up the grey suit.'

'Go ahead!'

'I've told your father, in Vilna . . . '

For the first time she tensed up. But she put on a grin straight away:

'If you want him to make the effort then you'd better send him the fare . . . '

Maigret didn't rise to the bait, but just carried on watching her — with interest, but also with some sympathy. You couldn't deny she had guts!

On first reading, her statement seemed insubstantial. The facts seemed to speak for themselves. But that's exactly the kind of situation where the police often lack sufficient solid evidence with which to confound the suspect's denials.

And in this case, they had no evidence at all! The revolver hadn't been supplied by any of the gunsmiths in Paris, so there was no way of proving it belonged to Anna Gorskin. Second: she'd been at the Majestic at the time of the murder, but it's not forbidden to walk in and around large hotels of that kind as if they were public spaces. Third: she claimed she'd been looking for someone, and that couldn't be ruled out.

Nobody had seen her pull the trigger. Nothing remained of the letter that Pietr had burned.

Circumstantial evidence? There was a ton of it. But juries don't reach a verdict on circumstantial evidence alone. They're wary of even the clearest proof for fear of making a judicial error, the ghost that defence lawyers are forever parading in front of them.

Maigret played his last card.

'Pietr's been seen in Fécamp . . . '

That got the response he wanted. Anna Gorskin shuddered. But she told herself he was lying, so she got a grip on herself and didn't rise to the bait.

'So what?'

'We have an anonymous letter — we're checking it out right now — that says he's hiding in a villa with someone called Swaan . . . '

Anna glanced up at him with her dark eyes. She looked grave, almost tragic.

★ ★ ★

Maigret was looking without thinking at Anna Gorskin's ankles and noticed that, as her mother feared, the young woman already had dropsy. Her scalp was visible through her thinning hair, which was in a mess. Her black dress was dirty. And there was a distinct shadow on her upper lip.

All the same she was a good-looking woman, in a common, feral way. Sitting sideways on the stool, or rather huddling up in self-defence, she fired daggers from her eyes as she scowled at the inspector.

'If you know all that already, why bother to ask me? . . . '

Her eyes flashed, and she added with an offensive laugh:

'Unless you're afraid of bringing *her* down too! . . . I'm right, aren't I? . . . Ha! Ha! . . . I don't matter ... I'm just a foreigner ... A ghetto girl living from hand to mouth ... But she's different! ... Oh well ... '

She was going to talk. Jealousy had done it. Maigret sensed that he might scare her off if he seemed too interested, so he put on a nonchalant air and looked away. But she screamed out:

'Well ... You get nothing! Did you hear me? Buzz off and leave me alone. I told you already, you get nothing! ... Not a thing!'

She threw herself to the floor in a way that could not have been forestalled even by men well acquainted with this kind of woman. She was having a fit of hysterics! Her face was all distorted, her arms and legs were writhing on the floor, and her body juddered with muscular spasms.

What had been a beautiful woman was now a hideous hag tearing whole tufts of hair off her head with no thought for the pain.

Maigret wasn't alarmed, he'd seen a hundred fits of this kind already. He picked the water jug off the floor. It was empty. He called a guard:

'Fill this up, quickly.'

Within minutes he'd poured cold water over the woman's face. She gasped, greedily opened her mouth, looked at Maigret without knowing who he was, then fell into a deep slumber. Now and again small spasms ran across the surface of her body.

Maigret let down the bed, which had been raised against the wall as required by regulations, smoothed out the wafer-thin mattress and with great effort picked up Anna Gorskin and laid her on the bed.

He did all that without the slightest resentment, with a gentleness you'd never think he was capable of. He pulled the unhappy woman's dress down over her knees, took her pulse and watched over her for a long while.

In this light she had the look of a worn-out woman of thirty-five. Her forehead was full of tiny wrinkles you couldn't usually see. Conversely her chubby hands, with cheap varnish clumsily painted on her nails, had a delicate shape.

Maigret filled his pipe slowly with his index finger, like a man not sure what to do next. For a while he paced up and down the cell, with its door still ajar.

Suddenly he turned around, for he could hardly believe his eyes.

Anna Gorskin had just pulled the blanket up over her face. She was just a shapeless lump underneath the ugly grey cotton cover. A lump that was heaving up and down in staccato. If you strained your ear you could hear her muffled sobs.

Maigret went out noiselessly, shut the door behind him, went past the guard then, when he had gone ten metres further on, came back on his tracks.

'Have her meals sent over from Brasserie Dauphine!' he blurted out, grumpily.

15

Two Telegrams

Maigret read them aloud to Monsieur Comeliau, the examining magistrate, who had a bored expression on his face.

The first was a wire from Mrs Mortimer-Levingston in response to the message informing her of her husband's murder.

Berlin. Hotel Modern. Am sick with a high temperature, cannot travel. Stones will deal with it.

Maigret smiled sourly.

'Do you see? Here's the message from Wilhelmstrasse, for contrast. It's in IPC, I'll translate it for you:

Mrs Mortimer arrived air, staying Hotel Modern, Berlin. Found message Paris on return from theatre. Took to bed and called American medic Pelgrad. Doctor claims confidentiality privilege. Query bring in second opinion? Hotel staff not aware any symptoms.

'As you can see, your honour, the lady is not keen to be questioned by French police. Mind you, I'm not claiming she's an accomplice. Quite the opposite, in fact. I'm sure Mortimer hid ninety-nine per cent of his activities from her. He wasn't the kind of man to trust a women, especially not his wife. But the bottom line is that she passed on a message one evening at Pickwick's Bar to a professional dancer who's now on ice in the morgue . . . That might be the only time that Mortimer used her, out of sheer necessity . . . '

'What about Stones?' the magistrate inquired.

'Mortimer's principal secretary. He was in charge of communications between the boss and his various businesses. At the time of the murder he'd been in London for a week, staying at the Victoria Hotel. I was careful to keep him out of the picture. But I called Scotland Yard and asked them to check the man out. Please note that when the English police turned up at the Victoria, news of Mortimer's death hadn't been released in the country, though it may have reached the news desks. Nonetheless the bird had flown. Stones did a bunk a few minutes before the police got there . . . '

The magistrate surveyed the pile of letters and telegrams cluttering his desk with a gloomy look on his face.

'Do you think we should foster the rumour that it was a love murder?' Comeliau asked, without conviction.

'I think that would be wise. Otherwise you'll set off a stock market panic and ruin a number of honourable businesses — first and foremost, those French companies that Mortimer had just bailed out.'

'Obviously, but . . . '

'Hang on a moment! The US Embassy will want proof . . . And you haven't got any! . . . And nor do I . . . '

The magistrate wiped his glasses.

'And the consequence is . . . ?'

'None . . . I'm waiting for news from Dufour, who's been in Fécamp since yesterday . . . Give Mortimer a fine funeral . . . Doesn't matter. With speeches and official delegations.'

The magistrate had been looking at Maigret with curiosity for the last few minutes.

'You look funny . . . ' he said suddenly.

The inspector smiled and put on a confidential air:

'It's morphine!' he said.

'Eh? . . . '

'Don't worry! I'm not hooked on it yet! Just a little injection in my chest . . . The medics want to remove two of my ribs, they say it's absolutely necessary . . . But it's a huge job! . . . I'll have to go into a clinic and stay there for God knows how many weeks . . . I asked for sixty hours' stay of execution . . . The worst outcome would be losing a third rib . . . Two more than Adam! . . . That's all! Now you're treating this like a tragedy as well . . . It's obvious you haven't gone over the pros and cons with Professor Cochet, who's fiddled about with the innards of almost all the world's kings and masters . . . He'd have told you as he told me that there are thousands of people missing all sorts of bits and pieces in their bodies . . . Take the Czech premier . . . Cochet removed one of his kidneys . . . I saw it . . . He showed me all sorts of things, lungs, stomachs . . . And the people who had them before are still around, all over the world, getting on with their lives . . . '

He checked the time on his wristwatch, muttering:

'Come on, Dufour! . . . '

He was now looking serious again. The air in the magistrate's office was blue with the smoke from Maigret's pipe. The inspector perched on the edge of the desk; he had made himself quite at home. After a pause:

'I think I'd better pop down to Fécamp myself!' he sighed. 'There's a train in an hour . . . '

'Nasty business!' Comeliau said, as if to bring the case to an end, pushing the file away.

Maigret was lost in contemplation of the pall of smoke all around him. The only noise that broke the silence, or rather gave it a rhythm, was the gurgling of his pipe.

'Look at this photograph,' he said all of a sudden.

He held out the Pskov photograph showing the tailor's white-gabled house, the hoist, the six steps and the seated mother, with the father posing and the two lads in their embroidered sailor collar shirts.

'That's in Russia! I had to look it up in an atlas. Not far from the Baltic Sea. There are several small countries in those parts: Estonia, Lithuania, Latvia . . . With Poland and Russia surrounding them. The national borders don't match ethnic boundaries. From one village to the next you change language. And on top of

146

that you've got Jews spread all over, constituting a separate race. And besides that, there are the communists! There are border wars going on all the time! And the armies of the ultra-nationalists . . . People live on pine-cones in the woods. The poor over there are poorer than anywhere else. Some of them die of cold and hunger. There are intellectuals defending German culture, others defending Slavic culture, and still others defending local customs and ancient dialects . . . Some of the peasants have the look of Lapps or Kalmyks, others are tall and blond, and then you've got mixed-race Jews who eat garlic and slaughter livestock their own special way . . . '

Maigret took the photograph back from the magistrate, who hadn't seemed very interested in it.

'What odd little boys!' was his only comment.

Maigret handed it back to the magistrate and asked:

'Can you tell me which of the two I'm looking for?'

Three-quarters of an hour remained before the train left. Magistrate Comeliau studied in turn the boy who seemed to be challenging the photographer and his brother, who could be turning towards the other one to ask for his advice.

'Photographs like that speak volumes!' Maigret continued. 'It makes you wonder why their parents and their teachers who saw them like that didn't guess right off what lay in store for these characters. Look closely at the father . . . He was killed in a riot one evening when the nationalists were fighting communists in the streets . . . He wasn't on either side . . . He'd just gone out to get a loaf of bread . . . I got the story by sheer chance from the landlord of the Roi de Sicile, who comes from Pskov . . . The mother's still alive and lives in the same house. On Sundays she puts on national dress, with a tall hat that comes down on the sides . . . And the boys . . . '

Maigret stopped. His voice changed entirely.

'Mortimer was born on a farm in Ohio and started out selling shoelaces in San Francisco. Anna Gorskin, who was born in Odessa, spent her early years in Vilna. Mrs Mortimer, lastly, is a Scot who emigrated to Florida when still a child. And the whole lot have ended up a stone's throw from Notre-Dame-de-Paris. Whereas I'm the son of a gamekeeper on a Loire Valley estate that goes back centuries.'

He looked at his watch again and pointed to the boy in the photograph who was staring admiringly at his brother.

'What I've got to do now is lay my hands on that boy there!'

He emptied his pipe into the coal bucket and almost began filling up the stove, out of habit.

A few minutes later Magistrate Comeliau was wiping his gold-rimmed spectacles and saying to his clerk:

'Don't you find Maigret changed? I thought he was . . . how should I put it . . . rather excited . . . rather . . . '

He couldn't find the right word, and then cut to the main point:

'What the hell are all these foreigners doing here?'

Then he abruptly pulled over the Mortimer file and began to dictate:

'Take this down: *In the year nineteen . . .* '

★ ★ ★

Inspector Dufour was in the very same nook in the wall where Maigret had kept watch on the man in the trenchcoat one stormy day, because it was the only niche to be found in the steep alleyway that led first to the handful of villas on the cliff and then turned into a track that petered out in a grazed meadow.

Dufour was wearing black spats, a short, belted cloak and a sailor's cap, like everyone else in these parts. He must have acquired it on arrival at Fécamp.

'So? . . . ' Maigret asked as he came upon him in the dark.

'All going fine, chief.'

He found that rather worrying.

'What's going fine?'

'The man hasn't come in or gone out . . . If he got to Fécamp before me and went to the villa, then that's where he is . . . '

'Give me the whole story, in detail.'

'Yesterday morning, nothing to report. The maid went to market. In the evening I had Detective Bornier relieve me. Nobody in or out all night long. Lights out at ten . . . '

'Next?'

'I returned to my post this morning, and

149

Bornier went to bed . . . He'll come back and relieve me . . . Around nine, same as yesterday, the maid went off to the market . . . About half an hour ago a young lady came out . . . She'll be back shortly . . . I guess she's gone to call on someone . . . '

Maigret kept quiet. He realized how far the surveillance fell short of the mark. But how many men would he need to make a job like this completely watertight?

To keep the villa under permanent observation he would need at least three men. Then he'd need a detective to tail the maid, and another one for the 'young lady', as Dufour called her!

'She's been gone thirty minutes?'

'Yes . . . Look! Here comes Bornier . . . My turn for a meal break . . . I've only had a sandwich all day and my feet are freezing . . . '

'Off you go . . . '

Detective Bornier was a young man just starting out with the Flying Squad.

'I met Madame Swaan . . . ' he said.

'Where? When?'

'At the dockside . . . Just now . . . She was going towards the outer pier . . . '

'On her own?'

'Yes, alone. I thought of tailing her . . . But then I remembered Dufour was expecting me . . . The pier's a dead end, so she can't get very far . . . '

'What was she wearing?'

'A dark coat . . . I didn't pay attention . . . '

'Can I go now?' Dufour asked.

'I told you already . . . '

'If anything comes up, you will let me know, won't you? . . . All you have to do is ring on the hotel bell three times in a row . . . '

What an idiot! Maigret was barely listening. He told Bornier: 'You stay here . . . ' and then took off quite abruptly for the Swaans' villa, where he tugged at the bell-pull at the gate so hard that it nearly came off. He could see light on the ground floor, in the room he now knew to be the dining room.

Nobody came for five minutes, so he climbed over the low wall, got to the front door, and banged on it with his fist.

From inside a terrified voice wailed:

'Who's there?'

He could hear children crying as well.

'Police! Open up!'

There was a pause and the sound of scuffling feet.

'Open up! Get a move on!'

The hallway was unlit, but as he went in Maigret made out a white rectangle that could only be the maid's apron.

'Madame Swaan?'

At that point a door swung open and he saw the little girl he'd noticed on his first visit. The maid stood stock still with her back to the wall. You could tell she was rigid with fright.

'Who did you see this morning?'

'Officer, I swear I . . . '

She collapsed in tears.

'I swear . . . I swear . . . '

'Was it Captain Swaan?'

'No! . . . I . . . It was . . . madame's

151

. . . brother-in-law . . . He gave me a letter to give to madame . . . '

'Where was he?'

'Opposite the butcher's . . . He was waiting for me there . . . '

'Was that the first time he's asked you to do jobs of that kind?'

'Yes, the first time . . . I never saw him before except in this house.'

' . . . Do you know where he planned to join up with Madame Swaan?'

'I don't know anything! . . . Madame has been in a nervous state all day . . . She asked me questions as well. She wanted to know how he looked . . . I told her the truth, I said he looked like he was on the edge . . . He scared me when he came up close.'

Maigret rushed out without closing the door behind him.

16

On the Rocks

Detective Bornier, a newcomer to the Squad, was quite horrified to see the chief run straight past, brushing him as he went without a word of apology and leaving the front door of the villa wide open. Twice he called out:

'Inspector Maigret! Inspector, sir!'

But Maigret did not turn back. He only slowed down a few minutes later, when he got to Rue d'Etretat, where there were some passers-by, then he turned to the right, sploshed through the mud at the dockside and started running again towards the outer pier.

He'd only gone 100 metres when he made out the figure of a woman. He switched to the other side so as to get nearer to her. There was a trawler with an acetylene lamp up in the rigging — that meant it was unloading its catch.

He stopped so as to allow the woman to reach the pool of light and he saw it was the face of Madame Swaan, in great distress. She was rolling her eyes and walking with a hurried and clumsy tread, as if she were hopping over deep ruts and by some miracle not falling into them.

The inspector was ready to tackle her and had already started to walk over. But the long black line of the deserted pier stretching out into the dark, with waves breaking over both sides, caught his eye. He rushed towards it. Beyond the trawler there wasn't a soul to be seen. The green and red flare of the harbour passage light cut through the night. The light was set on the rocks and every fifteen seconds it flashed over a wide stretch of water then lit up the outer cliff, which blinked on and off like a ghost.

Maigret stumbled over capstans as he found his way onto the pontoon, in the noise of crashing waves.

He strained his eyes to see in the dark. A ship's siren wailed a request to be let out of the lock.

In front of him was the blank and noisy sea. Behind him, the town with its shops and slippery pavements.

He strode on quickly, stopping at intervals to peer into the darkness, with increasing anxiety.

★   ★   ★

He didn't know the terrain and took what he thought was a short cut. The walkway on stilts led him to the foot of a lighthouse where there were three black cannonballs, which he counted without thinking why. Further on, he leaned over the railing and looked down on great pools of white foam settling between outcrops of rock.

The wind blew his hat off his head. He chased after it but couldn't stop it from falling into the sea. Seagulls screeched overhead, and every now and again he could make out a white wing flapping against the black sky.

154

Maybe Madame Swaan had found nobody waiting for her at the appointed place. Maybe her assignation had had time to get away? Maybe he was dead.

Maigret was hopping up and down, he was sure that every second counted.

He reached the green light and went round the steel platform on which it stood.

Nobody there! Waves raised their crests high, tottered, crashed down and retreated from the foamy hollow before renewing their attack on the breakwater. The sound of grinding shingle reached his ears in bursts. He could make out the vague outline of the deserted Casino.

Maigret was looking for a man!

He turned back and wandered along the shore among stones that in the dark all looked like huge potatoes. He was down at the waterline. Sea spray hit his face.

That was when he realized it was low tide, and that the pier stood on black rocks with swirling seawater in the hollows between them.

It was a complete miracle that he caught sight of the man. At first glance he looked like an inanimate object, just a blur among other blurry shapes in the dark.

He strained his eyes to see. It was something on the outermost rock, where breakers rose to their proudest height before collapsing into thousands of droplets.

But it was alive.

To get there Maigret had to slither through the struts holding up the walkway he'd run along a few minutes previously.

The rocks underfoot were covered in seaweed and Maigret's soles kept slipping and sliding. Hissing sounds came from all around — crabs fleeing in their hundreds, or air bubbles bursting, algae popping, mussels quivering on the wooden beams they'd colonized halfway to the top.

At one point Maigret lost his footing, plunging knee-deep into a rock pool.

He'd lost sight of the man but he knew he was going in the right direction. Whoever it was must have got to his spot when the tide had been even lower, because Inspector Maigret found himself held back by a pool that was now over two metres wide. He tested the depth with his right foot and nearly tipped right over. In the end he got across by hanging on to the ironwork supporting the stilts.

These are times when it's better not to be watched. You try out movements you've not been trained to do. You get them wrong every time, like a clumsy acrobat. But even so you make headway, pushed forwards by your own mass, so to speak. You fall and you get up again. There's no skill and no grace to it, but you splash on nonetheless.

Maigret got a cut in his cheek but he could never work out whether it was from a fall on the rocks or a graze from a nail in one of the beams.

He caught sight of the man again but wondered if he was seeing things: the man was so perfectly still that he could have been one of those rocks that from afar take on the shape of a human being.

He got to the point where he had water

slapping about between his legs. Maigret was not the sea-going type.

He couldn't help himself but hurry on forwards.

At last he reached the outcrop where the man was sitting. He was one metre higher than his target, and three or four metres away.

He didn't think of getting his gun out, but insofar as the terrain allowed it he tiptoed forwards, knocking stones down into the water, whose roar covered the noise.

Then, suddenly, without transition, he pounced on the stationary figure, put his neck in an arm-lock and pulled him down backwards.

The pair of them almost slipped and disappeared into one of the big rollers that break over those rocks. They were spared by sheer chance.

Any attempt to repeat the exploit would surely have ended in disaster.

The man hadn't seen who was attacking him, and he slithered like a snake. He could not free his head, but he wriggled with what must surely be counted in those circumstances as superhuman agility.

Maigret didn't want to strangle him. He was only trying to overpower him. He'd hooked one of his feet behind a stilt, and that foot was all that was keeping the pair of them from falling off.

His opponent didn't struggle for long. He'd only fought out of spontaneous reaction, like an animal.

As soon as he'd had time to think, at any rate once he'd seen it was Maigret, whose face was right next to his, he stopped moving.

He blinked his eyes to indicate surrender and when his neck was freed, he nodded towards the shifting and mountainous sea and blurted out in a still unsteady voice:

'Watch out . . . '

★ ★ ★

'Would you like to talk, Hans Johannson?'

Maigret was hanging on to a piece of slippery seaweed by his fingernails. When it was all over he confessed that at this precise moment his opponent could have easily kicked him into the water. It was only a second, but Johannson, squatting beside the last stilt of the pier, didn't take advantage of it. Later still, Maigret confessed with great honesty that he had had to hang on to his prisoner's foot to haul himself back up the slope.

Then the two of them began the return journey, without a word between them. The tide had risen further. A few metres from shore they were cut off by the same rock pool that had blocked the inspector on his way out, but it was deeper now.

Pietr went down first, stumbled when he was three metres in, slipped over, coughed up seawater, then stood up. It was only waist-deep. Maigret plunged in. At one point he closed his eyes as he felt he couldn't keep the huge weight of his body above the surface any more. But the two of them eventually found themselves dripping on the pebbles of the shore.

'Did she talk?' Pietr asked in a voice so blank that it seemed to be devoid of anything that might still harbour a will to live.

Maigret was entitled to lie but instead he declared:

'She told me nothing . . . But I know . . . '

They could not stay where they were. The wind was turning their wet clothes into an ice-jacket. Pietr's teeth started chattering. Even in the faint moonlight Maigret could see that the man's lips had turned blue.

He'd lost his moustache. He had the worried face of Fyodor Yurevich, the look of the little boy in Pskov gazing at his brother. But though his eyes were the same cloudy grey as before, they now stared with a harsh and unyielding gaze.

A three-quarters turn to the right would allow them to see the cliff and the two or three lights that twinkled on it. One of them came from Madame Swaan's villa.

Each time the beam of the harbour light went round, you caught a glimpse of the roof that shielded Madame Swaan, the two children and the frightened maid.

'Come on . . . ' Maigret said.

'To the police station?'

Maigret sounded resigned, or rather, indifferent.

'No . . . '

★   ★   ★

He was familiar with one of the harbour-side hotels, Chez Léon, where he'd noticed an entrance that was used only in the summer, for the handful of holiday-makers who spend the season by the sea at Fécamp. The entrance gave onto a room that was turned into a fairly grand dining room in high season. In winter, though, sailors were happy to drink and eat oysters and herring in the main bar.

That was the door Maigret used. He crossed the unlit room with his prisoner and found himself in the kitchen. A maid screamed in stupefaction.

'Call the *patron* . . . '

She stood still and yelled:

'Monsieur Léon! . . . Monsieur Léon! . . . '

'Give me a room . . . ' the inspector said when Léon came in.

'Monsieur Maigret! . . . But you're soaking! . . . Did you? . . . '

'A room, quickly! . . . '

'There's no fire made up in any of the rooms! . . . And a hot-water bottle will never . . . '

'Don't you have a pair of bathrobes?'

'Of course . . . My own . . . but . . . '

He was shorter than the inspector by three heads!

'Bring them down.'

They climbed a steep staircase with quaint bends in it. The room was decent. Monsieur Léon closed the shutters himself before suggesting:

'Hot toddy, right? . . . Full strength! . . . '

'Good idea . . . But get those bathrobes first . . . '

Maigret realized he was falling ill again, from

160

the cold. The injured side of his chest felt like a block of ice.

For a few minutes he and his prisoner got on like roommates. They got undressed. Monsieur Léon handed them his two bathrobes by stretching his arm around the door when it was ajar.

'I'll have the larger one,' the inspector said.

Pietr compared them for size. As he handed over the larger one to Maigret he noticed the wet bandage, and a nervous twitch broke out on his face.

'Is it serious?'

'Two or three ribs that'll have to be removed sooner or later . . . '

A silence ensued. It was broken by Monsieur Léon, who shouted from the other side of the door:

'Everything all right? . . . '

'Come in!'

Maigret's bathrobe barely covered his knees, leaving his thick, hairy calves for all to see.

Pietr, on the contrary, who was slim and pale with fair hair and feminine ankles, looked like a stylish clown.

'The toddy's on its way! I'll get your clothes dried, yes?'

Monsieur Léon gathered up the two soggy and dripping heaps on the floor and then shouted down from the top of the stairs:

'Come on then, Henriette . . . Where's that toddy?'

Then he tracked back to the bedroom and gave this advice:

'Don't talk too loud in here . . . There's a travelling salesman from Le Havre in the room next door . . . He's catching the 5 a.m. train . . . '

17

And a Bottle of Rum

It would be an exaggeration to say that in most criminal inquiries cordial relations arise between the police and the person they are trying to corner into a confession. All the same, they almost always become close to some degree (unless the suspect is just a glowering brute). That must be because for weeks and sometimes months on end the police and the suspect do nothing but think about each other.

The investigator strives to know all he can about the suspect's past, seeks to reconstitute his thinking and to foresee his reactions.

Both sides have high stakes in the game. When they sit down to a match, they do so in circumstances that are dramatic enough to strip away the veneer of polite indifference that passes for human relations in everyday life.

There have been cases of detectives who'd taken a lot of trouble to put a criminal behind bars growing fond of the culprit, to the extent of visiting him in prison and offering emotional support up to the moment of execution.

That partly explains the attitude that the two men adopted once they were alone in the hotel bedroom. The hotelier had brought up a portable charcoal stove, and a kettle was whistling on the hob. Beside it stood two glasses, a dish of sugar cubes and a tall bottle of rum.

Both men were cold. They huddled in their borrowed dressing gowns and leaned as close as they could to the little stove, which wasn't nearly strong enough to warm them up.

They were as casual with each other as if they were stuck in a dorm-room or a barracks, with the informality that arises between men only when social proprieties have become temporarily irrelevant.

In fact, it might have been simply because they were cold. Or more likely because of the weariness that overcame them at the same moment.

It was over! No words were needed to say that.

So each slumped into a chair and gazed at the blue enamel cooking stove that linked them together.

The Latvian was the one who took the bottle of rum and expertly mixed the toddy.

After taking a few sips, Maigret asked:

'Did you mean to kill her?'

The reply came straight away and it was just as straightforward:

'I couldn't do it.'

His face was all screwed up with nervous tics that gave the man no rest. His eyelids would bat up and down, his lips would go into spasms, his nostrils would twitch. The determined and intelligent face of Pietr started to dissolve into the face of Fyodor, the intensely agitated Russian vagrant. Maigret didn't bother to watch.

★ ★ ★

That's why he didn't realize that his opponent kept on taking the bottle of rum, filling his glass, and drinking it down. His eyes were beginning to shine.

'Was she married to Pietr? . . . He was the same as Olaf Swaan, wasn't he?'

The man from Pskov couldn't sit still, so he got up, looked for a packet of cigarettes but couldn't find any and seemed put out by that. As he came back past the table with the stove he poured himself some more rum.

'That's not the right starting point!' he said.

Then he looked Maigret straight in the eye:

'In a nutshell: you know the almost whole story already, don't you?'

'The two brothers of Pskov . . . Twins, I suppose? You're Hans, the one who was looking lovingly and tamely at the other one . . . '

'Even when we were kids he found it amusing to treat me as his servant . . . Not just between ourselves, but in front of classmates . . . He didn't call me his servant — he said: slave . . . He'd noticed I liked that . . . Because I did like it, I still don't know why . . . He was everything to me . . . I'd have got myself killed for his sake . . . When, later on . . . '

'Later on, when?'

He froze up. His eyelids flapped up and down. A swig of rum. Then he shrugged as if to say, what the hell. Then, controlling himself:

'When later on I came to love a woman, I don't think I was capable of any greater devotion . . . Probably less! I loved Pietr like . . . I can't find the word! . . . I got into fights with classmates who wouldn't grant that he was better than any of them, and as I was the least muscular boy in my class I got beaten up, and I got a kick out of it.'

'That kind of domination isn't uncommon between twins,' Maigret commented as he made himself a second glass of toddy. 'May I just take a moment?' He went to the door and called down to Léon to bring up the pipe he'd left in his clothes, together with some tobacco. Hans added:

'Can I have some cigarettes, do you mind?'

'And some cigarettes, Léon . . . Gauloises!'

He sat down again. They said nothing until the maid had brought up the supplies and withdrawn.

'You were both students at the University of Tartu . . . ' Maigret resumed.

The other man couldn't sit still or stop moving around. He nibbled the end of his cigarette as he smoked and spat out scraps of tobacco, jiggled from side to side, picked up a vase from the mantelpiece and put it down somewhere else, and got more and more excited as he talked.

'Yes, that's where it all began! My brother was top of the class. All the professors paid attention to him. Students came under his spell. So although he was one of the youngest, he was made Captain of Ugala.

'We drank lots of beer in the taverns. I did, especially! I don't know why I started drinking so young. I had no special reason. In a word, I've been a drinker all my life.

'I think it was mainly because after a few

glasses I could imagine a world to my own liking in which I would play a splendid part . . .

'Pietr was very hard on me. He called me a 'dirty Russian'. You can't know what that means. Our maternal grandmother was Russian. But in our part of the world, especially in the post-war years, Russians were treated as drunken dreamers and layabouts.

At that time the communists were stoking up riots. My brother led the Ugala Fraternity. They went to get weapons from a barracks and faced the communists head-on in the centre of town.

'I was scared . . . It wasn't my fault . . . I was frightened . . . I couldn't use my legs . . . I stayed in the tavern with the shutters closed and drank my way through the whole thing.

'I thought I was destined to become a great playwright, like Chekhov. I knew all his plays by heart. Pietr just laughed at me.

''You . . . You'll never make it!' he said.

'The disturbances and riots lasted a whole year, turning life upside down. The army wasn't up to maintaining order, so citizens got together in vigilante groups to defend the town.

'My brother, Captain of the Ugala Fraternity, became an important person, and he was taken seriously by people of substance. He didn't yet have any hair on his lip, but he was already being talked about as a potential leader of Free Estonia.

'But calm returned, and then a scandal erupted that had to be hushed up. When the accounts of the Ugala Club were done, it turned out that Pietr had used the group mainly to enrich himself.

'He was on several of the subcommittees and he'd fiddled all the books.

'He had to leave the country. He went to Berlin and wrote to ask me to join him there.

'That's where the two of us began.'

★ ★ ★

Maigret watched the man's face. It was too agitated by half.

'Which of you was the forger?'

'Pietr taught me how to mimic anybody's handwriting, and made me take a course in chemistry . . . I lived in a little room, and he gave me 200 marks a week to live on . . . But he soon bought himself a car, to take girls out for rides . . .

'Mainly, we doctored cheques . . . I could turn a cheque for ten marks into a cheque for ten thousand, and Pietr would cash it in Switzerland or Holland or even, one time, in Spain . . .

'I was drinking heavily. He despised me and treated me spitefully. One day I nearly got him caught accidentally, because one of my forgeries wasn't quite up to the mark.

'He beat me with his walking stick . . .

'And I said nothing! I still looked up to him . . . I don't know why . . . He impressed everyone, actually . . . At one point, if he'd wanted to, he could have married the daughter of a Reichsminister . . .

'Because of the dud forgery we had to get to France. To begin with I lived in Rue de l'École-de-Médecine . . .

'Pietr wasn't on his own. He'd linked up with several international gangs ... He travelled abroad a lot and he used me less and less. Only occasionally, for forgeries, because I'd got very good at that ...

'He gave me small amounts of money. He always said: 'You'll never do more than drink, you filthy Russian!' ...

'One day he told me he was going to America for a huge deal which would make him super-rich. He ordered me to go live in the country because I'd already been picked up several times in Paris by the immigration authorities. 'All I'm asking is for you to lie low! ... Not too much to ask, is it?' But he also asked me to supply him with a set of false passports, which I did.'

'And that's how you met the woman who became Madame Swaan ... '

'Her name was Berthe ... '

A pause. The man's Adam's apple was bouncing up and down. Then he blurted it all out:

'You can't imagine how much I wanted to *be something*! She was the cashier at the hotel where I was staying ... She saw me coming back drunk every night ... She would scold me ...

'She was very young, but a serious person. She made me think of having a house and children ...

'One evening she was lecturing me when I wasn't too drunk. I wept in her arms and I think I promised I would start over and become a new man.

'I think I would have kept my word. I was sick of everything! I'd had enough of the low life! . . .

'It lasted almost a month . . . Look! It was stupid . . . On Sundays we went to the bandstand together . . . It was autumn . . . We would walk back by way of the harbour and look at the boats . . .

'We didn't talk about love . . . She said she was my chum . . . But I knew that one day . . .

'That's right! One day my brother did come back. He needed me right away . . . He had a whole suitcase of cheques that needed doctoring . . . It was hard to imagine how he'd got hold of so many! . . . They were drawn on all the major banks in the world . . .

'He'd become a merchant seaman for the time being under the alias of Olaf Swaan . . . He stayed at my hotel . . . While I sweated over the cheques for weeks on end — doctoring cheques is tricky work! — he toured the Channel ports looking for boats to buy . . .

'His new business was booming. He told me he'd done a deal with a leading American financier, who would obviously be kept at arm's length from the scam.

'The aim was to get all the main international gangs to pull together.

'The bootleggers had already agreed to cooperate. Now they needed small boats to smuggle the alcohol . . .

'Do I need to tell you the rest? Pietr had cut off supplies of drink, to make me work harder . . . I lived alone in my little room with weaver's glasses, acids, pens and inks of every kind. I even had a portable printing press . . .

'One day I went into my brother's room without knocking. He had Berthe in his arms . . . '

He grabbed the almost empty bottle and poured the last dregs down his throat.

'I walked out,' he concluded in a peculiar tone. 'I had no option. I walked out . . . I got on a train . . . I tottered round every bar in Paris for days on end . . . and washed up in Rue du Roi-de-Sicile, dead drunk and sick as a dog!'

18

Hans at Home

'I suppose I can only make women feel sorry for me. When I woke up there was a Jewish girl taking care of me . . . She got the idea she should stop me drinking, just like the last one! . . . And she treated me like I was a child, as well! . . . '

He laughed. His eyes were misty. His restless fidgeting and twitching was exhausting to watch.

'Only this girl stuck it out. As for Pietr . . . I guess our being twins isn't insignificant, and we do have things in common . . .

'I told you he could have married a German society figure . . . Well, he didn't! He married Berthe, some while later, when she'd changed job and was working in Fécamp . . . He never told her the truth . . . I can see why not! . . . He needed a quiet, neat little place of his own . . . He had children with her! . . . '

That seemed to be more than he could bear. His voice broke. Real tears came to his eyes but they dried up straight away: maybe his eyelids were so hot they just evaporated.

'Right up to this morning she really believed she'd married the master of an ocean-going vessel . . . He would turn up now and again and spend a weekend or a month with her and the kids . . . Meanwhile, I was stuck with the other woman . . . with Anna . . . It's a mystery why she loved me . . . But she did love me, no doubt about that . . . So I treated her the way my brother had always treated me . . . I threw insults at her . . . I was constantly humiliating her . . .

'When I got drunk, she would weep . . . So I drank *on purpose* . . . I even took opium and other kinds of crap . . . *On purpose* . . . Then I would get ill, and she would look after me for weeks on end . . . I was turning into a wreck . . . '

He waved at his own body with an expression of disgust. Then he wheedled:

'Could you get me something to drink?'

Maigret hesitated only briefly, then went to the landing:

'*Patron*, send up some rum!' he shouted.

The man from Pskov didn't say thank you.

'I used to run away now and again, to Fécamp, where I prowled around the villa where Berthe lived . . . I remember her walking her first baby in the pram . . . Pietr had had to tell her I was his brother, because we looked so similar . . . Then I got an idea. When we were kids I'd learned to imitate Pietr, out of admiration . . . Anyway, one day, with all those dark thoughts in my mind, I went down to Fécamp dressed in clothes like his . . .

'The maid fell for it . . . As I went into the house the kid came up to me and cried 'Papa!' . . . What a fool I was! I ran away! But all the same it stuck in my mind . . .

'From time to time Pietr made appointments to see me . . . He needed me to forge things for him . . . And I said yes! Why? I hated him, but I was under his thumb . . . He was swimming in money, swanning around in five-star hotels and high society . . .

'He was caught twice, but he got off both times . . .

'I was never involved in what he was up to, but you must have seen through it as I did. When he'd been working on his own or with just a handful of accomplices, he only did things on a modest scale . . . But then Mortimer, whom I met only recently, got him in his sights . . . My brother had skills, cheek and maybe a touch of genius. Mortimer had scope and a rock-solid reputation the world over . . . Pietr's job was to get the top crooks to work in cahoots on Mortimer's behalf and to set up the scams. Mortimer was the banker . . .

'I didn't give a damn . . . As my brother had told me when I was a student at Tartu, I was a nobody . . . As I was a nobody, I drank, and alternated between moods of depression and periods of high spirits . . . Meanwhile there was one lifebuoy on these stormy seas — I still don't know why, maybe because it was the only time I'd ever glimpsed a prospect of happiness — and that was Berthe . . .

'I was stupid enough to come down to Fécamp last month . . . Berthe gave me some advice . . . Then she added: 'Why aren't you more like your brother?'

'Something suddenly occurred to me. I didn't understand why I hadn't thought of it before . . . I could *be* Pietr, whenever I liked!

'A few days later I got a message from him saying he was coming to France and would have need of me.

'I went to Brussels to wait for him. I crossed the tracks and boarded his train from the wrong side. I hid behind the luggage until I saw him get up from his seat to go to the toilet. I got there before he did.

'I killed him! I'd just drunk a litre of Belgian gin. The hardest part was to get his clothes off and then dress him up in mine.'

★ ★ ★

He was drinking greedily, with an appetite Maigret had never imagined possible.

'At your first meeting in the Majestic, did Mortimer suspect anything?'

'I think he did. But only vaguely. I had only one thing in my mind at that time: to see Berthe again . . . I wanted to tell her the truth . . . I had no real feelings of remorse, yet I felt unable to take advantage of the crime I'd committed . . . There were all sorts of clothes in Pietr's trunk . . . I dressed up as a tramp, the way I'm used to dressing . . . I went out by the back door . . . I sensed that Mortimer was on my tail, and it took me two hours to throw him off the scent . . .

'Then I got a car to drive me to Fécamp . . .

'Berthe was bewildered when I got there . . . And once I was standing in front of her, with her asking me to explain, I didn't have the heart to tell her what I'd done!

'Then you turned up . . . I saw you through the window . . . I told Berthe I was wanted for theft and I asked her to save me. When you'd gone, she said: 'Be off with you now! You are bringing dishonour on your brother's house . . . '

'That's right! That's exactly what she said! And I did go off! That's when you and I went back to Paris together . . .

'I went back to Anna . . . We had a row, obviously . . . Screaming and crying . . . Mortimer turned up at midnight, since he'd now seen through the whole thing, and he threatened to kill me unless I took over Pietr's place completely . . .

'It was a huge issue for him . . . Pietr had been his only channel of communication with the gangs . . . Without him, Mortimer would lose his hold over them.

'Back to the Majestic . . . with you right behind me! Someone said something about a dead policeman . . . I could see you'd got a bandage under your jacket . . .

'You'll never know how much life itself disgusted me . . . And the idea that I was condemned to acting the part of my brother for ever more . . .

'Do you remember when you dropped a photograph on the counter of a bar?

'When Mortimer came to the Roi de Sicile, Anna was up in arms . . . She saw it would put paid to her plan . . . She realized my new role would take me away from her . . . Next evening, when I got back to my room at the Majestic, I found a package and a letter . . . '

'A grey off-the-peg suit, and a note from Anna saying she was going to kill Mortimer,' Maigret said. 'And also making an appointment to see you somewhere . . . '

The air was now thick with smoke, which made the room feel warmer. Things looked less clear-cut in the haze. But Maigret spelled it out:

'You came here to kill Berthe . . . '

Hans was having another drink. He finished his glass, gripped the mantelpiece, and said:

'So as to be rid of everybody! Myself included! . . . I'd had enough! . . . All I had in my mind was what my brother would call a Russian idea — to die with Berthe, in each other's arms . . . '

He switched to a different tone of voice.

'That's stupid! You only get that kind of idea from the bottom of a bottle of spirits . . . There was a cop outside the gate . . . I'd sobered up . . . I scouted around . . . That morning I gave a note to the maid, asking my sister-in-law to meet me on the outer pier, saying that if she didn't come in person with some money, I'd be done for . . . That was base of me, wasn't it? But she came . . . '

★　★　★

All of a sudden he put his elbows on the marble mantelpiece and burst into tears, not like a man, but like a child. But, despite his sobs, he went on with his story.

'I wasn't up to it! We were in a dark spot . . . The roar of the sea . . . She was looking worried . . . I told her everything. All of it!

177

Including the murder . . . Yes, changing clothes in the cramped train toilet . . . Then, because she looked like she was going mad with grief, I swore to her that it wasn't true! . . . Wait a moment! I didn't deny the murder! . . . What I retracted was that Pietr was a piece of scum . . . I yelled that I'd made that up to get my own back on him . . . I suppose she believed me . . . *People always believe things like that* . . . She dropped the bag she'd brought with the money in it. Then she said . . . No! She had nothing else to say . . . '

He raised his head and looked at Maigret. His face was contorted, he tried to take a step but couldn't keep his balance and had to steady himself on the mantelpiece.

'Hand me the bottle, pal! . . . '

'Pal' was said with a kind of grumpy affection.

'Hang on! . . . Let me see that photo again . . . The one . . . '

Maigret got out the snapshot of Berthe. That was the only mistake he had made in the whole case: believing that at that moment Hans's mind was on the woman.

'No, not that one. The other one . . . '

The picture of the two boys in their embroidered sailor collar shirts!

The Latvian gazed on it like a man possessed. Inspector Maigret could only see it upside down, but even so the fairer boy's hero-worship of his brother stood out.

'They took my gun away with my clothes!' Hans blurted out in a blank and steady voice as he looked around the room.

Maigret had gone crimson. He nodded

awkwardly towards the bed, where his own service revolver lay.

The native of Pskov let go of the mantelpiece. He wasn't swaying now. He must have summoned up his last scrap of energy.

He went right past the inspector, less than a metre from him. They were both in dressing gowns. They'd drunk rum together.

Their two chairs were still facing each other, on opposite sides of the charcoal heater.

Their eyes met. Maigret couldn't bring himself to look away. He was expecting Hans to stop.

But Hans went on past him as stiff as a pike and sat on the bed, making its springs creak.

There was still a drop left in the second bottle. Maigret took it, clinking its neck against the glass.

He sipped it slowly. Or was he just pretending to drink? He was holding his breath.

Then the bang. He gulped his drink down.

★ ★ ★

Administratively speaking, the events were as follows:

On ... 19 November ... at 10 p.m. verified, an individual by the name of Hans Johannson, born Pskov, Russian Empire, of Estonian nationality, unemployed, residing at Rue du Roi-de-Sicile, Paris, after confessing to the murder of his brother, Pietr Johannson, on ... November of the same year in the train Étoile du Nord, took

179

his own life by shooting himself in the mouth shortly after his arrest in Fécamp by Detective Chief Inspector Maigret of the Flying Squad.

The 6 mm bullet traversed the palate and lodged in the brain. Death was instantaneous.

As a precaution the body has been taken to the morgue. Receipt of corpse has been acknowledged.

19

The Injured Man

The male nurses left, but not before Madame Maigret had treated them to a glass of plum liqueur, which she made herself every year on her summer holiday back home in the country in Alsace.

When she'd closed the door behind them and heard them going down the stairs, she went back into the bedroom with the rose-pattern wallpaper.

Maigret was lying in the double bed under an impressive red silk eiderdown. He looked rather tired; there were little bags under his eyes.

'Did they hurt you?' his wife inquired as she went around, tidying things up in the room.

'Not a lot . . . '

'Can you eat?'

'A bit . . . '

'It's amazing you had the same surgeon as crowned heads and people like Clemenceau and Courteline . . . '

She opened a window to shake out a rug on which a nurse had left the mark of his shoe. Then she went to the kitchen, moved a pot from one ring to another and put the lid at a slant.

'I say, Maigret . . . ' she said as she came back into the bedroom.

'What?' he asked.

'Do you really believe that it was a crime of passion?'

'What are you talking about?'

'About the Jewish woman, Anna Gorskin, who's on trial today. A woman from Rue du Roi-de-Sicile who claims she was in love with Mortimer and killed him in a fit of jealousy . . . '

'Ah, that starts today, does it?'

'The story doesn't hold water.'

'Mmm . . . You know, life is a complicated thing . . . You'd better raise my pillow.'

'Might she get an acquittal?'

'Lots of other people have been acquitted.'

'That's what I mean . . . Wasn't she connected to your case?'

'Vaguely . . . ' he sighed.

Madame Maigret shrugged.

'A fat lot of use it is being married to an inspector!' she grumbled. With a smile, all the same. 'When there's something going on, I get my news from the door-lady . . . One of her nephews is a journalist, so there!'

Maigret smiled too.

Before having his operation he'd been to see Anna twice, at the Saint-Lazare prison.

The first time she had clawed his face.

The second time she had given him information that led to the immediate arrest at his lodgings in Bagnolet of Pepito Moretto, the murderer of Torrence and José Latourie.

★ ★ ★

Day after day, and no news! A telephone call now and again, from God knows where, then one fine morning Maigret turns up like a man at the end of his rope, slumps into an armchair and mumbles:

'Get me a doctor . . . '

Now she was happy to be bustling around the flat, pretending to be grumpy just for show, stirring the crackling Swiss fries in the pan, hauling buckets of water around, opening and closing windows and asking now and again:

'Time for a pipe?'

Last time she asked she got no answer.

Maigret was asleep. Half of him was buried under the red eiderdown, and his head was sunk deep in a feather pillow, while all these sounds fluttered over his resting face.

In the central criminal court Anna Gorskin was fighting for her life.

In the prison, in a top-security cell, Pepito Moretto knew what fate awaited him. He walked in circles around his cell under the glum gaze of the guard, whose face could only be seen through the grid pattern on the wire screen over the hatch.

In Pskov, an old lady in a folk hat that came down over both cheeks must have been on her way to church in a sled behind a drunken coachman whipping a pony trotting across the snow like a mechanical toy.

The Late Monsieur Gallet

Translated by ANTHEA BELL

1

A Chore

The very first contact between Detective Chief Inspector Maigret and the dead man with whom he was to spend several weeks in the most puzzling intimacy was on 27 June 1930 in circumstances that were mundane, difficult and unforgettable all at the same time.

Unforgettable chiefly because for the last week the Police Judiciaire had been getting note after note announcing that the King of Spain would be passing through Paris on that day and reminding them of the precautions to be taken on such an occasion.

It so happened that the commissioner of the Police Judiciaire was in Prague, at a conference on forensics. His deputy had been called home to his villa in Normandy, where one of his children was ill.

Maigret, as the senior inspector, had to take everything on in suffocating heat, with manpower reduced by the holiday season to the bare minimum.

It was also early in the morning of 27 June that the body of a murdered woman, a haberdasher, was found in Rue Picpus.

In short, at nine in the morning all available inspectors had left for Gare du Bois-de-Boulogne,

187

where the Spanish monarch was expected.

Maigret had told his men to open the doors and windows, and in the draughts doors slammed and paper flew off tables.

At a few minutes past nine, a telegram arrived from Nevers:

> Émile Gallet, commercial traveller, home address Saint-Fargeau, Seine-et-Marne, murdered night of 25, Hôtel de la Loire, Sancerre. Many curious details. Please inform family for identification of corpse. Send inspector from Paris if possible.

Maigret had no option but to set off in person to Saint-Fargeau, a place thirty-five kilometres from the capital even the name of which had been unknown to him an hour earlier.

He did not know how the trains ran. As he arrived at Gare de Lyon, he was told that a local train was just about to leave. He began to run and was just in time to fling himself into the last carriage. That was quite enough to drench him in sweat, and he spent the rest of the journey getting his breath back and mopping his face, for he was a large, thick-set man.

At Saint-Fargeau he was the only traveller to get out, and he had to wander about on the softened asphalt of the platform for several minutes before he managed to unearth one of the station staff.

'Monsieur Gallet? Right at the end of the central avenue of the housing development. There's a sign outside the house with its name on it, 'Les Marguerites'. In fact it's almost the only house to be finished so far.'

Maigret took off his jacket, slipped a handkerchief under his bowler hat to protect the back of his neck, because the avenue in question was about 200 metres wide, and you could walk only right down the middle of it, where there was no shade at all.

The sun was an ominous coppery colour, and midges were stinging furiously in advance of the coming storm.

Not a soul in sight to brighten the scene and provide a traveller with any information. The housing development was nothing but a huge forest which must have been part of the grounds of a large manor house. All anyone had done to it yet was to mark out a geometrical network of streets, like the stripes left by a lawnmower, and to lay the cables that would provide the future houses with electric light.

Opposite the railway station, however, there was a square laid out with mosaic-lined fountains. Over a wooden shack was a sign reading 'Sales Office. Plots of Land for Development'. Beside it, there was a map on which the empty streets already bore the names of politicians and generals.

Every fifty metres, Maigret took out his handkerchief to mop his face again, and then put it back over the nape of his neck, which was beginning to sizzle. He saw embryonic buildings here and there, sections of wall that the builders must have abandoned because of the heat. At least two kilometres from the station he found

'Les Marguerites', a house that was faintly English in appearance, with red tiles, complicated architecture and a rustic wall separating the garden from what for a few years yet would still be the forest.

Looking up through the first-floor windows, he saw a bed with a mattress folded in two on top of it, while the sheets and blankets were airing over the window-sill.

He rang the bell. A maidservant about thirty years old with a squint looked at him through a peephole first, and while she was making up her mind to open the door Maigret put his jacket back on.

'I'd like to see Madame Gallet, please.'

'Who shall I say it is?'

But a voice inside the house was already asking her, 'Who is it, Eugénie?'

And Madame Gallet appeared on the steps in person, chin in the air as she waited for the intruder to explain himself.

'You've dropped something,' she said in unfriendly tones, as he took off his hat, forgetting the handkerchief, which now fell to the ground.

He picked it up, mumbling something unintelligible, and introduced himself. 'Detective Chief Inspector Maigret of the Flying Squad. I would like a few words with you, madame.'

'With me?' And she added, turning to the maid, 'What are you waiting about for?'

Maigret knew what he thought about Madame Gallet, at least. She was a woman of around fifty, and there were no two ways about it: she was disagreeable. In spite of the time of day, the heat, the solitude of the house, she was already wearing a mauve silk dress, and not one of her grey hairs ventured out of the rigidity of her set. Her neck, bosom and hands were laden with gold necklaces, brooches and rings that clicked against each other. Unwillingly, she preceded her visitor into the sitting room. As he passed an open door, Maigret saw a white kitchen sparkling with copper and aluminium pans.

'May I start waxing the floor, madame?'

'Of course! Why not?'

The maid disappeared into the dining room next door and could soon be heard spreading wax polish on the floor where she knelt, while an invigorating smell of turpentine spread through the house. There were pieces of embroidery on all the furniture in the sitting room. On the wall hung an enlarged photograph of a tall, thin adolescent boy with jutting knees, dressed for his First Communion.

A smaller photo on the piano showed a man with thick hair, a salt-and-pepper goatee beard, wearing a jacket with poorly cut shoulders. The oval of his face was as long as the boy's. Another detail brought Maigret up short, and it was several moments before he realized that the man's lips, which almost cut his face in half, were abnormally thin.

'Your husband?'

'Yes, my husband! And I am waiting to hear what the police think they are doing here . . . '

During the conversation that followed, Maigret had to keep looking back at the photograph, and that could really be described as his first point of contact with the dead man.

'I'm afraid I have bad news to break, madame . . . your husband is away, isn't he?'

'Well, go on! Out with it . . . has something . . . ?'

'Yes, there has been an accident. Well, not strictly speaking an accident. I must ask you to be brave . . . '

She was standing in front of him, her back very straight, her hand resting on a pedestal table with a reproduction bronze on it. Her face was hard, distrustful, and nothing about her moved except her podgy fingers. What made Maigret think that she had certainly been slim, maybe very slim, for the first half of her life, and had put on weight only with age?

'Your husband was killed in Sancerre on the night of 25 June. I have the painful task of informing you . . . '

The inspector turned to the portrait photo and asked, pointing to the boy dressed for his First Communion, 'You have a son, I believe?'

For a moment Madame Gallet looked as if the straight back that she thought indispensable to her dignity might be about to bend. She said, reluctantly, 'A son, yes,' and then she immediately added, in a triumphant tone, 'You did say Sancerre, didn't you? And this is the 27th. In that case you've made a mistake. Wait a minute . . . '

She went into the dining room, where Maigret could see the maid on all fours. When Madame Gallet came back, she held a postcard out to her visitor.

'This card is from my husband. It's dated the

192

26th and postmarked Rouen.'

She had some difficulty in suppressing a smile betraying her delight in humiliating a police officer who was bold enough to intrude on her privacy.

'It must be some other Gallet, not that I know anyone of that name.' She was almost on the point of opening the door, and couldn't keep her eyes off it. 'My husband represents the firm of Niel et Cie all over Normandy.'

'I'm afraid, madame, that your relief is unfounded. I must ask you to accompany me to Sancerre. For both your sake and mine . . . '

'But since . . . '

She shook the postcard, which showed the Old Market in Rouen. The door of the dining room was still open, and Maigret could see now the maid's behind and feet, now her head and the hair falling over her face. He heard the sound of the rag, greasy with polish, being wiped over the wooden floor.

'Believe me, I wish with all my heart that there was some mistake. However, the papers found in the dead man's pockets are definitely your husband's.'

'They could have been stolen from him . . . ' But despite herself, a note of anxiety was beginning to creep into her voice. She followed Maigret's eyes as he looked at the smaller portrait and said, 'That photo was taken when he had begun dieting.'

'If you would like to eat lunch first,' suggested the inspector, 'I could come back for you in an hour's time.'

'Certainly not. If you think that . . . that it's

193

necessary . . . Eugénie! My black silk coat, my bag and my gloves.'

⋆   ⋆   ⋆

Maigret was not interested in this case; it had all the hallmarks of a particularly distasteful investigation. And if he remembered the picture of the man with the goatee beard — who was dieting! — and the boy dressed for his First Communion, it was unintentionally.

Everything he did today felt like a chore. First going back up the central avenue in an increasingly stifling atmosphere, and this time unable to take his jacket off. Then waiting thirty-five minutes at Melun station, where he bought a picnic basket containing sandwiches, fruit and a bottle of Bordeaux.

At 3 p.m. he was sitting opposite Madame Gallet in a first-class compartment, in a train on the main line to Moulins, stopping at Sancerre. The curtains were drawn, the windows lowered, but there was only a very occasional breath of fresh air.

Maigret had taken his pipe out of his pocket; but when he looked at his companion he gave up any idea of smoking in front of her. The train had been going along for a good hour when she asked, in a voice that at last sounded more human, 'How would you explain all this?'

'I can't explain anything yet, madame. I don't know anything. As I told you, the crime was committed on the night of 25 June, at the Hôtel de la Loire. This is the holiday season, and in addition the provincial prosecutors' offices aren't always in a hurry. We weren't told at police head-quarters in Paris until this morning . . . Was your husband in the habit of sending you postcards?'

'Whenever he was away.'

'He was away a great deal?'

'About three weeks a month. He went to Rouen and stayed at the Hôtel de la Poste . . . he's been staying there for twenty years! He based himself there and went out all over Normandy, but he managed to get back to Rouen in the evening as often as possible.'

'You have only the one son?'

'One son, yes! He works in a bank in Paris.'

'Rather than living with you in Saint-Fargeau?'

'It's too far for him to come home every day. He always spends Sundays with us.'

'May I suggest that you have something to eat?'

'No thank you,' she said, in the same tone that she might have used to reply to an impertinent remark. And indeed, he had difficulty in imagin-ing her nibbling a sandwich like the first to arrive at a party, and drinking warm wine from the catering company's oiled paper cup. You could tell that dignity meant a great deal to her. She could never have been pretty, but she had regular features, and if she had not been so expression-less she would not have been without charm, thanks to a certain melancholy in her face which was emphasized by her way of holding her head on one side.

'Why would anyone kill my husband?' she wondered aloud.

'You don't know of any enemies he may have had?'

'No enemies, no friends either! We live very quietly, like everyone who's known a time before all the brutality and vulgarity you find now that the war is over.'

'I see.'

The journey seemed interminable. Several times Maigret went out into the corridor for a few puffs at his pipe. His detachable collar had gone limp owing to the heat and his profuse perspiration. He envied Madame Gallet, who didn't even notice temperatures of 33 or 34 degrees in the shade and stayed in exactly the same position as at the start of the journey, as if for a bus trip, handbag on her knees, head slightly turned to the window.

'How was th . . . that man killed?'

'The telegram doesn't say. I gathered that he was found dead in the morning.'

Madame Gallet jumped, and it took her a moment to get her breath back as she sat with her mouth half open.

'It can't possibly be my husband. Surely that card proves it? I shouldn't even have had to go to all this bother.'

Without knowing just why, Maigret regretted not bringing the photo from the piano, because he was already having trouble reconstructing the top part of the face in his mind. On the other hand, he clearly visualized the over-long mouth, the small, thick beard, the poorly cut shoulders of the jacket.

It was seven in the evening when the train stopped at Tracy-Sancerre station, and they still had to walk a kilometre along the main road and cross the suspension bridge over the River Loire, which did not offer the majestic view of a river but the sight of a great many streams of water running fast between sandbanks the colour of over-ripe wheat. A man in a nankeen suit was fishing on one of these islets. And now the Hôtel de la Loire came into view, its yellow façade running along the bank. The rays of the sun slanted more now, but it was still difficult to breathe the air, thick with so much water vapour.

Madame Gallet was in the lead now, and seeing a man who must be a colleague of his pacing up and down outside the hotel, Maigret disliked the thought that he and his companion looked a perfectly ridiculous couple.

People on holiday, mostly families, wearing pale clothes, were sitting at tables under a glazed roof, with waitresses in aprons and white caps walking around.

Madame Gallet had seen the sign bearing the name of the hotel surrounded by the crests of several clubs. She made straight for the door.

'Police Judiciaire?' asked the man pacing up and down, stopping Maigret.

'Yes, what is it?'

'He's been taken to the town hall. You'd better hurry up — the post-mortem is at eight. You'll be just in time.'

★ ★ ★

Just in time to get acquainted with the dead man. At that moment, Maigret was still dragging himself about like a man doing a difficult and unattractive task.

Later, he had time to remember the second point of contact at his leisure. It could not be followed by another.

The village was glaring white in the stormy light of that late afternoon. Chickens and geese crossed the main road, and fifty metres away two men in aprons were shoeing a horse.

Opposite the town hall, people were sitting at tables on a café terrace, and from the shade of red and yellow striped awnings rose an atmosphere of cool beer, ice cubes floating in sweet-smelling drinks and newspapers just arrived from Paris.

Three cars were parked in the middle of the square. A nurse was looking for the pharmacy. In the town hall itself, a woman was washing down the grey-tiled corridor.

'Excuse me. The body?'

'Back there! In the school playground. The gentlemen are over there . . . you can come this way.'

She pointed to a door with the word 'Girls' over it; it said 'Boys' above the other wing of the building.

Madame Gallet went ahead with unexpected self-assurance, but all the same Maigret thought she was more likely in some kind of daze.

In the school yard, a doctor in a white coat was smoking a cigarette and walking about like a man expecting something. Sometimes he rubbed his very delicate hands together. Two other people were talking under their breath, near a table with a body stretched out on it under a white sheet.

The inspector tried to slow his companion down, but he had no time to get there first. She was already in the yard, where she stopped in front of the table, held her breath and suddenly raised the sheet over the dead man's face.

She did not cry out. The two men who were talking had turned to her in surprise. The doctor put on rubber gloves, went over to a door and asked, 'Isn't Mademoiselle Angèle back yet?'

While he took off one of his gloves to light another cigarette Madame Gallet stood there motionless, very stiff, and Maigret prepared to go to her aid.

She abruptly turned to him, her face full of hatred, and cried, 'How could this happen? Who dared to . . . ?'

'Come this way, madame . . . it is him, isn't it?'

Her eyes moving fast now, she looked at the two men, the doctor in white, the nurse who was on her way, waddling.

'What do we do now?' she managed to say, her voice hoarse.

And when Maigret, embarrassed, hesitated to reply, she finally flung herself on her husband's body, cast a furious glance of anger and defiance at the yard and everyone in it and shouted, 'I don't want to! I don't want to!'

She had to be forcibly removed and handed over to the concierge, who abandoned her buckets of water. When Maigret returned to the yard the doctor had a surgical knife in his hand

and a mask over his face, and the nurse was handing him a frosted glass bottle.

Unintentionally, the inspector kicked a small black silk hat, decorated with a mauve bow and an imitation diamond gemstone.

★ ★ ★

He did not watch the post-mortem. Dusk was near, and the doctor had announced that he had seven guests coming to dinner at Nevers. The two men were the examining magistrate and the clerk of the court. After shaking the inspector's hand, the magistrate merely said, 'As you can see, the local police have begun their investigations. It's a terribly confused case.'

The body was naked under the sheet laid over it, and the dismal conversation lasted only a few seconds. The corpse was much as Maigret would have imagined from the photo of the living man: long, bony, with a bureaucrat's hollow chest, a pale skin that made his hair look very dark, while the body hair on his chest was reddish.

Only half his face was still intact; the left cheek had been blown away by a gunshot.

His eyes were open, but the mid-grey irises looked even more lifeless than in his photograph.

He was dieting, Madame Gallet had said.

Under his left breast there was a neat, regular wound retaining the shape of a knife-blade.

Behind Maigret, the doctor was dancing on the spot with impatience. 'Do I send my report to you? Where are you staying?'

'At the Hôtel de la Loire.'

The magistrate and his clerk looked elsewhere and said nothing. Maigret, looking for the way out, tried the wrong door and found himself among the benches in one of the school classrooms. It was pleasantly cool in there, and the inspector lingered for a moment in front of some lithographs entitled 'Harvest', 'A Farm in Winter' and 'Market Day in Town'. On a shelf all the measures of weight and volume, made of wood, tin and iron, were arranged in order of size.

The inspector mopped his face. As he left the room again, he met the police inspector from Nevers, who was looking for him.

'Oh, good, there you are! Now I can join my wife in Grenoble. Would you believe it . . . yesterday morning when the phone call came I was about to go on holiday!'

'Have you found anything out?'

'Nothing at all. As you'll see, it's a most improbable case. If you'd like we can dine together, and I'll give you the details, if you can call them details. Nothing was stolen. No one saw or heard anything! And it would be a clever fellow who could say why the man was killed. There's only one oddity, but I don't suppose it will get us very far. When he stayed at the Hôtel de la Loire, as he did from time to time, he checked in under the name of Monsieur Clément, a man of private means, from Orleans.'

'Let's go and have an aperitif,' suggested Maigret.

He remembered the tempting atmosphere of the terrace. Just now it had looked to him like the refuge he dreamed of. However, when he was sitting in front of an ice-cold beer, he did not feel the satisfaction he had anticipated.

'This is the most disappointing imaginable case,' sighed his companion. 'You just take a look at it! Nothing to give us a lead! And what's more, nothing out of the ordinary, except that the man was murdered . . . '

He went on in this vein for several minutes, without noticing that the inspector was hardly listening.

There are some people whose faces you can't forget even if you merely passed them once in the street. All that Maigret had seen of Émile Gallet was a photograph, half of his face, and his pale body. Again, it was the photo that lingered in his mind. And he was trying to bring it to life, to imagine Monsieur Gallet having a private conversation with his wife, in the dining room at Saint-Fargeau, or leaving the villa to catch his train at the station.

In fits and starts, the top part of the man's face took clearer shape in his mind. Maigret thought he remembered that he had ashen bags under his eyes.

'I'll bet he had liver trouble,' he suddenly said under his breath.

'Well, he didn't die of it, anyway!' said his companion tartly, annoyed. 'Liver trouble doesn't blow off half your face and stab you through the heart!'

The lights of a funfair came on in the middle of the square, where a carousel of wooden horses was being dismantled.

2

A Young Man in Glasses

There were only two or three groups of hotel guests still sitting at their tables. Howls of indignation from children being made to go to bed came from the rooms on the first floor.

From the other side of an open window, a woman's voice asked, 'See that big man, did you? He's a policeman! He'll put you in prison if you're naughty . . . '

Still eating, and letting his eyes wander over the scene before him, Maigret heard a persistent droning sound. It was Inspector Grenier from Nevers, talking for the sheer pleasure of talking.

'Now if only he'd had something stolen from him. Then the case would be child's play. This is Monday . . . the crime was committed on the night of Saturday into Sunday . . . it was a holiday. These days, as well as the travelling showmen, and I distrust them on principle, you see all sorts of people prowling round. You don't know what the countryside's like, inspector! You may well be able to find nastier characters here than among the dregs of Paris . . . '

'The fact is,' said Maigret, interrupting him, 'if it hadn't been for the holiday the crime would have been discovered at once.'

'What do you mean?'

'I mean it was because of the rifle range on the fairground and the firecrackers going off that no one heard the gunshot. Didn't you tell me that Gallet didn't die of the injury to his head?'

'So the doctor says, and the post-mortem will confirm that hypothesis. The man got a bullet in his head, but it seems that he could have lived another two or three hours. Directly after the shot, however, he was stabbed in the heart with a knife, and death was instantaneous. The knife has been found.'

'How about the revolver?'

'We haven't found that.'

'The knife was in the room with him?'

'Within a few centimetres of the body, and there are bruises on Gallet's left wrist. It looks as if, knowing he was wounded, he raised the knife in the air as he made for his attacker, but he was weakened . . . Then the murderer grabbed his wrist, twisted it, and ran the blade through his heart. That's not just my own opinion, the doctor thinks so too.'

'So if it hadn't been for the fair, Gallet wouldn't be dead!'

Maigret was not trying to indulge in ingenious deductions or startle his provincial colleague, but the idea struck him and now he was thinking it through, curious to see where it would lead him.

But for all the noise of the wooden carousel horses, the rifle range and the firecrackers, the detonation would have been heard. People from the hotel would have come running, and might have intervened before the knife went into the victim.

Night had fallen now; all you could see were a few reflections of moonlight on the river and the two lamps at the ends of the bridge. Inside the café, guests were playing billiards.

'A strange story,' concluded Inspector Grenier. 'It's not eleven yet, is it? My train leaves at eleven thirty-two, and it will take me quarter of an hour to get to the station. I was saying that if anything had gone missing . . . '

'What time do the fairground stalls close?'

'Midnight. That's the law!'

'Which means that the crime was committed before midnight, and that in turn means that not everyone in the hotel will have been in bed.'

While both officers pursued their own trains of thought, the conversation went on in desultory fashion.

'Like that false name he gave, Monsieur Clément. The proprietor should have told you . . . he stayed here from time to time. About every six months, I'd say. It must be ten years ago that he first came here. He always used the name of Clément, a man of private means, from Orleans.'

'Did he have a case with him — the kind of thing commercial travellers use for their samples?'

'I didn't see anything like that in his room . . . but the hotel proprietor can tell you. Monsieur Tardivon! Come here a minute, would you? This is Inspector Maigret from Paris, and he'd like to ask you a question. Did Monsieur Clément usually have a commercial traveller's case with him?'

'Containing silverware,' Inspector Maigret added.

'Oh no. He always had a travelling bag for his personal things, because he was very careful about looking after himself. Wait a minute! I didn't see him much in an ordinary jacket. Most of the time he wore a waisted one with tails, either black or dark grey.'

'Thank you.'

Maigret thought about the firm of Niel et Cie, which Monsieur Gallet represented all over Normandy. It specialized in gold and silverware for gifts: rattles, reproduction mugs, silver place settings, fruit baskets, sets of knives, cake slices . . .

He ate the tiny piece of almond cake that a waitress had put in front of him and filled his pipe.

'A little glass of something?' asked Monsieur Tardivon.

'I don't mind if I do.'

Monsieur Tardivon went in search of the bottle himself and then sat down at the table with the two police officers.

'So you'll be in charge of the inquiries, inspector? What a thing, eh? Right at the beginning of the season, too! What would you say if I told you seven guests left this hotel this morning to go to the Commercial Hotel instead! Your very good health, gentlemen! Now, as for this Monsieur Clément . . . I'm used to calling him that, you see . . . and who could have known it wasn't his real name?'

More and more people were leaving the

terrace. A waiter was taking the bay trees in wooden containers that stood among the tables and lining them up against the wall. A goods train passed along the opposite bank, and the eyes of the three men automatically followed the reddish light as it moved along the foot of the hill.

Monsieur Tardivon had begun his career as a cook in a big house and still had a certain air of solemnity from those days, a very slightly contrived way of bowing towards the person he was talking to.

'The really extraordinary thing,' he said, cradling his glass of Armagnac in the palm of his hand, 'is that the crime was within a hair's breadth of not being committed at all . . . '

'Yes, the funfair,' Grenier quickly put in, glancing at Maigret.

'I don't know what you mean . . . no, when Monsieur Clément arrived on Saturday morning I gave him the blue room, the one that looks out on what we call the nettle lane. It's the lane over there on the left. We call it that because now it's not used for anything it's been invaded by nettles . . . '

'Why isn't it used for anything?' asked Maigret.

'See that wall just beyond the lane? It's the wall of Monsieur de Saint-Hilaire's villa. Well, here in the country we usually call it the little chateau, to distinguish it from the big one, the old chateau of Sancerre above the hill. You can see its turrets from here, and it has very fine grounds. Well, in the old days, before the Hôtel de la Loire was built, the grounds came up to here, and the grand front entrance with a wrought-iron gate was at the end of the nettle lane. The gate is still there, but no one uses it, because they've made another entrance on the riverbank 500 metres away . . . In short, I gave Monsieur Clément the blue room with windows looking out this way. It's quiet, no one ever goes along the lane because it doesn't lead anywhere. I don't know why, but the afternoon when he came back he asked if I didn't have a room with a view of the yard. But I didn't have another vacancy. There's a big choice in the winter because I get hardly anyone then but the regulars, commercial travellers going round at fixed times, but the summer . . . that's different! Believe it or not, most of my guests come from Paris! There's nothing like the air of the Loire . . . Well, so I told Monsieur Clément that I couldn't oblige him, and I did point out that his room was the best in the hotel. With a view of the yard you get chickens and geese, and water being drawn from the well at all sorts of times. And no matter how much grease we put on it, that chain makes a screeching noise. He didn't persist . . . but if only I *had* had a room with a view of the yard, just think . . . he wouldn't be dead now!'

'Why not?' murmured Maigret.

'Didn't anyone tell you that the shot was fired from at least six metres away? And the room is only five metres wide, so the murderer must have been outside, taking advantage of the fact that the nettle lane is deserted. He couldn't have got into the yard to fire his gun, and besides, people would have heard it. Another little drink, gentlemen? It's on the house, of course.'

'So that makes two!' said the inspector.

'Two what?' asked Grenier.

'Two coincidences. First the fair had to be in full swing, to muffle the sound of the shot. And then all the rooms looking out on the yard had to be occupied . . . ' He turned to Monsieur Tardivon, who had just refilled their glasses. 'How many guests do you have here at the moment?'

'Thirty-four, counting the children.'

'And none of them have left since the crime was committed?'

'Yes, I told you. Seven have left: a family from the suburbs of Paris — Saint-Denis, I think. A mechanic of some kind, with his wife, his mother-in-law, his sister-in-law and their kids. Not very well-educated people, incidentally. I can't say I was sorry to see them move to the Commercial. We all have our own kinds of regulars, and here, as everyone will agree, you meet only a nice class of guests . . . '

'How did Monsieur Clément spend his days?'

'I couldn't really say . . . he went for walks. Wait a moment, I had an idea that he has a child somewhere around here . . . a child out of wedlock. That's just an idea, because in spite of yourself you try to work things out. He was very polite, and there was always a sad look about him. I never saw him eating at the table d'hôte — we do have a table d'hôte in winter, but he liked to sit in a corner dining by himself . . . '

Maigret had taken a notebook out of his pocket, an ordinary notebook with a black waxed cover, the kind a laundrywoman would use. He made some notes in pencil.

1. Send telegram to Rouen;
2. Send telegram to Niel et Cie;
3. Look at hotel yard;
4. Find out about Saint-Hilaire property;
5. Take fingerprints from knife;
6. Get list of guests;
7. Mechanic and family at Commercial Hotel;
8. People who left Sancerre on Sunday the 26th;
9. Get the town crier to announce a reward for anyone who met Monsieur Gallet on Saturday the 25th.

His colleague from Nevers, a forced smile on his lips, was following Maigret's every movement with his eyes.

'Well? Have you come up with an idea already?'

'No, nothing of the sort! I have two telegrams to send now, and then I'm going to bed.'

The only people left in the café were the locals finishing their game of billiards. Maigret glanced at the nettle lane, which had once been the central avenue going up to the little chateau and still had two rows of fine oak trees lining it. These days dense vegetation had invaded everything, and there was nothing to be seen at this hour.

Grenier prepared to set off for the station, and Maigret retraced his steps to shake hands and say goodbye.

'Good luck,' said Grenier. 'Between ourselves, this is a brute of a case, don't you agree? Nothing sensational, and no kind of useful lead either. Sooner you than me, to be frank with you.'

Maigret was shown to a room on the first floor, where mosquitoes began to whine around his head. He was in a bad temper. The job ahead was a gloomy prospect, a nondescript case with nothing interesting about it.

And yet once he was in bed, instead of going to sleep he began seeing Gallet's face in his mind's eye, sometimes only one cheek, sometimes only the lower part of the face.

He tossed and turned awkwardly in the damp sheets. He could hear the murmuring of the river as it lapped against the sandbanks.

Every criminal case has a feature of its own, one that you identify sooner or later, and it often provides the key to the mystery.

He thought that the feature of this one was, surely, its sheer mediocrity.

Mediocrity in Saint-Fargeau! A mediocre house! Undistinguished interior decoration, with the portrait photo of the boy about to take his First Communion and the one of his father in an overly tight jacket, both on the piano.

More mediocrity in Sancerre! A low-budget holiday resort! A second-class hotel!

All these details added to the dull, grey atmosphere surrounding the case.

A commercial traveller for the firm of Niel:

fake silverware, fake luxury, fake style!

A funfair, and one with a rifle range and firecrackers into the bargain . . .

And then there was the distinction lent to it all by Madame Gallet, whose hat adorned with paste diamonds had fallen into the dust of the school playground.

It was a relief to Maigret to find out, in the morning, that the widow had taken the first train back to Saint-Fargeau, and the coffin containing the remains of Émile Gallet was on its way back to Les Marguerites in a hired van.

He was in a hurry to get this case over and done with. Everyone else had left: the magistrate, the doctor with his seven guests coming to dinner, and Inspector Grenier.

As a result, Maigret was left alone with some precise tasks to carry out.

First, he must wait for replies to the two telegrams he had sent the previous evening.

Then examine the room where the crime had been committed. Finally, think about all those who *could have* committed the crime and who were therefore suspects.

He did not have to wait long for the reply from Rouen. It came from the police of that city:

Have questioned staff of Hôtel de la Poste. Cashier, Irma Strauss, said a man called Émile Gallet sent her an envelope containing postcards to be forwarded. Received 100 francs a month for her trouble. Has been doing this for five years, and thinks that the cashier before her did the same.

212

Half an hour later, at ten o'clock, a telegram from the firm of Niel arrived:

Émile Gallet has not worked for our firm since 1912.

This was the moment when the town crier began doing his rounds. Maigret, who had just finished breakfast, was examining the hotel yard (which had nothing in particular about it) when he was told that the road-mender would like a word with him.

'I was on the road to Saint-Thibaut,' he explained, 'when I saw that Monsieur Clément. I knew him, see, because I'd met him a few times, and I knew his jacket. There was a young man just coming down the road from the farm, and they met face to face. I was sort of like a hundred metres from them, but I could see they were arguing . . . '

'And did they walk away from each other at once?'

'Oh no, they like went up the hill at the end of the road. Then the old man came back on his own, and it wasn't 'til half an hour later in the square that I saw the young man again at the Commercial.'

'What did he look like?'

'Tall, thin . . . with a long face and glasses.'

'What was he wearing?'

'Couldn't rightly say. Might've been something grey . . . or black. So do I get the fifty francs?'

Maigret gave him the money and set off for

213

the Commercial Hotel, where he had drunk his aperitif the evening before.

Yes, he was told, the young man had had lunch there on Saturday 25 June, but the waiter who served him was now on holiday at Pouilly, some twenty kilometres away.

'Are you sure he didn't spend the night here?'

'He'd be in our register if he had.'

'And no one remembers him?'

The cashier recollected that someone had asked for pasta without any butter, and she added that it had to be cooked specially for him.

'It was a young man sitting over there, to the left of that pillar. He had an unhealthy complexion.'

It was beginning to get hot, and Maigret no longer felt the same bored indifference as he had early in the morning.

'Did he have a long face? Thin lips?'

'Yes, a kind of a wide mouth with a scornful look to it. He didn't want coffee or a liqueur or anything . . . some guests are like that, you know . . . '

What had made Maigret think of the photograph of the lad dressed for his First Communion?

The inspector was forty-five years old. He had spent half his life in various branches of the police force: Vice Squad, Traffic, Drug Squad, Railway Police, Gambling Squad. It was quite enough to dispel any vaguely mystical ideas and kill faith in intuition stone dead.

But all the same, for almost twenty-four hours he had been haunted by those two portrait photographs, father and son, and also by an ordinary little phrase from Madame Gallet: 'He was on a diet . . . '

It was without any very clear idea in his mind that he made for the post office and a telephone, and asked for the town hall of Saint-Fargeau.

'Hello. Police Judiciaire . . . can you tell me when Monsieur Gallet's funeral is taking place?'

'At eight o'clock tomorrow.'

'In Saint-Fargeau?'

'Here, yes.'

'One more question! Who am I speaking to?'

'The Saint-Fargeau schoolteacher.'

'Do you know Monsieur Gallet junior?'

'Well, I've seen him several times. He came for the papers this morning.'

'What does he look like?'

'How do you mean?'

'Is he tall, thin?'

'Yes . . . yes, rather.'

'Does he wear glasses?'

'Wait a minute. Yes, now I remember. Horn-rimmed glasses.'

'You don't happen to know if he's unwell?'

'How would I know? He's pale, certainly.'

'Thank you very much.'

Ten minutes later, the inspector was back at the Commercial.

'Madame, can you tell me whether your guest at lunch on Saturday wore glasses?'

The cashier searched her memory and finally shook her head. 'Yes . . . well, no, I can't remember. We get so much passing trade in the summer! It was his mouth I noticed most. In

215

fact, I even said to the waiter, that man has a mouth like a toad's . . . '

It took Maigret longer to track the road-mender down, because he was busy drinking his fifty francs away with some friends in a little bistro tucked away behind the church.

'You told me that the man you saw wore glasses.'

'The young one, that's right. Not the old one.'

'What sort of glasses?'

'Well, round, know what I mean? With dark rims . . . '

On getting up that morning, Maigret had been glad to hear that the body had been taken away. And Madame Gallet, the magistrate, the doctor and the local police officers had also left. He hoped that now he could focus on an objective problem at last, and put the strange appearance of the old man with the beard out of his mind.

He took the train for Saint-Fargeau at three in the afternoon.

For a start all he had seen of Émile Gallet was a photograph. Then he had seen half his face.

Now all he would find would be a coffin permanently closed. And yet, as the train moved away, he had the disagreeable feeling that he was running after the dead man.

Back in Sancerre a disappointed Monsieur Tardivon told his regulars as he offered them a glass of Armagnac:

'A man who looked the serious kind . . . a man of our own age! And he heads off without even going into the room! Do you want to see the place *where he died?* Funny thing, that.

216

However, the Nevers police are no better . . . when they took the body away they drew its outline on the floor first, in chalk. Mind you don't touch anything . . . huh! You never know where a thing like this will lead you.'

3

Henry Gallet's Replies

Maigret, who had spent the night at home in the Boulevard Richard-Lenoir, arrived in Saint-Fargeau on the Wednesday a little before eight in the morning. He was already out of the station when he had second thoughts, retraced his steps and asked the clerk in the ticket office, 'Did Monsieur Gallet often travel by train?'

'Father or son?'

'The father.'

'He went away for three weeks every month. He travelled second class to Rouen.'

'What about the son?'

'He arrives from Paris almost every Saturday evening on a third-class return ticket, and goes back by the last train on Sunday . . . Who could ever have foreseen that . . . I can still see him opening the fishing season . . . '

'Father or son?'

'The father, for heaven's sake! By the way, the blue skiff you can see among the trees is his. Everyone's going to want to buy that skiff. He made it himself out of best oak, thinking up all sorts of little improvements. It was like the gadgets he made . . . '

Conscientiously, Maigret added this little detail to the still very sketchy idea he had of the

218

dead man. He looked at the skiff, the Seine, tried to imagine the man with the goatee beard sitting perfectly still for hours with a bamboo fishing rod in his hand.

Then he set off for Les Marguerites, noticing that an empty, fairly well-appointed hearse was travelling the same way. There was no one to be seen near the house, except for a man pushing a wheelbarrow, who stopped at the sight of the hearse, no doubt interested to see the funeral procession.

The bell on the gate had been wrapped in a linen cloth, and the front door was draped in black, with the dead man's initials picked out in silver embroidery.

Maigret had not expected so much pomp and ceremony. To the left, in the corridor, there was a tray with a single card on it, one corner turned down, from the Mayor of Saint-Fargeau.

The sitting room where Madame Gallet had received the inspector had been turned into a temporary chapel of rest. Its furniture must have been moved into the dining room. Black hangings covered the walls, and the coffin stood in the middle of the room, surrounded by candles.

It was hard to say why the scene seemed so odd. Perhaps because there were no visitors, and you could guess that there would not be any, although the hearse was already at the door.

That lone visiting card, a fake lithograph! All those silver tears! And two silhouettes, one on each side of the coffin: Madame Gallet on the right in full mourning, a crape veil over her face, a rosary of matt beads in her fingers; Henry Gallet on the left, also entirely in funereal black.

Maigret moved forward in silence, dipped a sprig of box into the holy water and sprinkled the water over the coffin. He felt that mother and son were following him with their eyes, but no one said a word. Then he moved back into a corner, on the alert for sounds from outside and at the same time watching the young man's facial expressions. Sometimes one of the horses drawing the hearse pawed the path with a hoof. The undertakers' men were talking under their breath out in the sunlight, close to the window. In the funereal room, lit only by the candles, young Monsieur Gallet's irregular face looked even more irregular because all the black emphasized the unhealthy pallor of his skin. His hair, separated by a parting, clung close to his scalp. He had a high, bumpy forehead. It was difficult to catch his troubled gaze as he peered short-sightedly through the thick lenses of his horn-rimmed glasses.

Sometimes Madame Gallet dabbed her eyes with her mourning handkerchief. Henry's gaze never focused on anything for long. It slid over things, always avoiding the inspector, who was relieved to hear the steps of the undertaker's men.

A little later, the stretcher bumped into the corridor walls as it was carried in. Madame Gallet uttered a small sob, and her son patted her on the shoulder while still looking elsewhere.

There was a great contrast between the ostentatious splendour of the hearse and the two figures who began to walk after it, preceded by a puzzled master of ceremonies.

It was still as hot as ever. The man with the wheelbarrow made the sign of the cross, and went off along another path, while the funeral procession, taking small steps, went down the avenue, which was wide enough for regiments to march down it.

★ ★ ★

A small group of locals gathered in the square as the religious ceremony took place, but Maigret went off into the town hall, where he found no one. He had to go and fetch the schoolteacher, whose classroom was next to the town hall, and the children were left to their own devices for a little while.

All I can tell you,' said the teacher, 'is what's recorded in our registers. Wait, here we are:

'Gallet, Émile Yves Pierre, born Nantes, 1879, married Aurore Préjean in Paris, October 1902 . . . A son, Henry, born in Paris 1906, registered at the town hall of the IXth arrondissement . . . '

'Don't the local people like them?'

'It's just that the Gallets, who had the villa built in 1910 when the forest was sold off in plots, never wanted to see anyone . . . they're very proud. I've been known to spend a whole Sunday fishing in my skiff less than ten metres away from Gallet's. If I needed something he'd let me have it, but I wouldn't get the slightest bit of conversation out of him afterwards . . . '

'How much do you think this lifestyle cost?'

'I can't say exactly, because I don't know what he spent when he was away, but they'll have needed at least 2,000 francs a month just for the upkeep of their household. If you've seen the villa, you'll know that it has every convenience. They send to Corbeil or Melun for almost everything they need . . . and that's another thing that . . . '

But looking out of the window, Maigret saw the funeral procession going round the church and into the graveyard. He thanked the teacher and, once out in the road again, heard the first spadeful of earth falling on the coffin.

He did not let the mourners see him but went a long way round back to the villa and was careful to arrive a little while after the Gallets. The maid opened the door to him and looked at him hesitantly.

'Madame can't . . . ' she began.

'Tell Monsieur Henry that I need to talk to him.'

The squinting maidservant left him outside. A few moments later, the figure of the young man appeared in the corridor. He came towards the doorway and asked, looking past Maigret, 'Couldn't you postpone this visit to another day? My mother is absolutely devastated.'

'I have to talk to you today. Please forgive me if I insist.'

Henry half turned, thus implying that the police officer had only to follow him. He hesitated at the doors on the ground floor and finally opened the door to the dining room, where the sitting-room furniture had been

222

stacked so that you could hardly get round it. Maigret saw the portrait photo of Henry as a boy ready for his First Communion, but looked in vain for the photo of Émile Gallet. Henry did not sit down or say anything, but he took off his glasses to clean the lenses with a gesture of annoyance, while his eyelashes fluttered as he adjusted to the bright light.

'I'm sure you know that it is my job to find whoever killed your father.'

'Yes, which is why I'm surprised to see you here, at a time when it would be more proper to leave my mother and me alone!'

And Henry put his glasses back on, pulling up a double cuff that had slipped down over a hand covered with the same reddish hairs as the chest of the dead man in Sancerre. There was not so much as a twitch on his bony and rather horsy face, with its strong features and gloomy expression. He was leaning his elbow on the piano, which had been moved sideways, showing its green baize back.

'I'd like to ask you for some information about both your father and the whole family.'

Henry did not open his mouth or move a muscle but stood in the same place, icy and funereal.

'Please would you tell me where you were on Saturday 25 June, around four in the afternoon?'

'Before that I'd like to ask you a question. Am I obliged to see you and reply to you at a time like this?' He spoke in the same neutral voice suggesting boredom, as if every syllable tired him.

'You're at liberty not to answer. However, let me point out that . . . '

'At what point in your inquiries did you find out who I was?'

Maigret did not reply to that, and to tell the truth he was stunned by this unexpected turning of the tables. It was all the more unexpected because it was impossible to detect the least subtlety on the young man's features. Henry let several seconds pass, and the maid could be heard downstairs replying to a summons from the first floor. 'Just coming, madame!'

'Well?'

'Since you know it already, I was there.'

'In Sancerre?'

Henry still did not move a muscle.

'And you were having a discussion with your father on the lane leading to the old chateau.' Maigret was the more nervous of the two of them, since he felt that his remarks were getting nowhere. His voice sounded flat, there was no echo of response to his suspicions. But the most unnerving thing about it was Henry Gallet's silence; he was not trying to explain himself, just waiting.

'Can you tell me what you were doing in Sancerre?'

'Going to visit my mistress, Éléonore Boursang, who is on holiday and staying at the Pension Germain on the road from Sancerre to Saint-Thibaut.' He almost imperceptibly raised his eyebrows, which were as thick as Émile Gallet's.

'You didn't know your father was in Sancerre?'

224

'If I'd known I'd have avoided meeting him.' Still the minimum of explanation, forcing the inspector to repeat his questions.

'Did your parents know you were having an affair?'

'My father suspected. He was against it.'

'What was the subject of your conversation?'

'Are you making inquiries about the murderer or his victim?' asked the young man deliberately slowly.

'I'll know who the murderer was when I know enough about the victim. Was your father angry with you?'

'Sorry . . . I was the angry one — I was angry with him for spying on me.'

'And then?'

'Then nothing! He treated me like a disrespectful son. How kind of you to remind me of that today.'

To his relief, Maigret heard footsteps on the stairs. Madame Gallet appeared, as dignified as ever, her neck adorned by a triple necklace of heavy dark stones.

'What is going on?' she asked, looking at Maigret and her son in turn. 'Why didn't you call me, Henry?'

There was a knock, and the maid came in. 'The upholsterers have come to take the draperies away.'

'Keep an eye on them,' said Madame Gallet.

'I came in search of information which I consider indispensable for finding out who the murderer is,' said Maigret, in a voice that was becoming rather too dry. 'I recognize that this is not the ideal moment, as your son has pointed out. But every hour that passes will make it more difficult to arrest the man who killed your husband.' His eyes moved to Henry, who was still looking gloomy.

'When you married Émile Gallet, madame, did you have a fortune of your own?'

She stiffened slightly, and then, with a tremor of pride in her voice, announced, 'I am the daughter of Auguste Préjean!'

'Forgive me, but I . . . '

'The former secretary to the last Bourbon prince and editor of the legitimist journal *Le Soleil*. My father spent all he had on publishing that journal, which went on fighting the good fight.'

'Do you still have any family?'

'I must have, but I haven't seen them since my marriage.'

'You were advised against marrying Monsieur Gallet?'

'What I've just told you ought to help you to understand. All my family are royalists. All my uncles occupied prominent positions, and some of them still do. They did not like it when I married a commercial traveller.'

'Then you were penniless on your father's death?'

'My father died a year after my marriage. At the time when we married my husband had some 30,000 francs . . . '

'What about his family?'

'I never knew them. He avoided mentioning them . . . all I know is that he had an unhappy childhood and that he spent several years in Indochina.'

There was the suggestion of a scornful smile on her son's lips.

'I am asking you these questions, madame, because for one thing I have just heard that your husband has not in fact worked for the firm of Niel for the last eighteen years.'

She looked at the inspector, and then Henry, and protested emphatically, 'Monsieur . . . '

'I have the information from Monsieur Niel himself.'

'Perhaps, monsieur, it would be better . . . ' began the young man, moving towards Maigret.

'No, Henry! I want to prove that what he says is false, it's an odious lie! Come with me, inspector. Come along, follow me!'

And, showing some liveliness for the first time, she made for the corridor, where she came up against the piles of black draperies being rolled up by the upholsterers. She took the inspector up to the first floor, through a bedroom with polished walnut furniture, where Émile Gallet's straw hat still hung on a hook, as well as a cotton drill outfit that he must have worn for fishing. Next came a small room furnished as a study.

'Look at that! Here are his samples. And those place settings, for instance, in that dreadful Art Deco style, you wouldn't say they were eighteen years old, would you? Here's the book of orders that my husband wrote up at the end of every month. Here are some letters that he received regularly, on the Niel letterhead . . . '

Maigret was paying very little attention to this.

He felt sure that he would have to come back to this room and just now he preferred to let its atmosphere sink in. He tried to imagine Émile Gallet sitting here in the swivel chair at his desk. On the desk itself there was a white metal inkwell and a glass globe acting as a paperweight. Through the window you could see the central avenue and the red roof of another uninhabited villa.

The letters on the Niel letterhead were typed in an almost regular typeface:

Dear sir,

We have received your letter of the 15th inst., as well as the statement of orders for January. We shall expect you at the end of the month to settle our account, as usual, and we will then give you some information about the expansion of your sphere of activity.

With good wishes,
Signed: Jean Niel

Maigret picked up some of the letters and put them into his wallet.

'So what do you think now?' asked Madame Gallet, with a touch of defiance.

'What's that?'

'Oh, nothing ... my husband liked to do things with his hands. Here's an old watch that he took apart ... and out in the shed there are all kinds of things that he made himself, including fishing gear. Every month he had a full week to spend here, and writing up his accounts

228

and so forth took him only an hour or two in the morning . . . '

Maigret was opening drawers at random. He saw a large pink file in one of them, with the word 'Soleil' written on it.

'Some of my father's papers,' explained Madame Gallet. 'I don't know why we kept them. There are copies of all the numbers of the journal in that cupboard, right up to the last one. My father sold his bonds to bring that out.'

'May I take this file away?'

She turned to the door as if to consult her son, but Henry had not followed them. 'But what can it possibly tell you? It's a kind of relic . . . Still, if you think . . . Oh, but listen, inspector, it surely must be impossible that Monsieur Niel said . . . I mean, it's like those postcards! I had another one yesterday, and in his writing, I'm sure of it. Sent from Rouen, like the other card. Read it! *All going well. Will be home on Thursday . . .* ' Once again some emotion broke through, but with difficulty. 'I shall almost be expecting him. Thursday is tomorrow.' And she suddenly burst into a fit of tears, but an extraordinarily brief one, just two or three hiccups. She raised her black-bordered handkerchief to her mouth and said in a muted voice, 'Well, let's not stay here.'

They had to go through the bedroom again with its walnut furniture — ordinary but of good quality: a wardrobe with a full-length mirror on it, two bedside tables and an imitation Persian carpet.

Down in the ground-floor corridor, Henry was watching the upholsterers loading the draperies into a van without seeming to see them. He did not even turn his head when Maigret and his mother descended the polished staircase, causing the stairs to creak.

There was an untidy look to the house. The maid came into the sitting room, carrying a litre of red wine and glasses. Two men in overalls were dragging the piano back into it.

'Won't do us any harm!' one of the men was saying indifferently.

Maigret had an impression that he had never had before, and it unnerved him. It seemed to him that the whole truth was here, scattered round him, and everything he saw had its meaning. But to understand it, he would have had to see it clearly, not through a sort of fog that distorted the view. And the fog persisted, created by this woman who resisted her emotions, by Henry whose long face was as impregnable as a safe, by the black draperies now on their way out, in fact by everything and most of all by Maigret's own discomfort, out of place as he was in this house.

He felt ashamed of the pink file that he was taking away like a thief, and he would have had difficulty in explaining why it might come in useful. He would have liked to stay upstairs for some time, alone in the dead man's study, and wander round the shed where Émile Gallet worked on perfecting his fishing equipment.

There was a moment of wavering, with everyone coming and going in the corridor at once. It was lunchtime, and it was obvious that the Gallets were only waiting for the police officer to leave. A smell of fried onions came from the kitchen. The maid was as distraught as the others. All anyone could do was watch the upholsterers restoring the sitting room to its usual state. One of them found the photo of Gallet underneath a tray of liqueurs.

'May I take that with me?' Maigret intervened, turning to the widow. 'I may need it.'

He sensed that Henry's eyes were following him with more scorn than ever.

'If you must ... I don't have many photographs of him.'

'I promise to let you have it back.'

He could not bring himself to leave. At the moment when the workmen were unceremoniously carrying in an enormous fake Sevres vase, Madame Gallet hurried forwards.

'Careful! You're going to collide with the mantelpiece.'

And the same mixture of grief and the grotesque, the dramatic and the petty, was still weighing down on Maigret's shoulders in this desolate house, where he felt as if he could see Émile Gallet, whom he had not known alive, wandering in silence, his eyes ashen with his liver trouble, his chest hollow, wearing his poorly cut jacket.

He had slipped the portrait photo into the pink file. He hesitated.

'Please forgive me again, madame ... I'm leaving, but I'd be glad if your son would come a little way with me.'

Madame Gallet looked at Henry with an anxiety that she could not repress. For all her dignified manner, her measured gestures, her triple necklace of black stones, she too must be feeling *something* in the air.

But the young man himself, indifferent to anything of the kind, went to collect his hat with its crape hatband from a hook.

Their departure seemed more like an escape. The file was heavy. It was only a cardboard folder, and the papers threatened to fall out.

'Would you like some newspaper to wrap that in?' asked Madame Gallet.

But Maigret was already out of the house, and the maid was making for the dining room with a tablecloth and some knives. Henry was walking towards the station, tall and silent, his expression inscrutable.

When the two men were 300 metres away from the house, and the upholsterers were starting the engine of their van, the inspector said, 'I only want to ask you for two things: first Éléonore Boursang's address in Paris, and second your own, and the address of the bank where you work.'

He found a pencil in his pocket and wrote on the pink cover of the file he was holding:

Éléonore Boursang, 27 Rue de Turenne. Banque Sovrinos, 117 Boulevard Beaumarchais. Henry Gallet, Hôtel Bellevue, 19 Rue de la Roquette.

'Is that all?' asked the young man.

'Thank you, yes.'

'In that case I hope you'll be putting your

mind to the murderer now.'

He did not try to judge the effect of this remark, but touched the brim of his hat and set off back up the central avenue.

The van passed Maigret just before he reached the station.

The last fact he picked up that day was by sheer chance. Maigret arrived at the station an hour before the train was due in and found himself alone in the deserted waiting room, in the middle of a swarm of flies. Then he saw a postman with the purple neck of an apoplectic arrive on a bicycle and put his bags down on the table for luggage.

'Do you call at Les Marguerites?' asked the inspector.

The postman, who had not noticed him, swung round. 'What did you say?'

'Police! Do you get a lot of mail to be delivered to Monsieur Gallet?'

'A lot, no. Letters from the firm the poor gentleman worked for. They always came on a certain day. And then there were newspapers . . . '

'What newspapers?'

'Provincial papers, mostly from the Berry and Cher regions. And magazines: *Country Lifestyles, Hunting and Fishing, Country Homes . . .* '

The inspector noticed that the postman was avoiding his eyes.

'Is there a poste restante office in Saint-Fargeau?'

'How do you mean?'

'Didn't Monsieur Gallet get any other letters?'

The postman suddenly seemed flustered.

'Well, seeing as you know, and seeing as he's dead,' he stammered. 'And anyway it's not like I was even breaking the rules . . . he just asked me not to put some letters into the box but keep them until he was back, when he went away . . .'

'What letters?'

'Oh, not many . . . hardly one every two or three months. Blue envelopes, the cheap sort, with the address typed.'

'They didn't have the sender's address on them?'

'Not the address, no. But I couldn't go wrong because it said on the back, and that was typed too, *From: Monsieur Jacob.* Did I do wrong?'

'Where did these letters come from?'

'Paris.'

'I suppose you didn't notice the arrondissement?'

'I did look . . . but it changed every time.'

'When did the last one arrive?'

'Let's see . . . today is the 29th, right? Wednesday. Well, it was Thursday evening, but I didn't see Monsieur Gallet until Friday morning, when he was going fishing . . .'

'So he went fishing?'

'No, he went home after he gave me five francs, same as usual. I came over all funny when I heard he'd been killed . . . do you think that letter . . . ?'

'Did he leave that same day?'

'Yes . . . hey, is it the train from Melun you're waiting for? They just rang the bell at the level crossing . . . Will you have to mention this to anyone?'

Maigret had no time to do anything but run to the platform and jump into the only first-class carriage.

4

The Crook among the Legitimists

Arriving for the second time at the Hôtel de la Loire, Maigret responded without warmth to Monsieur Tardivon, who received him with a confidential air, took him to his room and showed him some large yellow envelopes that had arrived for him. They contained the coroner's report and the reports of the gendarmerie and the Nevers municipal police. The Rouen police had sent further information about the cashier Irma Strauss.

'And that's not all!' said the hotel manager exultantly. 'The sergeant from the gendarmerie came to see you. He wants you to phone him as soon as you arrive. And then there's a woman who's already turned up three times, no doubt because of the town crier and his sales pitch.'

'What woman?'

'Mother Canut, the wife of the gardener opposite. I told you about the little chateau, remember?'

'Didn't she say anything, then?'

'She's not that stupid! Since there's a reward on offer she's not about to give anything away, but for all that she may know something.'

Maigret had put the pink file on the table along with the photograph of Gallet.

'Ask someone to find the woman and get me the gendarmerie on the phone.'

A little later he was speaking to the sergeant, who told him that, according to instructions, he had picked up all the vagrants in the neighbourhood and was holding them at Maigret's disposal.

'Anyone interesting among them?'

'They're vagrants,' was all the sergeant said to that.

Maigret stayed alone in his room for three or four minutes, facing a pile of paperwork. And there was more of it to come! He had sent a telegram to Paris asking for information about Henry Gallet and his mistress, and just in case he had alerted Orleans to find out if there was a Monsieur Clément in that city.

Finally, he hadn't had time yet to look at the room where the crime was committed, or the clothing worn by the dead man, which had been placed in that room after the post-mortem.

At first the case had looked like nothing to speak of. A man who did not seem out of the ordinary had been killed by someone unknown in a hotel room. But each new item of information complicated the problem instead of simplifying it.

'Do I get her to come in and see you, inspector?' called a voice in the yard. 'I've got Mother Canut here.'

A strong, dignified old lady, who had probably cleaned herself up more thoroughly than usual for the occasion, came in, immediately looking for Maigret with the wary glance of a countrywoman.

'Do you have something to tell me?' he asked.

'About Monsieur Clément?'

'It's about the gent who died and got his picture in the paper. You're handing out fifty francs, right?'

'Yes, if you saw him on Saturday 25 June.'

'Suppose I saw him twice?'

'Well, maybe you'll get a hundred! Come on, out with it!'

'First you've got to promise not to say a word to my old man. It's not so much that he likes to be the boss as on account of the hundred francs. All the same, I'd not like Monsieur Tiburce to know I been talking, because it was with him I saw the gent who got killed. First time was in the morning, about eleven, when they were walking in the grounds.'

'Are you sure you recognized him?'

'Sure as I'd recognize you! There aren't so many look like him. Well, they were chatting for maybe an hour. Then I saw them through the sitting-room window in the afternoon, and it looked like they were arguing.'

'What time was that?'

'It had just struck five . . . so that makes twice, right?'

Her eyes were fixed on Maigret's hand as he took a hundred-franc note out of his wallet, and she sighed as if she was sorry she hadn't stuck close to Monsieur Clément's trail all that Saturday.

'And could be I saw him a third time,' she said hesitantly, 'But I s'pose that doesn't count. A few minutes later I saw Monsieur Tiburce taking him back to the gate.'

'You're right, it doesn't count,' agreed Maigret, impelling her towards the door.

He lit a pipe, put his hat on and stopped opposite Monsieur Tardivon in the café. 'Has Monsieur de Saint-Hilaire lived in the little chateau for long?'

'About twenty years.'

'What kind of man is he?'

'Very pleasant fellow! A little, fat man, cheerful, straightforward. When I have guests in summer we hardly see him, because, well, they're not his class. But he often drops in here in the hunting season.'

'Does he have any family?'

'He's a widower. We almost always call him Monsieur Tiburce, because that's not a common first name. He owns all the vines you can see on the slope there. He tends them himself, goes to live it up in Paris now and then and comes back to get his hobnailed boots. What did Mother Canut have to tell you?'

'Do you think Monsieur Tiburce is at home now?'

'Could be. I didn't see his car pass this morning.'

Maigret went to the barred gate and rang the bell, noticing that as the Loire described a bend just outside the hotel, and the villa was the last property in the area, you could go in and out of it at any time without being seen.

Beyond the gate, the wall surrounding the vineyard went on for another three or four hundred metres, and after that there was nothing but undergrowth.

A man with a drooping moustache, wearing a gardener's apron, came to open the gate, and the inspector concluded, from the strong smell of alcohol about him, that he was probably Madame Canut's husband.

'Is your master here?'

At the same moment, Maigret caught sight of a man in shirtsleeves inspecting a mechanical sprinkler. The gardener's glance told him that this was indeed Tiburce de Saint-Hilaire, and moreover, abandoning the device, he turned to the visitor and waited.

Then, as Canut looked awkward, to say the least of it, he finally picked up the jacket that he had left on the grass and came over.

'Is it me you want to see?'

'Detective Chief Inspector Maigret of the Police Judiciaire. Would you be kind enough to give me a moment of your time?'

'That crime again, is it?' The owner of the property jerked his chin at the Hotel de la Loire. 'What can I do for you? Come this way. I won't invite you into the drawing room, because the sun's been beating on the walls all day. We'll be more comfortable under that arbour. Baptiste! Glasses and a bottle of the sparkling wine . . . the row at the back.'

He was just as the hotelier had described him, small and stout, red-faced, with short hands not very well cared for, wearing an off-the-peg khaki hunting and fishing outfit.

'Did you know Monsieur Clément?' asked Maigret, sitting down on one of the wrought-iron chairs.

'According to the newspaper that wasn't his real name, he was called . . . what was it? . . . Grelet? Gellet?'

'Gallet, yes. It doesn't matter. Were you in business with him?'

At that moment, Maigret could have sworn that the other man was not entirely at his ease. Furthermore, Saint-Hilaire felt a need to lean forwards out of the arbour, murmuring, 'That fool Baptiste is perfectly capable of bringing us the demi-sec, and I'm sure you'd rather have the sec, like me. It's our own wine, made by the champenoise method . . . Now, about this Monsieur Clément — might as well go on calling him that — what shall I say? It would be exaggerating to say I was in business with him! But it wouldn't be exactly true to say I'd never seen him either . . . '

As he was talking, Maigret thought of another interrogation, the questions he had asked Henry Gallet. The two men had entirely different attitudes. The murder victim's son did nothing to appear likeable, and he didn't care about the oddity of his attitude either. He waited for questions with a suspicious air, took his time and weighed up his words.

Tiburce talked away with animation, smiled, gestured with his hands, paced up and down, appeared extremely friendly — and yet there was the same latent anxiety in each of them: perhaps the fear of being unable to hide something.

'Well, you know how it is. We country landowners come into contact with all sorts. And I'm not just talking about vagrants, commercial travellers, peripatetic salesmen. Now, to return to this Monsieur Clément . . . Ah, here comes the wine! That's fine, Baptiste. Right, you can be off now. I'll come and look at that sprinkler soon. Whatever you do don't touch it.'

As he spoke, he slowly removed the cork and filled the glasses without spilling a drop.

'So to cut a long story short, he came here once, it's some time ago now. I expect you know that the Saint-Hilaires are a very old family, and at the moment I'm the last offshoot of the family tree. In fact it's a miracle that I'm not a clerk in some office in Paris or further afield. If I hadn't inherited money from a cousin who made his fortune in Asia . . . but never mind, I was going to tell you that my name features in all the yearbooks of the aristocracy. My father, some forty years ago, was noted for his legitimist opinions . . . but so far as I myself am concerned, well, you know!'

He smiled, drank his sparkling wine, clicking his tongue in a distinctly democratic way and waited for Maigret to empty his own glass before refilling it.

'So this Monsieur Clément, whom I don't know from Adam or Eve, came looking for me, got me to read his references from Royal Highnesses in France and elsewhere and then gave me to understand that he was, so to speak, the official representative of the legitimist movement in France. I let him go on talking, and he took his chance to get what he wanted: he was asking me for 2,000 francs for the propaganda fund. And when I said no, he carried on about

242

— oh, some ancient family or other reduced to penury, and a subscription that had been opened for it . . . We began at 2,000 francs, and haggled the sum down to a hundred. In the end I gave him fifty.'

'How long ago was this?'

'Oh, several months. I can't say exactly. It was in the hunting season. The beaters were at work in the grounds of one of the local chateaux here almost every day. I heard about that fellow everywhere and I felt sure he was a specialist in that kind of swindle. But I wasn't about to sue him over fifty francs, was I? To your very good health! Only the other day he had the nerve to come back . . . that's all I know!'

'What day was it?'

'Erm . . . at the weekend.'

'On Saturday, yes. In fact he called twice, if I remember correctly . . . '

'You're brilliant, inspector! Yes, you're right, twice. I refused to see him in the morning. But he buttonholed me in the grounds that afternoon.'

'He was after money?'

'You bet he was, but I'd be hard put to it to say what for. However, he was still on about the restoration of the monarchy. Come on, drink up! It's not worth leaving any in the bottle. Good lord . . . you don't think he committed suicide, do you? He must have been at the end of his tether . . . '

'The shot was fired from seven metres away, and the revolver hasn't been found.'

'In that case, then he didn't. What do you

think of it? A vagrant who happened to be passing and . . . ?'

'That's difficult to accept. The windows of the room look out on a lane that leads only to your property.'

'By a disused entrance,' objected Monsieur de Saint-Hilaire. 'It's many years since the gate to the nettle lane was last opened, and I'd be hard put to it to say where the key is . . . How about getting another bottle brought out?'

'No, thank you . . . I don't suppose you heard anything?'

'What kind of thing?'

'The gun being fired on Saturday evening.'

'No, nothing like that. I go to bed early. I didn't hear about the crime until the next morning, when my manservant told me.'

'And you didn't think of mentioning Monsieur Clément's visit to the police?'

'Good heavens, no . . . ' He tried to laugh, covering up for his uneasiness. 'I told myself the poor devil had been punished enough anyway. When you have a name like mine, you don't much like seeing it in the papers anywhere but the society column.'

Maigret still had the same vague and annoying sensation, coming back again and again like a musical chorus: the sensation that everything touching on the death of Émile Gallet creaked, sounded out of tune and wrong, from the dead man himself to his son's voice, and Tiburce de Saint-Hilaire's laughter.

'You're staying at old Tardivon's place, aren't you? Did you know he used to be a cook at the chateau? He's made a packet since then. Are you sure you won't have another little glass? . . . That fool of a gardener has done something or other to the mechanical sprinkler, and I was just trying to put it right when you turned up . . . out here in the country we have to do everything for ourselves. Well, if you're here for a few days, inspector, come and have a chat with me in the evening now and then. Life in the hotel must be tedious with all those tourists . . . '

At the gate, he took the hand that Maigret had not offered him and shook it with excessive cordiality.

Walking along the side of the Loire, Maigret made a mental note of two points. First, Tiburce de Saint-Hilaire, who must know about the town crier's announcement and thus the importance that the police ascribed to what Monsieur Clément did on the Saturday, had expected to be interrogated and had not in fact said anything until he realized that his interrogator was up to date with the facts already.

Second, he had lied at least once. He had said that on Saturday morning he had refused to see the visitor, who then *buttonholed him in the grounds*.

However, it was the morning when the two men went walking in the grounds. And in the afternoon they had certainly been engaged in conversation *in the drawing room of the villa*.

So the rest of it could also be untrue, the inspector concluded. He was just reaching the nettle lane. On one side of him was the whitewashed wall enclosing Saint-Hilaire's grounds. On the other rose a single-storey building, part of the Hôtel de la Loire. The ground here was over-grown with long grass, brambles and dead nettles, and the wasps were revelling in it all. The oak trees cast a comfortable shade on the avenue, which ended at an old, beautifully worked gate.

Maigret felt curious enough to go up to this gate, which, according to the owner of the property, had not been opened for years and had lost its key. As soon as he looked at the lock, covered with a thick layer of rust, he noticed that in some places that rust had recently been chipped away. This was better! He took out a magnifying glass and saw, without a shadow of doubt, that a key had left scratch marks as it went into the complicated wards of the lock.

I'll get that photographed tomorrow, he thought, making a mental note.

He retraced his steps, head bent, rearranging the picture he had of Monsieur Gallet in his mind's eye, bringing it to light, so to speak. But instead of filling out and becoming more comprehensible, was it not more evasive than ever? The face of the man in the tight-fitting jacket was blurred to the point of having nothing human about it.

Instead of the portrait photo, the only tangible and theoretically complete picture of the murder victim that Maigret had, he saw fleeting images which ought to have made up nothing but one and the same man, but refused to be superimposed into a single whole.

Once again the inspector saw the half of his face, the thin and hairy chest, as he had seen it in the school playground while the doctor danced up and down with impatience behind his back. He also called up images of the blue skiff that Émile Gallet had made in Saint-Fargeau, and the perfectly fashioned fishing tackle, Madame Gallet in mauve silk and then in full mourning, the quintessence of the discreet and formal middle class.

He thought of the wardrobe with the full-length mirror. Gallet must have stood in front of it as he put on his jacket . . . And all that correspondence on the letterheads of the firm that he didn't work for any longer. The monthly statements that he drew up carefully, eighteen years after giving up his job as a commercial traveller!

Those goblets and cake slices *that he had to buy himself*!

Wait a minute, his case of samples hasn't been found yet, thought Maigret in passing. He must have left it somewhere . . .

He had automatically stopped a few metres from the window through which the murderer had aimed at his victim. However, he was not even looking at the window. He was feeling slightly feverish because, at certain moments, he had the impression that with a bit of effort he would be able to reunite all the aspects of Émile Gallet into a single image.

But then he thought of Henry again, both as he knew him, stiffly upright and disdainful, and as a boy with an asymmetrical face ready for his First Communion.

This case, described by Inspector Grenier of

Nevers as 'an annoying little case', and one that Maigret had tackled reluctantly, was visibly growing larger as the dead man was transformed to the point of becoming a truly outlandish figure.

Ten times, Maigret brushed aside a wasp hovering close to his head with a noise like a miniature aeroplane.

'Eighteen years!' he said under his breath.

Eighteen years of forged letters signed Niel, of postcards sent on from Rouen, and all the time he was living his ordinary little life at Saint-Fargeau, without luxuries, without any emotional complications!

The inspector knew the mentality of malefactors, criminals and crooks. He knew that you always find some kind of passion at the root of it.

And that was exactly what he was looking for in the bearded face, the leaden eyelids, the excessively wide mouth.

He made perfectly constructed fishing tackle, and he took old watches apart!

At this point Maigret rebelled.

You don't tell lies for eighteen years just for that, he thought. You don't tie yourself to a double life that is so difficult to organize!

That wasn't the most disturbing part of it. There are difficult situations in which you can manage to live for several months, even several years. But eighteen years! Gallet had grown old! Madame Gallet had put on weight and assumed an air of too much dignity! Henry had grown up . . . he had taken his First Communion, passed his school-leaving exams, come of age, gone to

248

live in Paris, found a mistress . . .

And Émile Gallet went on sending himself letters from the firm of Niel, wrote postcards addressed to his wife in advance, patiently copied out fake lists of orders!

He was on a diet . . .

Maigret could still hear Madame Gallet's voice. He was so deep in his thoughts — thoughts that made his pulse beat faster — that he had let his pipe go out.

Eighteen years without being detected!

It was so unlikely. The inspector, who knew the business of crime, was better aware of that than anyone! But for the murder, Gallet would have died peacefully in his bed, after leaving all his papers in order. And Monsieur Niel would have been astonished to get an announcement of his death.

It was so extraordinary that the picture the inspector was constructing for himself made him feel an indefinable anxiety, as if it evoked certain phenomena that shake our sense of reality. So it was pure chance that, as he looked up, the inspector saw a darker mark on the white wall round the property, opposite the room that was the scene of the crime.

He went over and saw that the mark was a space between two stones that had recently been enlarged and scuffed by the toe of a shoe. There was a similar mark a little higher up, but less visible. Someone had climbed up the wall, using a branch that hung down to help him . . .

At the very moment when he was about to reconstruct the climb, the inspector swung round. He had the impression that there was an unexpected presence at the end of the road, near the Loire.

He was just in time to see a feminine figure, tall and quite strong,with blonde hair and the regular, clear-cut profile of a Greek statue. The young woman had begun walking on when Maigret turned round, which suggested that she had previously been watching him.

A name sprang to the detective's mind of its own accord: Éléonore Boursang! Up to this point he had not tried to imagine Henry Gallet's mistress. Yet he was suddenly as good as certain that this was the lady.

He quickened his pace and reached the embankment just as she was turning the corner of the main road.

'Back in a minute!' he told the hotelier, who tried to stop him as he was passing.

He ran for a little way while he was out of the fugitive's sight, to reduce the distance between them. Not only did the woman's figure suit the name of Éléonore Boursang, she was exactly the woman that a man like Henry would have chosen.

But on arriving at the crossroads himself, Maigret was annoyed. She had disappeared. He looked into the dimly lit window of a small grocery store and then into the forge next to it.

But it did not matter much, since he knew where to find her.

5

The Thrifty Lovers

The sergeant from the gendarmerie must have formed a seductive idea that morning of the kind of life led by a police officer from Paris. He himself had been up at four in the morning and had already cycled some thirty kilometres, first in the early-morning cold, then in increasingly hot sunlight, when he reached the Hôtel de la Loire for the periodic check carried out on the register of its guests.

It was now 10 a.m. Most of the guests were walking beside the water or bathing in the river. Two horse dealers were talking on the terrace, and the hotelier, a napkin in his hand, was making sure that the tables and the bay trees in their containers were lined up properly.

'Aren't you going to say good morning to the inspector?' asked Monsieur Tardivon, and then, lowering his voice to a confidential tone, 'He's in the room that was the scene of the crime at this very moment. He's had all kinds of papers sent to him from Paris, and big photographs too . . . '

It worked; a little later the sergeant knocked on the door and said, apologetically, 'It was Monsieur Tardivon, inspector. When he told me you were examining the scene I was tempted . . . I know you have special methods in Paris

. . . if I'm not in the way I'd really like to learn from seeing how you do it.'

He was an amiable man whose round, pink face showed an ingenuous wish to please, and he made himself as small as possible, not entirely easy in view of his hobnailed boots and his gaiters. He couldn't decide where to put his kepi.

The window was wide open, the morning sun fell right on the nettle lane so that against the light the room was almost dark. And Maigret, in his shirtsleeves, pipe between his teeth, detachable collar unbuttoned, tie loose, gave an impression of well-being that was bound to strike the local policeman.

'Sit down, do, by all means. But there's nothing interesting to see, you know.'

'Oh, you're too modest, inspector.'

It was so naive that Maigret turned his head to hide a smile. He had brought everything to do with the case into the room with him. After making sure that the table, covered with an Indian tablecloth that had a reddish leaf pattern, could tell him nothing, he had spread out all his files on it, from the medical examiner's report to photos of the scene and the victim sent to him from Criminal Records that very morning. Finally, giving way to a feeling that was superstitious rather than scientific, he had put the picture of Émile Gallet on the black marble mantelpiece, which had a copper candlestick on it by way of an ornament.

There was no carpet on the varnished oak boards of the floor, on which the first officers to come on the scene had drawn the outline of the

252

body they found there in chalk.

In all the greenery outside the window there was a confused murmuring made up of birdsong, rustling leaves, the buzzing of flies and the distant clucking of chickens on the lane, all of it punctuated by the rhythmic blows of the hammer on the anvil in the forge. Confused voices sometimes came up from the terrace, or the sound of a cart crossing the suspension bridge.

'Well, you're not short of documents! I'd never have thought . . . '

But the inspector wasn't listening. Calmly, taking little puffs at his pipe, he put a pair of black trousers on the floor where the corpse's legs had lain. The fabric was such a fine weave that, after having been worn for some ten years, judging by their shininess, they could surely have been worn for another ten.

Maigret also laid out a percale shirt and, in its usual place, a starched shirt-front. However, there was no shape to this collection, and it was only when he put a pair of elastic-sided shoes at the ends of the trouser legs that it became both absurd and touching.

In fact it did not look like a body, it was more of a caricature, and it was so unexpected that the sergeant glanced at his companion and uttered an embarrassed little laugh.

Maigret did not laugh. Heavy and bent on his task, he was walking up and down slowly, conscientiously. He examined the jacket and put it back in the travelling bag, after making sure that there was no hole in the fabric where the blade of the knife had gone in. The waistcoat, which was torn level with its left pocket, took its place on the shirt-front.

'That's how he was dressed,' he said under his breath.

He consulted one of the police photographs and adjusted his handiwork by giving his imaginary dummy a very high detachable celluloid collar and a black satin tie.

'See that, sergeant? He dined at eight on Saturday — he had some pasta because he was on a diet. Then he read the paper and drank mineral water, as usual. A little while after 10 p.m. he entered this room and took off his jacket, keeping on his shoes and his detachable collar.'

In fact Maigret was talking not so much to the sergeant, who was listening intently and thought it his duty to nod approval of every remark, as to himself.

'Now where would his knife have been at that moment? It was a pocket flick-knife, the kind a lot of people carry on them. Wait a minute . . .'

He folded back the blade of the knife that was lying on the table with the other exhibits and slipped it into the left-hand pocket of the black trousers.

'No, that makes creases in the wrong place.' He tried the right-hand pocket and seemed satisfied. 'There we are! He has his knife in his pocket. He's alive. And between eleven and twelve thirty at night he died. There's chalk and stone dust on the toes of his shoes. I've found marks left by the same kind of shoes opposite the window, on the wall surrounding Tiburce de Saint-Hilaire's property. Did he take off his jacket to climb the wall? We have to remember that he wasn't a man to make himself comfortable, even at home.'

Maigret was still walking round the room, leaving some of his sentences unfinished and never glancing at the listener sitting motionless on his chair.

'I've found some remnants of burned paper in the fireplace — they'd taken the stove out of it for the summer. Now let's go over the movement he must have made: he takes off his jacket, burns the papers, crushes out the ashes with the foot of that candlestick (I found sweat on the copper), he climbs the wall opposite after getting out over the window-sill, and he climbs back in the same way. Then he takes the knife out of his pocket and opens it. It's not much, but if we knew the order in which those things happened . . . Between eleven and twelve thirty he's back here again. The window is open, and someone shoots him in the head. There's no doubt about that — the bullet came before the knife wound, and it was fired from outside. So Gallet took out his knife. He didn't try to get out, which would suggest that the murderer came into the room, because you don't fight someone seven metres away from you with a knife. And there's more to come: Gallet had half his face blown away. The wound was bleeding, and there's not a drop of blood to be found near the window. The bloodstains we do find show that, once wounded, he moved in a circle with a diameter of no more than two metres. *Severe ecchymosis on left wrist*, writes the doctor who performed the post-mortem. So our man is holding his knife in his left hand, and the murderer seized that hand to turn the weapon against him. The blade pierces his heart, and he falls all at once, dropping the knife. That doesn't bother the murderer, *who knows that it will have only the victim's own fingerprints on it*. Gallet's wallet is still in his pocket; nothing has been stolen from him. However, Criminal Records claims that there are tiny traces of rubber on the travelling bag in particular, as if someone had been holding it with rubber gloves on.'

'Strange! Very strange!' said the delighted sergeant, although he would not have been able to repeat a quarter of what had been said.

'The strangest thing of all is that as well as those traces of rubber they found some powdered rust.'

'Maybe the revolver was rusty!'

Maigret said nothing in reply to this but went to stand at the window, where, looking somewhat unkempt, with the sleeves of his white shirt billowing out, his outline looked enormous against the lighted rectangle. A thin trail of blue smoke rose in the air above his head. The sergeant stayed in his corner, hesitating even to change the position of his legs.

'Didn't you want to see my vagrants?' he asked timidly.

'Oh, are they still there? You can let them go again.'

Maigret went back to the table, rubbing his hair up the wrong way, tapped the pink file, changed the place of the photos and looked at the other man.

'Did you come on a bicycle? Would you go to the railway station and ask what time Henry Gallet — young man of about twenty-five, tall, thin, pale, dark clothes, horn-rimmed glasses — took the train to Paris on Saturday? And by the way, have you ever heard of a Monsieur Jacob?'

'Only the one in the Bible,' ventured the sergeant.

Émile Gallet's clothes were still on the floor, like the caricature of a corpse. Just as the sergeant was making for the door, someone knocked. It was Monsieur Tardivon, who said, 'Someone to see you, inspector! A lady called Boursang who says she'd like a word with you.'

The sergeant would have liked to stay, but his companion did not invite him to do so. After a satisfied glance round the room, Maigret said, 'Show her in.'

And he leaned down to his insubstantial tailor's dummy, hesitated, smiled, planted the knife in the place where the heart would have been and tamped the tobacco down in his pipe with one finger.

★   ★   ★

Éléonore Boursang was wearing a pale, well-cut skirt suit, well cut although, far from making her appear youthful, it made her look nearer to thirty-five than thirty. Her stockings fitted nicely, her shoes were well chosen, and her fair hair was carefully arranged under a white straw toque. She was wearing gloves.

Maigret had withdrawn into a shady corner, interested to see how she would present herself. When Monsieur Tardivon left her at the door she stopped, apparently taken aback by the sharp contrasts of light and shadow inside the room.

'Detective Chief Inspector Maigret?' she asked at last, taking a few steps forwards and turning to the silhouette against the window, at whose identity she could so far only guess. 'I'm so sorry to disturb you.'

He came over to her, entering the light. When he had closed the door again, he said, 'Please sit down.'

And he waited. His attitude gave her no help at all; on the contrary, he assumed a cantankerous manner.

'Henry must have mentioned me to you, and so when I found myself in Sancerre I hoped it would be all right to speak to you.'

He still said nothing, but he had not managed to upset her. She spoke with composure, with a certain dignity that almost reminded him of Madame Gallet. A younger Madame Gallet, and no doubt a little prettier than Henry's mother had been, but just as representative of the same social class.

'You must understand my situation. After that . . . that dreadful tragedy, I wanted to leave Sancerre, but Henry wrote a letter advising me to stay here. I've seen you two or three times, and the local people told me that you were in charge of the attempts to track down the murderer. So I decided to come and ask if you had found anything out. I'm in a delicate situation, given that officially I don't have any connection with Henry or his family . . . '

It didn't sound like a speech she had prepared in advance. The words came easily to her lips, and she spoke with composure. Several times her eyes had gone to the knife placed on the bizarre shape traced by the clothes lying on the floor, but she had not flinched at the sight of it.

'*So* your lover has told you to pick my brains?' said Maigret suddenly, his voice intentionally harsh.

'He didn't tell me to do anything! He's devastated by what happened. And one of the worst things about it is that I couldn't be at the funeral with him.'

'Have you known him for long?'

She did not seem to notice that the conversation had turned into an interrogation. Her voice remained level.

'Three years. I'm thirty, while Henry is only twenty-five. And I'm a widow.'

'Are you a native of Paris?'

'No, I'm from Lille. My father is chief accountant in a textile factory, and when I was twenty I married a textiles engineer who was killed in an accident by a machine a month after our wedding. I ought to have been paid a pension at once by the firm that employed him, but they claimed that the accident was because of my husband's own carelessness. So as I had to earn my own living, and I didn't want to take a job in a place where everyone knew me, I went to Paris and started work as a cashier in a shop in Rue Reaumur. I brought an action against the textiles factory. The case went on and on through the courts, and it was settled in my favour only two years ago. Once I knew that I would not be in want I was able to leave my job.'

'So you were working as a cashier when you met Henry Gallet?'

'Yes, he's a direct marketing agent, and he often came to see my employers on behalf of the Sovrinos Bank.'

'Didn't the two of you ever think of marrying?'

'We did discuss it at first, but if I had married again before my case was decided in court I wouldn't have been in such a good position over the pension.'

'So you became Henry Gallet's mistress?'

'Yes, I'm not afraid of the word. He and I are united just as much as if we'd gone through a wedding ceremony at the town hall. We've been seeing each other daily for the last three years, and he eats all his meals at my place . . . '

'But he doesn't actually live with you in Rue de Turenne?'

'That's because of his family. They have very strict principles, like my own parents. Henry decided he'd rather avoid friction with his by leaving them in ignorance of our relationship. But all the same it's always been agreed that when there are no more obstacles and we have enough to go and live in the south of France we'll get married.'

She showed no embarrassment even when faced with the most indiscreet questions. Now and then, when the inspector's eyes went to her legs, she simply pulled her skirt down.

'I have to go into all the details. So Henry was eating his meals with you . . . did he contribute to the expenses?'

'Oh, that's very simple! I kept accounts, as you do in any well-organized household, and at the end of the month he gave me half of what had been spent on our food and drink.'

'You mentioned going to live in the south of the country. Was Henry managing to put some money aside?'

'Yes, just like me! You must have noticed that his constitution isn't very strong. The doctors say he needs good fresh air. But you can't live out of doors when you have to earn a living and you don't have a manual job. I love the country too. So we live modestly. As I told you, Henry is a direct marketing agent for Sovrinos — a small bank concentrating mainly on speculation. So he was at the source of it here, and we used everything we could save one way or another to invest on the stock exchange.'

'You have separate accounts?'

'Of course! We never know what the future has in store for us, do we?'

'And what capital have you built up in this way?'

'It's hard to say exactly, because the money is in securities, and they change value from one day to the next. Around 40,000 to 50,000 francs.'

'And Gallet?'

'Oh, more than that! He didn't always like to let me embark on risky speculations like the mines of Plata last August. At the moment he must have about 100,000 francs.'

'Have you decided the figure at which you'll stop?'

'Five hundred thousand . . . we expect to work in Paris for three more years.'

Maigret was now looking at her with feelings verging on admiration. But a particular kind of admiration, with more than a touch of revulsion in it. She was thirty! Henry was twenty-five! They were in love, or at least they had decided to spend their lives together. Yet their relationship was like that of two partners in a business enterprise! She spoke of it simply, even with a certain pride.

'Have you been in Sancerre for long?'

'I arrived on 20 June to stay for a month.'

'Why didn't you go to stay at the Hôtel de la Loire, or the Commercial?'

'Too expensive for me! I'm paying only twenty-two francs a day at the Pension Germain, at the far end of the village.'

'So Henry came on the 25th? What time?'

'He has only Saturday and Sunday off, and it had been agreed that he'd spend the Sunday at Saint-Fargeau. He came here on Saturday morning, and left by the last train that evening.'

'And that was when?'

'Eleven thirty-two p.m. I went to the station with him.'

'Did you know that his father was here?'

'Henry told me he'd met him. He was furious, because he was sure his father had come here just to spy on us, and Henry didn't want his family getting involved in what's no one's business but our own.'

'Did the Gallets know about that 100,000 francs?'

'Of course! Henry has come of age — he had a right to live his own life, didn't he?'

'In what terms did your lover usually speak of his father?'

'He thought poorly of him for his lack of ambition. He said it wasn't right, at his age, for him still to be selling junk jewellery. But he was always very respectful to his parents, especially his mother.'

'So he didn't know that in reality Émile Gallet was nothing but a crook?'

'A crook? Him . . . ?'

'And that for the last eighteen years he hadn't been selling 'junk jewellery' at all?'

'That can't be true!'

Was she playing a part as she looked at the lugubrious dummy corpse on the floor with a kind of wonderment?

'I'm stunned, inspector! Him! With his odd ways, his ridiculous clothes? He looked just like a poor pensioner!'

'What did you two do on Saturday afternoon?'

'We went for a walk in the hills, Henry and I. It was when he left me to go back to the Commercial that he met his father. Then we met again at eight and we went for another walk, on the other side of the water this time, until it was time for Henry to catch the train.'

'And you didn't come close to this hotel?'

'It was better to avoid a meeting.'

'Then you came back from the station by yourself. You crossed the bridge . . . '

'And I turned left at once to get back to the Pension Germain. I don't like walking on my own at night.'

'Do you know Tiburce de Saint-Hilaire?'

'Who's he? I've never heard the name . . . Inspector, I hope you don't suspect Henry of anything.' Her expression was animated, but she was as composed as ever. 'I'm here because I know him. He's almost always been ill, and that's made him gloomy and distrustful. We can sometimes spend hours together without talking. It's pure coincidence that he met his father here. Although I realize it might seem an odd coincidence. He's too proud to defend himself . . . I don't know what he told you. Did he answer your questions at all? What I can swear is that he never left me from eight in the evening to the time when he caught his train. He was nervous. He was afraid his mother would hear about our relationship, because he's always been very fond of her, and he foresaw that she'd try to turn him against me . . . I'm not a young girl any more! There are five years between us. And, after all, I've been his mistress. I can't wait to hear that the murderer is behind bars, especially for Henry's sake. He's clever enough to know that his meeting with his father could give rise to terrible suspicions.'

Maigret went on looking at her with the same surprise. He was wondering why this behaviour, which after all did her some credit, did not move him. Even as she uttered those last phrases with a certain vehemence, Éléonore Boursang was still in control of herself. He moved the papers to show a large photo from Criminal Records of the corpse as it had been found, and the young woman's eyes moved over the disturbing image without lingering on it.

'Have you found out anything yet?' she asked.

'Do you know a Monsieur Jacob?'

She raised her eyes to him as if inviting him to see the sincerity in them. 'No, I don't know the name. Who is he? The murderer?'

'Perhaps,' he said, as he went towards the door.

Éléonore Boursang left in much the same way as she had come into the room. 'May I come to see you now and then, inspector, to ask if you have any news?'

'Whenever you like.'

The sergeant was waiting patiently in the corridor. When the visitor had disappeared, he cast an inquiring glance at the inspector.

'What did you find out at the station?' Maigret asked.

'The young man took the Paris train at eleven thirty-two with a third-class return ticket.'

'And the crime was committed between eleven and half past twelve,' murmured the inspector thoughtfully. 'If you hurried you could get from here to Tracy-Sancerre in ten minutes. The murderer could have done the deed between eleven and eleven twenty. If it takes ten minutes to reach the station, then you wouldn't need any longer to get back . . . so Gallet could have been killed between eleven forty-five and half past twelve *by someone coming back from the station* . . . Except there's that business of the barred gate! And what the devil was Émile Gallet doing on the wall?'

The sergeant was sitting in the same place as before, nodding his approval and waiting to hear what followed. But nothing followed.

'Come on, let's go and have an aperitif!' said Maigret.

6

The Meeting on the Wall

'Still nothing?'

' . . . *bution!*'

'What word did you say just now?'

'*Preparations*. At least, I suppose so. The *ions* bit is missing. Or it could be *preparation*, singular. Or *preparatory*.'

Maigret sighed, shrugged his shoulders and left the cool room, where a tall, thin, red-haired young man with a tired face and the phlegmatic manner typical of northerners had been bending over a table since that morning, devoting himself to work that would have discouraged even a monk. His name was Joseph Moers, and his accent showed that he was of Flemish origin. He worked in the labs of Criminal Records and had come to Sancerre at Maigret's request, to set up shop in the dead man's hotel room, where he had arranged his instruments, including a strange kind of spirit stove.

He had hardly looked up since seven in the morning, except when the inspector entered the room abruptly or stood at the window looking out on the nettle lane.

'Anything?'

'I . . . you . . . '

'Huh?'

'I've just found an *I* and a *you*, except that the *u* is missing too.'

He had spread out some very thin sheets of glass on the table, and as he went along with his work was coating them with liquid glue heated on the spirit stove. From time to time he went over to the fireplace, delicately picked up one of the pieces of burned paper and put it on one of the sheets of glass. The ash was fragile and brittle, ready to crumble to bits. Sometimes it took five minutes to soften it by surrounding it with water vapour, and then it was stuck on the glass.

Opposite him, Joseph Moers had a small case which was a veritable portable laboratory. The larger pieces of charred paper measured seven to eight centimetres. The smaller pieces were mere dust.

. . . bution . . . prepara . . . I . . . yo

That was the result of two hours of work, but, unlike Maigret, Moers was not impatient and did not flinch at the thought that he had examined only about one-hundredth of a part of the contents of the fireplace. A large purple fly was buzzing as it circled round his head. It settled on his frowning brow three times, and he didn't even raise a hand to brush it away. Perhaps he didn't even notice it.

However, he did tell Maigret, 'The trouble is that when you come in through the doorway you set up a draught! You've already lost me some ash like that.'

'Oh, all right! I'll come in through the window!'

It was not a joke. He did it. The files were still in this room, which Maigret had chosen as a study, and where the clothes spread on the floor with a knife piercing them had not even been touched. The inspector was impatient to know the result of the expertise he had summoned to his aid, and as he waited he could hardly keep still.

For quarter of an hour, he could be seen walking up and down the lane with his head bent, hands clasped behind his back. Then he straddled the window-sill, his skin burning in the sunlight and shiny; he mopped his brow and growled, 'Slow work, if you ask me!'

Did Moers even hear him? His movements were as precise as a manicurist's, and his mind was entirely on the sheets of glass that he was covering with irregularly outlined black marks.

The main reason why Maigret was agitated was that he had nothing to do, or rather he thought it was better not to try doing anything before he had a clear idea of what was on the paper burned on the night of the crime. And as he paced up and down the lane, where the oak leaves cast dappled light and shade on him, he kept going over the same ideas.

Henry and Éléonore Boursang could have killed Gallet before going to the station, he thought. Éléonore could have come back on her own to kill him after seeing her lover off on the train . . . and then there's that wall, and that key! What's more, there was a certain Monsieur Jacob, the man whose letters Gallet was fearfully hiding . . .

He went back ten times to examine the lock of the barred gate, without finding anything new. Then, as he was passing the spot where Émile Gallet had climbed the wall, he suddenly went into action himself, took off his jacket and put the toe of his right shoe into the first join between the stones. He weighed a good hundred kilos, but he had no difficulty in grasping the hanging branches, and once he had a hold on them it was child's play to finish the climb.

The wall was made of irregular stones covered with a coat of whitewash. On top of it was a row of bricks set edgeways. Moss had invaded them, and there was even grass growing and flourishing.

From his perch, Maigret had an excellent view of Moers deciphering something through his magnifying glass.

'Anything new?' he called.

'An s and a comma.'

Above his head the inspector now had not oak leaves, but the foliage of an enormous beech tree, its trunk coming up from the property on the other side of the wall.

He knelt down, because the top of the wall was not wide, and he was not sure of keeping his balance on his feet, examined the moss to right and left of him and murmured, 'Well, well!'

Not that his discovery was sensational. It consisted solely of the fact that the moss had been scuffed and even partly removed at a spot directly above the scratches on the stone, but nowhere else.

As the moss was fragile, as he quickly

established, he felt absolutely certain that Émile Gallet had not walked along the wall, not even as much as a metre either way.

So now to find out if he came down on the side of the Saint-Hilaire property . . .

Strictly speaking, this place was not really part of the grounds, no doubt because the area was hidden behind a great many trees and served as a kind of outdoor lumber room. A dozen metres from Maigret, there were piles of old barrels, empty, stove in or minus their hoops. There were also old bottles, several of which had held pharmaceuticals, crates, a decrepit mower, rusty tools and packages of old numbers of a comic magazine tied up with string. Soaked with rain, dried and discoloured by the sun, stained by the soil, they were a sad sight.

Before climbing down from the wall, Maigret made sure that just below him, in fact just below the place that Gallet must have occupied on the wall himself, there were no markings on the ground. He jumped so as not to risk scratching the wall and was rewarded by landing on all fours.

There was nothing to be seen of Tiburce de Saint-Hilaire's villa apart from a few light-coloured patches in the filigree pattern of the foliage. An engine was chugging, and Maigret now knew that it was pumping water from the well into stocks for the household.

This corner of the park was full of flies because of all the rubbish. The inspector had to keep shooing them away, and did so in an increasingly bad temper.

First for the wall, he thought.

The examination of the wall was easy. It had been given a coat of whitewash on both sides in spring. Maigret could see that there was no trace of any mark or scratch underneath the place where Émile Gallet had climbed the wall, and no footprints for ten metres anywhere near.

However, near the casks and bottles the inspector noticed that a barrel had been dragged two or three metres and then stood on end at the foot of the wall. It was still there. He got up on it, and his head came above the top of the wall exactly ten and a half metres from the place where Gallet had been stationed. Furthermore, from where he was he saw Moers still at work, not even taking time off to mop his face.

'Found anything?'

'*Clignancourt* . . . but I think I have a better fragment here.'

The moss on the wall above the barrel had not been torn away, but looked as if it had been crushed by arms pressing on it. Maigret tried leaning on his elbows and got the identical result a little further along.

In other words, he reflected, Émile Gallet gets up on the wall *but does not come down on the side of Saint-Hilaire's property.* On the other hand, someone coming from inside the Saint-Hilaire property hauls himself up on that barrel *but goes no higher and does not leave the enclosure of the grounds, or at least not that way.*

For that to make any sense, the couple going for a nocturnal expedition would have had to be a young man and a girl. And whichever of them had stayed inside the wall could have brought the barrel as close to the other as possible.

But this couldn't have been a lovers' meeting! One of the couple must certainly have been Monsieur Gallet, who had taken off his jacket before embarking on an exercise which was far from compatible with his character.

Was the other one Tiburce de Saint-Hilaire?

The two men had seen each other first that morning, then in the afternoon, quite openly. It was not very likely that they had decided on such a roundabout way of seeing each other again after dark!

And at a distance of ten metres from one another they wouldn't even have been able to hear each other if they spoke in an undertone.

Unless, thought Maigret, they had come separately, first one and then the other . . . but which of the two had hoisted himself up on the wall first? And had the two men met?

It was about seven metres from the barrel to Gallet's room — the distance at which the gun had been fired.

When Maigret turned round he saw the gardener, who was looking at him with an interested expression.

'Oh, it's you,' said the inspector. 'Is your master here?'

'Gone fishing.'

'You know I'm from the police, don't you? Well, I'd like to get out of these grounds without jumping the wall. Would you open the gate at the end of the nettle lane for me?'

'No problem!' said the man, making off in that direction.

'Do you have the key?'

'No, you'll see!' And when he reached the gate he put his hand unhesitatingly into the gap between two stones and cried out in surprise.

'Good heavens!'

'What?'

'It isn't there any more! And I put it back myself last year, that's when three oak trees were chopped down and we got them out this way.'

'Did your master know?'

'Course he did!'

'You don't remember seeing him go that way?'

'Not since last year.'

Another version of the facts automatically began taking shape in the inspector's mind: Tiburce de Saint-Hilaire up on top of the barrel, firing the gun at Gallet, going round by way of the gate, leaping into his victim's room . . .

But it was so improbable! Even supposing that the rusty lock hadn't put up any resistance, it would take three minutes to get along the lane separating the two points. And in those three minutes Émile Gallet, with half his face blown away, had not cried out, had not fallen over, had done nothing but take his knife out of his pocket in case someone came along to attack him! It all sounded wrong! It creaked the way the gate ought to have creaked. Yet it was the only theory that made sense in terms of logical deduction from the material clues!

Anyway, thought Maigret, there was a man on the other side of the wall. That was a definite fact. But nothing indicated that the man was Saint-Hilaire other than the lost key and the fact that the unknown stranger was in his property.

On the other hand, two more people closely connected with Émile Gallet, a couple who might have an interest in his death, were in Sancerre at that moment, and there was no firm alibi to show that they had not set foot in the nettle lane. That couple was Henry Gallet and Éléonore.

Maigret crushed a horsefly that had settled on his cheek and saw Moers leaning out of the window.

'Inspector!'

'Anything new?'

But the Fleming had disappeared into the room again.

Before deciding to go the long way round by the bank again, Maigret shook the gate, and contrary to his expectations it gave way.

'Hey, it's not locked after all!' said the gardener in surprise, leaning over the lock. 'Funny thing, that!'

Maigret almost recommended him not to mention his visit to Saint-Hilaire, but looking the man up and down he thought him too stupid to heed it and decided not to make matters more complicated.

'Why did you call me just now?' he asked Moers a little later.

Moers had lit a candle and was looking through the sheet of glass almost entirely covered with black. 'Do you know a Monsieur Jacob?' he asked, putting his head back to examine his work as a whole with satisfaction.

'Good heavens! What have you found?'

'Nothing much. One of the burned letters was signed Monsieur Jacob.'

'Is that all?'

'Just about. The letter was written on squared paper torn out of a notebook or some kind of register. I've only found a few words on that kind of paper. *Absolutely*, or I suppose so because the *ab* is missing. Then *Monday* . . . '

Maigret waited for more, frowning, teeth clenched on his pipe.

'After that?'

'There's the word *prison* underlined twice. Unless something's lost and the word is *prisoner*. Then there's *cash*, or it could be *cashier*. And there's also a number written in words, *twenty thousand* . . . '

'No address?'

'I told you just now, *Clignancourt*. The trouble is that there's no way I can reconstruct the order of the words.'

'Any clue in the handwriting?'

'There isn't any — it was done on a typewriter.'

Monsieur Tardivon was in the habit of serving Maigret's meals himself, and he did so making a great show of discretion together with a touch of conspiratorial familiarity. Now, before knocking, he called from outside the door, 'A telegram, inspector!'

He very much wanted to enter the room, as Moers and his mysterious work intrigued him. Seeing that the officer was about to close the door again, he asked cheerfully, 'And what can I bring you for lunch, inspector?'

'Nothing,' said Maigret curtly. He had opened the telegram. It was from headquarters in Paris; Maigret had asked for certain information. It said:

Émile Gallet left no will. Estate consists of Saint-Fargeau house, estimated value a hundred thousand with furniture, three thousand five hundred francs deposited in bank.

Aurore Gallet gets life insurance three hundred thousand taken out by husband with Abeille company 1925.

Henry Gallet back at work Sovrinos bank.

Éléonore Boursang out of Paris on holiday in Loire valley.

'Good heavens,' muttered Maigret, looking into space for a moment and then, turning to Moers, said, 'Do you know anything about life insurance?'

'That depends,' said the young man modestly. He was wearing a pair of pince-nez fitting so tightly that his whole face looked contracted.

'In 1925 Gallet was over forty-five. And he had liver trouble. How much a year do you think he had to pay for life insurance worth 300,000 francs?'

Moers moved his lips silently. The arithmetic took him less than two minutes.

'About 20,000 francs a year,' he said at last. 'All the same . . . it can't have been easy to persuade a company to take the risk!'

The inspector cast a furious glance at the portrait photo, still standing on the mantelpiece at the same angle as on the piano in Saint-Fargeau.

'Twenty thousand! And he was spending barely 2,000 a month! In other words, about half of what he was painfully squeezing out of the supporters of the Bourbons!'

His eyes moved on from the photograph to the shapeless black trousers, baggy at the knees and shiny, stretched out on the floor. And he summoned up the image of Madame Gallet with her mauve silk dress, her jewellery, her cutting voice.

He might almost have been about to ask the photograph, 'Did you love her as much as all that?'

Finally, shrugging his shoulders, he turned to the brightly sunlit wall up which, exactly eight days earlier, Émile Gallet had hoisted himself in his shirtsleeves, his starched shirt-front jutting out of his waistcoat.

'There are still some ashes left,' he told Moers, sounding rather weary. 'Try to find me something else about this Monsieur Jacob. Who's that idiot who said he only knew the Jacob in the Bible?'

A boy with a freckled face had his elbows propped on the window-sill, grinning from ear to ear, as a man's voice called up half-heartedly from the terrace, 'You let those gentlemen get on with their work, Émile!'

'Oh no, not another Émile!' grumbled

278

Maigret. 'At least this one's alive! Whereas the other . . . '

But he had enough control over himself to leave the room without looking at the photograph again.

7

Joseph Moers' Ear

The temperature was still scorching. Every morning, the papers had reports of storms breaking in many different parts of France, but it was three weeks since a drop of rain had fallen in and around Sancerre. In the afternoon, the rays of the sun shone directly into the room where Émile Gallet had stayed, making it uninhabitable.

That Saturday afternoon, however, all Moers did was to lower the cream-coloured blind over the open window. Less than half an hour after lunch, he was leaning over his glass sheets and bits of blackened paper, working with the regularity of a metronome.

Maigret prowled round him for several minutes, touching everything, dragging his feet, looking hesitant. At last he sighed, 'Listen, old fellow, I can't take this any more! I admire you, but you don't weigh as much as I do. I must go and get some fresh air.'

But where could he go on a day like this? There was a little fresh air on the terrace, but he would have to put up with the hotel guests and their children. And it was unusual for half an hour to go by in the café without the irritating click of billiard balls being heard.

Maigret went into the courtyard, half of which was in shade, and called to a young waitress passing by, 'Bring me a lounger, will you?'

'Do you want to sit here? You'll be close to all the noise from the kitchens.'

He preferred that, and the clucking of chickens into the bargain, to other people's conversations. He took his lounger over to near the well, spread a newspaper over his face to protect himself from the flies and was soon overcome by a delightful sleepiness. Little by little, the noise of plates being washed in the scullery became unreal, and the drowsy Maigret escaped his obsession with the late Monsieur Gallet.

Exactly when did he notice what sounded like two loud bangs? They did not entirely rouse him from his torpor, because a dream explaining those misplaced sounds surfaced in his mind . . .

He was sitting on the hotel terrace. Tiburce de Saint-Hilaire was passing by in a bottle-green suit, followed by a dozen long-eared hounds . . .

'Weren't you asking the other day if there's any game to be found in this part of the country?' he said.

Raising his gun to shoulder level, he fired it at random, and a whole flock of partridges looking like autumn leaves fell to the ground . . .

'Inspector! Quick!'

He jumped and saw a chambermaid in front of him.

'It's in the bedroom . . . someone's firing a gun!'

The inspector was ashamed of feeling so

heavy. People were already running into the hotel, and he was far from being the first to reach Gallet's room, where he saw Moers standing by the table with both hands over his face.

'Everyone out of here!' he ordered.

'Shall I call a doctor?' asked Monsieur Tardivon. 'Look . . . there's blood!'

'Yes, go!'

Once the door was closed he went over to the young man from Criminal Records. He was feeling remorseful.

'What's the matter, lad?' Although, as he could see, there was blood — blood everywhere! On Moers' hands, on his shoulders, on the sheets of glass and on the floor.

'It's nothing serious, inspector . . . just my ear, look!'

He let go of his left earlobe for a moment, and blood immediately spurted out. Moers was pale, but all the same he tried to smile and above all to stop his jaws moving convulsively.

The shutter was still down, filtering the sunlight and giving the air an orange tinge.

'It's not dangerous, is it? There's nothing like an ear for bleeding . . . '

'Calm down and get your breath back.' For the Fleming's teeth were chattering so much that he could hardly speak.

'I ought not to get myself into such a state,' he said. 'But I'm not used to this sort of thing! I had just got up to fetch some new plates . . . '

He dabbed his wounded ear with his bloody handkerchief, leaning on the table with his free hand.

282

'And so I was standing just here when I heard a bang. I swear I felt the draught of a bullet passing through the air, so close to my eyes that I thought it had taken my pince-nez off. I flung myself backwards, and then at the same time, at once, I mean after the first shot a second one was fired. I thought I was a dead man . . . there was such a racket in my head, as if my brain were boiling!'

His smile was less forced now.

'Well, as you can see, it was nothing, just a little nick in my ear. I ought to have run to the window, but I simply couldn't move. I thought more shots might be fired — I had no idea what it felt like to be under fire before . . . '

He had to sit down. In some sort of delayed reaction, the shock had hit him, and he had gone weak at the knees. 'Don't worry about me,' he told Maigret. 'Find whoever was firing that gun.'

Drops of sweat suddenly stood out on his forehead, and Maigret, seeing that he was about to faint, ran to the door.

'Tardivon!' he called. 'See to Monsieur Moers here. Has a doctor come?'

'He's not at home. But one of the guests staying here is a male nurse at the Hôtel-Dieu hospital in Paris . . . '

Maigret pulled aside the blind and went out over the window-sill, automatically putting the stem of his empty pipe in his mouth. The nettle lane was deserted, half of it in the shade, the other half vibrant with light and warmth. The Louis XIV gate at the end of it was closed.

The inspector could see nothing unusual

283

about the white wall facing the room. As for footprints, it would be no use looking for any in the dry grass, which, like places where the soil was too stony, did not preserve prints. He made for the bank, where some twenty people had gathered, but hesitated to go any further.

'Were any of you on the terrace when those shots were fired?'

Several voices replied, 'I was!' Their delighted owners stepped forward.

'Did you see anyone starting off along this road?'

'No, no one! Not for the last hour, anyway.'

'I never moved from the spot, inspector!' said a thin little man in a multi-coloured sweater.

'Go back to Mama, Charlot! I was here, inspector. If the murderer had gone along the nettle lane I'd have been bound to see him. It could have been fatal!'

'Did you hear the shots?'

'Everyone did . . . I thought they were hunting in the property next door. I even took a few steps . . . '

'And you didn't see anyone on the road?'

'No one at all.'

'But of course you wouldn't have looked behind every tree trunk.' Maigret did exactly that, to put his mind at rest, and then made for the front entrance of the chateau, where he saw the gardener pushing a wheelbarrow full of gravel along a path.

'Your master's not in, is he?'

'No, he'll be at the notary's place. This is the time of day when they play cards.'

'Did you see him leave?'

'I saw him as clearly as I see you now! It was about an hour and a half ago.'

'And you didn't see anyone in the grounds?'

'Not a soul. Why?'

'Where were you ten minutes ago?'

'Right beside the water, loading up this gravel.'

Maigret looked into his eyes. The man appeared to be telling the truth — in fact he looked too stupid to be telling a plausible lie.

Without bothering about him any more, the inspector went over to the barrel propped against the wall enclosing the property, but he saw no indication that the murderer had gone that way. He had no more luck when he examined the rusty barred gate. It did not look as if it had been opened since he himself had pushed it back into place that morning.

'Yet someone fired a gun, twice!'

The people at the hotel were sitting down again now, but the conversation was general.

'I don't expect it means anything.' Monsieur Tardivon came over to the inspector. 'But I've just heard that the doctor has gone to see Petit, the notary. Should I send someone for him?'

'Where's the notary's house?'

'In the square beside the Commercial.'

'Whose is that bicycle?'

'I don't know, but you can take it . . . are you going yourself?'

The bicycle was too small for him, but Maigret mounted it, making the springs of the saddle groan under him. Five minutes later he was setting off a chime of bells at the front door of a huge house, very neat and clean, and an old maidservant in a blue checked apron was looking out at him through a peephole.

'Is the doctor here?'

'Who's it for?'

But a half-open window was flung wide, and a man of jovial appearance holding playing cards in his hands leaned out.

'Is it for the guard's wife? I'm just coming!'

'No, there's a man wounded, doctor! Would you go straight to the Hôtel de la Loire, please?'

'Not another crime, at least I hope not!'

Three other men, sitting at a table with gleaming crystal glasses on it, rose to their feet. Maigret recognized Saint-Hilaire among them.

'Yes, a crime! Come on, quick!'

'Anyone dead?'

'No . . . and make sure you bring something to dress a wound.' Maigret was keeping his eyes on Saint-Hilaire, and he realized that the owner of the little chateau was absolutely thunderstruck.

'One question, gentlemen,' he began.

'Just a moment!' the notary interrupted. 'Why hasn't anyone let you in?'

Hearing this, the maid finally opened the door. The inspector went along a corridor and into the sitting room, where there was a pleasant smell of cigars and well-aged spirits.

'What has happened?' asked the master of the house, a well-groomed old man with silky hair and skin as clear as a baby's.

Maigret pretended not to have heard him. 'Gentlemen, I'd like to know how long you have been playing cards.'

The notary glanced at a pendulum clock. 'A good hour.'

'And none of you has left this room during that time?'

They looked at each other in astonishment.

'Good heavens, no! There are only four of us — just the right number for bridge.'

'Are you *absolutely certain?*'

Saint-Hilaire was crimson in the face.

'Who is the victim?' he asked. His throat was evidently dry.

'An officer from Criminal Records. He was working in the room where the late Émile Gallet had stayed, concentrating on a part of the case involving the identity of one Monsieur Jacob . . . '

'Monsieur Jacob,' repeated the notary.

'Do you know anyone of that name?'

'Why, no. Sounds like a Jewish surname.'

'Monsieur de Saint-Hilaire, I'm going to ask you a favour. I'd like you to move heaven and earth to find the key of that barred gate. If necessary I'll lend you officers to search the villa.'

The owner of the chateau tossed the contents of a glass of spirits down his throat in a single gulp, something that did not escape Maigret's notice.

'I'm sorry to have disturbed you, gentlemen.'

'Won't you take a glass of something with us, inspector?'

'Not now, thank you . . . maybe another time.'

He set off on the bicycle again, turned left and soon came to a rather dilapidated house with a barely legible board outside giving its name: Pension Germain.

It was a poor sort of place, and Maigret doubted its cleanliness. A little boy, not very well washed, was standing in the doorway, where a dog was gnawing a bone picked up from the dusty road outside.

'Is Mademoiselle Boursang here?' he asked.

A woman carrying a baby in her arms appeared at the back of the room. 'She's gone out, same as every afternoon, but you'll probably find her on the hill near the old chateau. She took a book with her, and that's her favourite place.'

'Does this road lead there?'

'Yes, turn right after the last house.'

Halfway up the hillside, Maigret had to get off the bicycle and push it. He was feeling more nervous than he would have liked, perhaps because once again he had the impression that he was on the wrong track.

It wasn't Saint-Hilaire who fired those shots, that's for sure, he told himself. Yet all the same . . .

The road he was following crossed a kind of public garden. On the left, where the ground sloped, a little girl was sitting near three goats tethered to stakes. The road went round a sudden bend, and just above him, a hundred metres uphill, Maigret saw Éléonore sitting on a bench with a book in her hands. He called to the girl, who looked about twelve.

'Do you know the lady sitting up there?'

'Yes, sir.'

'Does she often come to sit on that bench and read?'

'Yes, sir!'

'Every day?'

'I think so, sir, but when I'm at school I don't see her.'

'What time did you arrive here today?'

'Oh, ages ago, sir. I left home as soon as I'd had something to eat.'

'And where do you live?'

'In the house you can see down there.'

It was half a kilometre away, a low-built house with something of the look of a farmhouse about it.

'Was the lady already there then?'

'No, sir.'

'When did she arrive?'

'I can't say exactly, sir, but it would be about two hours ago.'

'And she hasn't moved since then?'

'No, sir.'

'Not even to go for a little walk along the road?'

'No, sir.'

'Does she have a bicycle?'

'No, sir!'

Maigret took a two-franc coin out of his pocket and put it into the child's hand. She closed her fingers on the coin without looking at it and stayed there motionless in the middle of the road, her eyes following him, as he mounted the bicycle again and rode off towards the village.

He stopped outside the post office and drafted a telegram to Paris.

Urgent. Need to know where Henry Gallet was 15 hours Saturday. Maigret, Sancerre.

'I should let that be for now, old fellow!'

'You told me yourself it was urgent, inspector. Anyway I hardly feel a thing!'

Good man, Moers! The doctor had given his ear a dressing as complicated and thick as if he had six bullets in his head. The sparkling bright glass of his pince-nez looked strange in the middle of all that white linen.

Maigret had not felt anxious about him until seven in the evening, knowing that his injury was not a severe one — and now he found him just where he had spent the morning, in front of his sheets of glass, his candle and his spirit stove.

'I haven't found out anything else about Monsieur Jacob. I've just reconstructed a letter signed *Clément* addressed to I don't know whom, and talking about a present intended for a prince in exile. The word *bution* comes in twice, and *loyalism* once.'

'That's of minor interest now,' said Maigret. For all this was obviously to do with the swindle on which Gallet had embarked. The pink file had provided him with information on that subject, as well as several phone calls to the owners of chateaux and manor houses in the Berry and Cher areas. At some time or other, probably three or four years after his marriage, and one or two years after his father-in-law's death, Émile Gallet had decided that it would be a good idea to make use of the old documents relating to the *Le Soleil* material that he had inherited.

The journal, its text from the pen of Préjean himself, had a very small print run, reserved almost exclusively for the few who subscribed to it, and it kept the hope of seeing a Bourbon back on the throne of France alive in the hearts of a few country squires.

Maigret had leafed through the *Soleil* material, noticing that half a page was always devoted to subscription lists, sometimes on behalf of an old family that had fallen on hard times, sometimes for the propaganda fund, or again in the cause of celebrating an anniversary worthily.

That was what had given Gallet the idea of swindling the legitimists. He had their addresses, he even knew from the lists what sum of money could be got from them and how to appeal to each of them individually for contributions.

'Have you found the same handwriting on the other papers?' Maigret asked.

'Yes, the same,' said Moers. 'In fact Professor Locard, who trained me, would tell you more. Calm, careful handwriting, but with signs of agitation and discouragement at the ends of words. A graphologist would say unhesitatingly that the man who wrote those letters was ill and knew it.'

'Good heavens, that'll do, Moers! You can take a rest now!'

Maigret was looking at two holes in the canvas blind — the holes made as the bullets passed through it. 'Would you go and sit back where you were just now?'

He had no difficulty in reconstructing the trajectory of the bullets.

'The same angle,' he concluded. 'Firing from the same place on top of the wall . . . good heavens, what's that noise?'

He raised the blind and saw the gardener raking the ground of the path where the nettles and tall grass grew.

'What are you doing?' Maigret called.

'It was my master . . . he told me to . . . '

'Look for the key?'

'That's right!'

'And he sent you to look for it here?'

'He's searching the grounds himself. And the cook and the manservant, they're searching inside the house.'

Maigret abruptly pulled the blind down and alone in the company of Moers again he whistled.

'Well, well,' he said. 'Want to bet, old fellow? He'll be the one who finds the key.'

'What key?'

'Never mind, it would take too long to explain. What was the time when you lowered the blind?'

'As soon as I got back here, about one thirty.'

'And you didn't hear any sounds on the lane outside?'

'I wasn't listening for any. I was absorbed in my work . . . it may look silly, but it's a very delicate job.'

'I know it is, I know! Come to think of it, who could have heard me talking about Monsieur Jacob? The gardener, I think. And Saint-Hilaire, who was out fishing, came home for lunch, changed his clothes and went out for his card game. Are you sure that the handwriting on all the other charred papers belongs to Monsieur Clément?'

'Absolutely sure.'

'Then they're of no interest. The only one that counts is the letter signed by Monsieur Jacob speaking of cash, mentioning Monday and looking very much as if it's threatening the recipient of the letter with prison if 20,000 francs is not received by that day. The crime was committed on Saturday . . . '

Sometimes the rake outside hit a stone.

'It wasn't Éléonore or Saint-Hilaire who fired the shots, it was . . . '

'Well, who'd have believed it!' said the gardener's voice outside.

Maigret smiled with pride and went to raise the blind. 'I'll take that!' he said, holding out his hand.

'If I'd expected to find it here . . . '

'I said I'll take that.'

It was the key, an enormous key, the kind you would never find anywhere except an antique dealer's. Like the lock, it was rusty and had some scratches on it.

'All you have to do is tell your master that you handed it over to me. Off you go!'

'But I . . . '

'Off you go!'

And Maigret pulled the blind down and threw the key on the table.

'You might say that, apart from your ear, we've had a wonderful day. Don't you agree, Moers? Monsieur Jacob! The key! Those two shots and all the rest of it. Well . . . '

'Telegram for you!' announced Monsieur Tardivon.

293

'What was I saying, old fellow?' the inspector finished, after glancing at the telegram. 'We're going backwards, not forwards. Listen to this:

At three p.m. Henry Gallet was with his mother at Saint-Fargeau. Still there at six p.m.

'*So?*'
'So nothing! There's only Monsieur Jacob left who could have fired on you, and so far Monsieur Jacob has been as hard to pin down as a soap bubble.'

8

Monsieur Jacob

'Wait a moment, Aurore! There's no point in showing yourself in such a state!'

And a muffled voice replied, 'I can't help it, Françoise. That visit reminds me of the other one a week ago. And the journey . . . oh, you don't understand.'

'What I don't understand is how you can mourn for a man like that, a man who dishonoured you, who lied to you all his life. The only good thing he ever did was to take out life insurance . . . '

'Oh, do be quiet!'

'And there's more! He made you live what was almost a life of poverty, swearing that he earned only 2,000 francs a month. The insurance proves that he was making at least twice that and hiding it from you. Who knows if he wasn't earning even more? If you ask me that man was leading a double life, with a mistress and maybe children somewhere else . . . '

'Oh, please don't, Françoise!'

Maigret was alone in the small sitting room of the house in Saint-Fargeau. The maid had shown him in, forgetting to close the door. The two women's voices came to him from the dining room, where the door, opening on to the same corridor, was also only half closed. The furniture and other items were back in their old places, and the inspector couldn't look at the large oak table without remembering that a few days earlier, covered with a black sheet, it had had a coffin and candles on it.

The atmosphere was dismal, the weather oppressive. There had been a storm during the night, but you could feel that there was more rain to come.

'Why should I keep quiet? Do you think it's none of my business? I'm your sister. Jacques is about to be offered an important political post. Suppose the local people find out that his brother-in-law was a crook?'

'Why did you come, then? You've gone twenty years without . . . '

'Without seeing you, because I didn't want to see him! I didn't hide my opinion when you wanted to get married, and nor did Jacques! When your name is Aurore Préjean, when you have a brother-in-law who's managing director of one of the largest tanneries in the Vosges area and another who's going to be principal private secretary to a government minister, you don't marry a man like Émile Gallet. I mean, the name alone tells you . . . A commercial traveller! I wonder how our father ever gave his consent to it! Or rather, between ourselves, I can guess just what happened. In his last days Father thought of only one thing: how to bring out his journal at all costs — and Gallet had a little money. So it was decided to involve him in *Le Solei!* Don't you dare to say that's not true! But as for you, sister, you had the same education as me, you even look like Mama, and you chose a man who was nothing. Don't look at me like that! I only want you to understand that you've lost no one to shed tears about! Were you happy with him? Frankly, were you?'

'I don't know . . . I don't know any more.'

'Admit that you had more ambition than that!'

'I always hoped he would try something else. I encouraged him to . . . '

'Might as well try encouraging a pebble! And you resigned yourself to it! You didn't even know that you wouldn't be left in poverty on the day he died! Because but for that insurance . . . '

'He did think of that,' said Madame Gallet slowly.

'That's all we need! To hear you talk, I'll end up thinking you loved him!'

'Hush — the inspector might hear us. I must go in and see him.'

'What's he like? I'll come with you. That will be best, considering the state you're in. And please, Aurore, don't look so miserable. The inspector might think you were his accomplice, that you're sad, that you're afraid . . . '

★ ★ ★

Maigret just had time to take a step back. The two women came through the communicating door, looking not quite as he had imagined them from the conversation he had just overheard.

Madame Gallet was almost as distant in her manner as at the time of their first interview. As for her sister, who was two or three years younger, with peroxide hair and a heavily made-up face, she made Maigret feel that she had twice Madame Gallet's amount of nerve and pretension.

'Have you found out anything more, inspector?' asked the widow wearily. 'Please sit down. Let me introduce you to my sister, who arrived yesterday from Epinal.'

'Where her husband is a tanner, I think?'

'He owns a number of tanneries, actually,' Françoise corrected him drily.

'Madame was not at the funeral, am I right? And now, three days ago the newspapers reported that you, Madame Gallet, are to receive a life insurance payment of 300,000 francs.'

He spoke slowly, looking right and left with apparent awkwardness. He had come to Saint-Fargeau for no precise reason, to sniff out the atmosphere and refresh his memory of the dead man. None the less, he would not have been sorry to meet Henry Gallet again.

'I'd like to ask you a question,' he said without turning to the two women. 'Your husband must have known that your marriage to him estranged you from your family.'

It was Françoise who answered. 'That's not true, inspector! At first we welcomed him. Several times, my husband advised him to find another job and offered to help him. It was only when we saw that he would always be someone of low achievement, incapable of making an effort, that we avoided him. He would have shown us in a poor light.'

'What about you, madame?' Maigret asked gently, turning to Madame Gallet. 'You encouraged him to change to a different profession? You blamed his lack of ambition?'

'It seems to me that anything like that belongs to our private life. Isn't it my right to keep that to myself?'

Hearing her just now through the door, Maigret had been able to imagine a woman made more human by her grief. A woman who had abandoned that scornful dignity that he now found neither more nor less robust than on the first day.

'Did your son get on with his father?'

Her sister intervened again. 'Henry will make something of himself! He's a Préjean, although physically he looks like his father. And he did right to get away from that atmosphere when he came of age. He was back at work this morning in spite of that attack of his liver trouble he had last night.'

Maigret looked at the table, trying to imagine Émile Gallet somewhere in this room, but he couldn't do it, perhaps because the inhabitants of this villa never set foot in the sitting room except when they were receiving a formal visit from someone.

'Did you have a message for me, inspector?'

'No . . . I'll leave you now, ladies, with my apologies for disturbing you. However . . . yes, I do have one question. Do you have a photograph of your husband in Indochina? I believe he lived there before his marriage.'

'No, I have no photograph of him then. My

husband almost never talked about that time of his life.'

'Do you know what he studied as a young man?'

'He was very clever . . . I remember that he talked to my father about Latin literature.'

'But you don't know the name of the school he attended?'

'All I know is that he was a native of Nantes.'

'Thank you very much. And I do apologize to you once again.'

He picked up his hat and stepped backwards into the corridor, still unable to identify the obscure anxiety he felt each time he set foot in that house.

'I hope my name will not be given to the press, inspector,' said Françoise, in a tone not far from impertinence. 'You may know that my husband is a departmental councillor. He has a great deal of influence in government circles, and as you are an official . . . '

Maigret did not feel brave enough to reply to this. He merely looked her between the eyes and then took his leave, sighing.

As he crossed the tiny garden, escorted by the maid with the squint, he murmured thoughtfully, 'You poor devil, Gallet!'

★ ★ ★

He briefly stopped at the Quai des Orfèvres to pick up his post, which included nothing bearing on the present case. On coming out of the building he looked in, on the off chance, at the

300

shop of the gunsmith who had examined the bullet taken from the dead man's skull as well as the two that had been aimed at Moers.

'Have you finished examining those bullets?'

'Yes, just this minute. I was going to write the report. All three bullets were fired from the same gun, no doubt about that. An automatic revolver, a precision weapon and one of the latest models, no doubt from the National Factory at Herstal.'

Maigret was feeling gloomy. He shook hands with the gunsmith and hailed a taxi. 'Rue Clignancourt, please.'

'What number?'

'Drop me off at either end of the street, it doesn't matter which.'

On the way he tried to banish from his mind the unpleasant memory of the Saint-Fargeau villa and the conversation between the two sisters. He wanted to concentrate only on the positive aspects of the problem. But as soon as he had put a few simple ideas together, back came the woman Françoise whose husband was a departmental councillor — as she had been careful to point out — and who had come running to Les Marguerites on discovering that Madame Gallet had inherited 300,000 francs.

He would have shown us in a poor light.

And early in the marriage Émile Gallet had been badly treated, just to get the idea into his head that he must do credit to the Préjeans, like their other sons-in-law. But he was only a commercial traveller in gift items!

Yet he had the courage to sign that life assurance agreement and pay the premium for five years, thought Maigret, intrigued. His feelings were contradictory; he was both attracted and repelled by the complex physiognomy of his murder victim. Did he do it because he loved his wife? She too must have given him a piece of her mind, more than once, about his humble station in life.

Funny sort of household! Funny sort of people, too. But in spite of everything hadn't Maigret felt, for a moment, that Madame Gallet felt genuine affection for her husband? True, he had heard her only through the door. That was all gone when she was in front of him. Once again she had been the pretentious and disagreeable petit bourgeois woman who had talked to him on that first visit of his, and who was very much Françcoise's sister.

Then there was Henry, who already had a thoughtful and suspicious expression when he was about to take his First Communion, and who at the age of twenty-two didn't marry Éléonore for fear of losing the pension she might get after her late husband's death! Henry who had suffered an attack of his liver trouble but still went straight back to work!

It began to rain. The taxi driver pulled in to the side of the pavement so that he could put up the top of the car.

The three bullets had been fired from the same revolver — from which one might deduce that they had been fired by the same person. However, neither Henry nor Éléonore nor Saint-Hilaire could have fired the last two shots.

Nor could a vagrant. A vagrant doesn't kill for

the sake of killing. He steals, and nothing had been stolen.

The lack of progress in this case, circling round the lacklustre and melancholy figure of the dead man, was getting Maigret down, and it was with a grumpy expression that he entered the first concierge's lodge in the Rue Clignancourt.

'Do you know a Monsieur Jacob?'

'What does he do?'

'No idea. But anyway, he gets letters addressed to that name . . .'

The rain was still falling heavily, but the inspector was quite glad of it, because in this atmosphere the busy road, full of small shops and run-down buildings, was more in tune with his own frame of mind. This traipsing from building to building was a job that could have been given to a junior officer, but Maigret didn't like the idea of getting a colleague mixed up in this case; he couldn't really have said why himself.

'Monsieur Jacob?'

'Not here. Try over there, you'll find some Jews.'

He had popped his head round the door or through the window of a hundred concierge lodges and questioned a hundred concierges, when one of them, a stout woman with tow-coloured hair, looked at him suspiciously.

'What do you want with Monsieur Jacob? You're police, aren't you?'

'Flying Squad, yes. Is he at home?'

'You wouldn't expect him to be at home at this time of day!'

'Where can I find him?'

'In his usual place, of course! Corner of Rue Clignan court and Boulevard Rochechouart. Here, I hope you're not going to bother him! Poor old fellow like that, I'm sure he never did anyone any harm. So maybe he didn't always have a trading permit — is that why you're here?'

'Does he get a lot of post?'

The concierge frowned. 'So that's what you're here for, eh?' she said. 'I might have known it. Not a nice story, that. You must know as well as me that he only got a letter once every two or three months.'

'By registered post?'

'No, more like a little package than a letter.'

'Containing banknotes, I expect?'

'How would I know?' she said tartly.

'I think you do! Yes, I think you do! You felt those envelopes and you, too, had an idea that there were banknotes inside.'

'And suppose there was? Monsieur Jacob wouldn't have been breaking no bank!'

'Where's his room?'

'His attic, you mean? Right up at the top. He has a hard time getting upstairs every evening with his crutches.'

'Has no one ever come looking for him?'

'Let's see . . . about three years ago. Old gentleman with a pointy beard, looked like a priest without a cassock. I told him, like I told you . . .'

'Was Monsieur Jacob already getting letters?'

'He'd just had one.'

'Did the man wear a close-fitting jacket?'

'He was all in black, like a priest.'

'Doesn't Monsieur Jacob ever have visitors?'

'There's only his daughter, she's a chambermaid in a furnished place in the Rue Lepic, got a baby on the way.'

'What's his profession?'

'You mean you don't know? And you from the police and all? Are you making fun of me? Monsieur Jacob, why, he's the oldest newspaper seller in the area. Old as the hills, everyone knows him . . . '

★ ★ ★

Maigret stopped on the corner of Rue Clignancourt and Boulevard Rochechouart, outside a bar called Au Couchant. There was a vendor of peanuts and toasted almonds at the end of the terrace who probably sold chestnuts in winter. On the side of Rue Clignancourt a little old man was sitting on a stool, reciting the names of newspapers in a hoarse voice which was lost in all the noise coming from the crossroads.

'*Intran . . . Liberté . . . Presse . . . aris-Soir . . . Intran . . . *'

A pair of crutches was propped against the front of his stall. One of the old man's feet had a leather shoe, but he wore only a shapeless slipper on the other.

At the sight of the newspaper seller, Maigret realized that 'Monsieur Jacob' was not his real name but a nickname, because the old man had a long beard divided into two with two pointed ends, and above it was a curved nose in the shape of those clay pipes known as Jacobs.

The inspector suddenly remembered the few words of a letter that Moers had been able to reconstruct: *twenty thousand . . . cash . . . Monday*. And suddenly, leaning over the lame man, he asked 'Have you got the latest consignment?'

Monsieur Jacob raised his head, opening and closing his reddened eyelids several times.

'Who are you?' he asked at last, handing a copy of *L'Intransigeant* to a customer and looking in a box-wood bowl for the right change.

'Police Judiciaire! Now, let's talk nicely, or I'll have to take you away. This is a nasty business.'

Monsieur Jacob spat on the pavement.

'Then what?'

'Do you have a typewriter?'

The old man cackled with laughter, this time spitting out a chewed cigarette end, of which he had quite a collection in front of him already.

'No point playing who's cleverest,' he said in a thick voice. 'You know it's not me. Though I'd have done best to stay away from trouble, for the little I've got out of it.'

'How much?'

'She gave me a hundred sous a letter. So it's a pathetic business.'

'A business likely to land those involved in it in court.'

'You don't say! So they really were notes of a thousand? I wasn't so sure. I felt the envelopes, they made a kind of silky sound. I held them up to the light, but I couldn't see inside, the paper was too thick.'

'What did you do with them?'

'Brought them here. Didn't even need to say when I'd be here . . . around five the little lady who bought an *Intran* off of me would turn up without fail, put the hundred sous in the bowl here and slip the package into her bag.'

'A small brunette?'

'No, no, a tall blonde. More strawberry blonde, and ever so nicely dressed, my word, yes! She'd come up out of the Métro . . . '

'When did she first ask you to do her this service?'

'It'll be about three years back . . . wait a minute. Yes, my daughter had had her first baby, he was out at Villeneuve-Saint-Georges with a wet-nurse . . . that's right, a little less than three years ago. It was getting late, I'd packed up the merchandise and was hoisting it on my back; she asked if I had a fixed address and if I could help her. We see all sorts around here. Well, so it was about getting letters addressed to me, not opening them, bringing them here in the afternoon.'

'Was it you who fixed the price at five francs a package?'

'It was her . . . I was just pointing out it was worth more — joking, like — what with the price of a litre of red these days, but she started going over to the peanut vendor . . . an Algerian, he is. Some folk'll work for nothing. So I said yes.'

'And you don't know where she lives?'

Monsieur Jacob winked. 'Not so stupid when it comes to it, eh? Even if you are police! There was someone else who tried to find out, early on that was. My concierge only told him I sold my papers here. She described him to me, and I reckoned he was the young lady's father. So he started hanging around when there was a package for me to deliver, but never said a word to me. Yes, wait a minute — he lay low over there, behind the fruit stall. And then he went chasing off after her, but he didn't have any luck. In the end he came to find me and offered me 1,000 francs for the young lady's address. He could hardly believe it when I said I had no more idea than he did. Seems like she led him a fine dance on who knows how many Métro trains and buses, and then she shook him off outside an apartment building with two exits. He wasn't a joker either, that one. I soon caught on that he wasn't her father. He tried his luck again, twice. I thought I ought to warn my customer, and I reckon she led him on another merry dance, because he didn't try again. Well, and so what else do you think I got instead of that man's 1,000 francs? A whole louis! And I had to pretend I didn't have any change or I'd only have got ten francs, and she went off muttering something that wasn't very polite, though I didn't understand it. She was a sly one! But talk about a cheapskate!'

'When did that last letter arrive?'

'I reckon three months back. You've got to move about a bit in case the customers don't see the papers any more. That all I can do for you, then? You've got to admit I'm the right sort, and I didn't try to do you down . . . '

Maigret put twenty francs in the bowl, made a

vague gesture of farewell and walked off with a thoughtful expression. As he passed the entrance to the Métro, he made a face of distaste at the thought of Éléonore Boursang going off with an envelope containing several 1,000-franc notes after throwing five francs to old Jacob, taking ten different Métro and bus lines, entirely at her ease, and to cap it all going through a building with two exits before heading back to her own apartment.

What could that have to do with Émile Gallet taking off his jacket and persisting in climbing a wall three metres high?

Monsieur Jacob, on whom Maigret had pinned his last hopes, was vanishing into thin air.

There was no Monsieur Jacob!

Was he to believe that, instead, there was a couple, Henry Gallet and Éléonore Boursang, who had found out Henry's father's secret and were making him pay for it?

Éléonore and Henry, who hadn't killed anyone!

Saint-Hilaire hadn't killed anyone either, in spite of his contradictions in the matter of the open gate and *the key that he himself had thrown on to the nettle lane, making sure that his gardener found it after the inspector had told him that he was going to get his hands on it at all costs!*

None of that made any difference to the fact that two bullets had been fired at Moers, and that Émile Gallet, whose sister-in-law implied that he was bringing shame on the whole family, had been murdered.

At Saint-Fargeau, they were consoling each other by heaping scorn on him, emphasizing the mediocrity of his character and his life, and by the thought that his death, after all, was worth 300,000 francs.

That morning, Henry had gone to deposit securities with the Sovrinos bank and put the 100,000 francs of savings to good account — the savings which must become 500,000 to allow him to go and live in the country with Éléonore.

While she, finally, as calm as when she was exchanging the newspaper seller's envelope for five francs, was in Sancerre, spying on Maigret, or was coming to see him with an unfurrowed brow and innocent eyes to tell him the story of her life.

And Saint-Hilaire was playing cards with the notary!

The only one absent was Émile Gallet. He was firmly in a coffin, half his face torn away by the bullet, maltreated by the forensic surgeon who had seven guests coming to dinner, a stab wound through his heart, and his grey eyes were open because no one had thought of closing their lids.

'Last avenue on the left, near the old mayor's pink marble monument,' said the verger doing duty as cemetery attendant.

And the undertaker in Corbeil was scratching his head as he looked at an order specifying 'a simple stone, sober lines, good taste, not too expensive but distinguished'.

Maigret had seen a good deal in his time. Yet he tried to consider the possibility that the tall woman with strawberry blonde hair was not necessarily Éléonore Boursang and that, if she was indeed Monsieur Jacob's customer, there was nothing to prove that Henry was her accomplice.

The simplest thing, he thought, would be to show the old man her photograph. That was why he had himself driven to Rue de Turenne, where he was almost sure to find a photograph of the young woman in her apartment.

'Madame Boursang isn't here, but Monsieur Henry is upstairs,' the concierge told him.

Evening was drawing in. Maigret bumped into the walls of the narrow staircase on the way up and opened the door indicated by the concierge without knocking.

Henry Gallet was leaning over a table, doing up a rather large parcel. He gave a start then managed to regain his self-control when he recognized the inspector. However, he could not say anything. His teeth were so firmly clenched that it must have hurt. The change in him after a week was alarming. His cheeks were hollow, his cheekbones jutted. Above all, his complexion was an appalling leaden hue.

'I hear that you had a terrible attack of liver trouble last night,' said Maigret, with more ferocity than he had intended. 'Move over, please.'

The parcel was the shape of a typewriter. The inspector tore off the wrapping paper, took a sheet of white paper out of his pocket, typed a few random words on it, took it out of the machine and slipped it into his pocket. Briefly, the noise of the typewriter had broken the silence in the apartment, where dustsheets covered the furniture and there was newspaper stuck to the windows for the holiday season.

Henry, leaning his elbows on a chest of drawers, was looking at the floor, his nerves so tense that it was painful to look at him.

Maigret, heavy, implacable, went on with what he was doing, opened drawers, searched their contents. Finally he found a photograph of Éléonore. Then, ready to leave, his hat pushed back on the nape of his neck, he stopped for a moment in front of the young man and looked him up and down, from head to foot.

'Is there anything you'd like to tell me?'

Henry swallowed and finally managed to say, 'No.'

Maigret was careful not to arrive at Rue Clignancourt, where Monsieur Jacob was still sitting in front of his newspapers, until an hour later. Did he want one more piece of evidence? Before he was even level with the old man, he saw Henry Gallet's long, discoloured face behind the windowpane of a bistro.

Next moment Monsieur Jacob told him, 'Yes, that's her all right. Got her!'

Maigret went off without a word but cast an aggressive glance at the bistro. He could have gone in and set off another attack of Henry's liver trouble simply by putting a hand on his shoulder.

And never mind that *they* didn't kill him, he thought.

Half an hour later, he was walking through the

Prefecture without greeting anyone, and in his office he found a letter from the inspector of indirect taxes in Nevers.

9

A Farcical Marriage

If you would care to go to the trouble of paying a discreet visit to my home at 17, Rue Creuse, in Nevers, I will give you some information concerning Émile Gallet that will interest you to a very high degree.

Maigret was in the Rue Creuse. In front of him, in a red and black drawing room, was the inspector of indirect taxes for Nevers, who had introduced himself with a conspiratorial air.

'I sent the maid away! As you will understand, that's for the best. And so far as anyone who may have seen you arrive is concerned, you are my cousin from Beaucaire.'

Was he winking at Maigret to emphasize his every word? Not really; instead of closing one eye at a time he was closing and opening them both, very fast, which ultimately made him look as if he had a nervous tic.

'Are you a former colonial yourself? No? I would have thought . . . well, that's a pity, because it would have been easier for you to understand.'

And he continued to bat his eyelids the whole time and adopted an ever more confidential tone; the expression on his face was simultaneously sly and frightened.

314

'I myself spent ten years in Indochina, at the time when Saigon didn't yet have wide boulevards like Paris. It was there that I met Gallet . . . and what set me thinking along those lines was the way he was stabbed with a knife, as you will see. I'll bet you've found out nothing yet! And you won't find anything out, because it's a story that only a colonial can understand. A colonial who has seen the *thing itself*.'

Maigret had already placed the tax inspector: he knew that with a man of this kind he must possess his soul in patience, be careful not to interrupt, nod now and then — which after all was the only way to gain time.

'He was a great fellow, our friend Gallet. He was some kind of clerk to a notary who's made his way since then, he's a senator. And he was mad on sport — even took it into his head to form a football team. He'd recruited us all, we couldn't resist him — only there was no other team for us to play against. Well, in short, he liked women even better than football, and there were plenty of chances to meet women out there. Ah, yes, he was a jolly companion. And the tricks he played on the fair sex . . . excuse me, please.'

On silent feet, he made for the door and abruptly flung it open to make sure there was no one on the other side.

'Right, well . . . Once he went too far, and I'm not proud of having played the part of his accomplice, without great enthusiasm, I might add. There was a planter who'd just imported two or three hundred Malay workers, and there were some women and children with them

— among others a girl, a little creature who might have been carved from amber. I don't remember her name now. But I do remember I was just finishing reading a book by Stevenson about the natives of the Pacific and I mentioned it to Gallet. It's about a white man who organizes a sham marriage, so that he can enjoy the charms of a wild native girl. And my friend Émile got rather carried away by the idea! In those days the Malays couldn't read, in particular the poorer sort who were transported round the place like brute beasts. So Gallet goes to put his request to the girl's father. He decks out his future in-laws in ridiculous garments, he gets together a wedding procession to lead the happy couple to this run-down little house that we'd repaired. Another friend played the part of mayor to marry them. He's dead now, although there'll be others still alive who remember the joke. He was a great joker, Gallet was, and he made sure the whole farce was as comic as possible. The speeches would have had you rolling in the aisles, and the marriage certificate, which we solemnly handed over to the girl, was complete gobbledegook from start to finish. What larks — at the expense of the head of the family, the witnesses and everyone else!'

The inspector of indirect taxes fell silent for a moment, to assume an expression of greater gravity.

'Well, then,' he concluded. 'Gallet lived with the girl as man and wife for three or four months. Then he went back to France, of course leaving the wife who wasn't his wife behind. We were still young, or we wouldn't have made such a joke of it, because the Malays don't forgive easily . . . you don't know them, inspector. The girl waited a long time for her husband to come back. I don't know what happened to her after that but years later I met her again — she'd aged a lot — in a poor quarter of Saigon. And when I read Gallet's name in the local Nevers newspaper . . . I hadn't seen him for twenty-five years, remember. I hadn't even heard anyone speak of him. But it was that knife wound, you see. Can you guess now? It was vengeance, sure enough. A Malay will go all round the world to get revenge. And they're used to knives. Suppose a brother of the girl, or even a son, more civilized now . . . suppose he began by using a revolver, because it's a practical weapon. But then instinct got the upper hand.'

Maigret was waiting, with a gloomy expression, listening with only half an ear to this torrent of words. It would be useless to interrupt. In a criminal case there are usually a hundred witnesses of the tax inspector's calibre, and if this time only one turned up it must be because the Parisian newspapers had devoted only a few lines to the case.

'Are you with me, inspector? You'd never have guessed, would you? I thought it better to ask you to come here, because if the murderer knew I was talking to you . . . '

'You were saying that Gallet used to play football?'

'He was mad about it! And what a joker! The best company you could find. Why, he was capable of telling funny stories all evening without giving you time to get your breath back.'

'Why did he leave Indochina?'

'He said he had ideas of his own, and they didn't include living on less than 100,000 a year — that was before the war. A hundred thousand francs! You see what I mean? Folk might laugh at him, but he was perfectly serious. He used to laugh and say, 'We'll see, we'll see!' He didn't get his 100,000 a year, did he? Now as for me, it was the fevers sent me away from Asia. They still give me shaking fits. You'll take something to eat and drink, won't you, inspector? I'll serve you myself, because I sent the maid out of town for the whole afternoon.'

Maigret did not feel up to accepting the tax inspector's hospitality, or to having to put up with any more of his knowing winks as he launched once again into his story of the vengeful Malay. He could hardly manage to thank the man with a smile — a pallid, civil smile.

Two hours later, he got off the train at Tracy-Sancerre station, where he already knew his way around. As he walked down the road leading to the Hôtel de la Loire, he was in the middle of a soliloquy:

'So suppose this is Saturday 25 June. And suppose I am Émile Gallet. The heat is stifling, my liver is giving me trouble. And in my pocket I have a letter from Monsieur Jacob threatening to tell the police everything if I don't give him 20,000 francs in cash on Monday. My legitimists would never come up with 20,000 francs at a time. The average amount I manage to get out of them is between 200 and 600 francs — very rarely 1,000! I get to the Hôtel de la Loire and I ask for a room *looking out on the courtyard* . . . why the courtyard? Because I'm afraid of being murdered? By whom?'

He was walking slowly with his head bent, trying hard to get inside the dead man's skin.

'Do I know who Monsieur Jacob really is? He's been blackmailing me for three years, I've been paying up for three years. I've interrogated the newspaper seller on the corner of Rue Clignancourt. I've followed a young blonde who shook me off at a building with two exits. I can't possibly suspect Henry because I know nothing about his affair. Nor do I know that he's already saved 100,000 francs and needs 500,000 to go and live down south. Which means that Monsieur Jacob remains a terrifying lurking entity behind the figure of the old street seller.'

He made a gesture like a teacher wiping the exercise off a blackboard with a duster. He would have liked to forget all he now knew and start his investigation again from scratch.

Émile Gallet was a jolly fellow. He made his friends form a football team.

He passed the hotel without going in and rang the bell at the main entrance to the Saint-Hilaire property. Monsieur Tardivon, who was standing in his doorway and whom Maigret had not greeted, watched him go disapprovingly.

The inspector had to wait some time out in the road. At last a manservant opened the door, and Maigret asked, point-blank, 'How long have you been living in this house?'

'A year ... but isn't it Monsieur de Saint-Hilaire you want to see?'

Monsieur de Saint-Hilaire himself gave Maigret a friendly wave from a ground-floor window. 'Well now, that key! We had it after all! Won't you come in a moment? How are the inquiries coming along?'

'How long has the gardener been working for you?'

'Oh, three or four years ... but do come in!'

The owner of the chateau too was struck by the change that had come over Maigret. His features were hard, there was a frown on his brow, and his eyes had a disturbing look of lassitude and malice.

'I'll just get a bottle brought in and we ... '

'What became of your old gardener?'

'He has a bistro a kilometre from here, on the Saint-Thibaut road. An old rogue who made his pile out of me before setting up on his own account.'

'Thank you.'

'Are you going?'

'I'll be back.'

He seemed to say that without a moment's thought, and with his mind preoccupied went back to the gate and off towards the main road.

So he needed 20,000 francs in a hurry, Maigret went on thinking. He didn't try getting it out of his usual victims, that's to say the local landowners. Saint-Hilaire was the only one he visited. Twice in the same day! Then he climbed the wall ...

He interrupted himself with an oath. 'Good lord above! And why, in that case, did he ask for a room *looking out on the yard?* If he'd got one, he couldn't have climbed the wall.'

The former gardener's bistro was near a lock on the canal joining the River Loire from the side, and was full of bargees.

'Can you help me, please? Police. I'm inquiring into the crime at Sancerre. Do you remember seeing Émile Gallet visiting your old boss when you worked for him?'

'You mean Monsieur Clément? That's what we called him. You bet I did!'

'Often?'

'Can't really say . . . maybe about once every six months. But that was enough to leave the boss in a bad mood for a couple of weeks.'

'Were his first visits long ago?'

'At least ten years ago, maybe fifteen. Can I offer you a glass of something?'

'No thank you. Did they sometimes argue?'

'Sometimes, no! Every time, yes! I even saw them come to blows like a couple of dockers!'

And yet, Maigret reasoned a little later, as he walked back to the hotel, it wasn't Saint-Hilaire who carried out the killing. First, he couldn't have fired those two shots at Moers, because he was playing cards at the notary's house. And then, on the night of the crime, why would he have gone the long way round by the barred gate?

He saw Éléonore not far from the church but turned his head away so as to avoid her. He didn't want to talk to anyone, her least of all. He heard rapid footsteps behind him and saw her catch up with him. She was wearing a grey dress, and her hair was smooth and tidy.

'Excuse me, please, inspector.'

He turned abruptly and looked her in the eyes with such an aggressive expression that it took her breath away for a moment.

'I only wanted to know whether . . . '

'No, nothing! I've found out nothing at all!'

And he walked away without another word, hands behind his back.

Suppose the room looking out on the courtyard had been free, he wondered, would he be dead just the same?

A little boy playing with a football collided clumsily with the inspector's legs. Maigret picked him up and put him down a metre away without even looking at him.

Anyway, he continued his train of thought, he didn't have the 20,000 francs. He couldn't get them together in time for Monday. And he couldn't have climbed the wall. It would have been impossible to fire on him from that wall. So, Maigret reasoned, *he wouldn't be dead now!*

He mopped his brow, although the temperature was much more tolerable than the week before. He had that annoying feeling of being close to the solution that he wanted, yet unable to reach it.

He had a great many facts: that business of the wall, the two gunshots fired a week later at Moers, the conduct of Monsieur Jacob, the visits to Saint-Hilaire fifteen years before, the lost key so providentially found by the gardener, the matter of the hotel room, the knife wound finishing off the work of the bullet with a few seconds between them, and finally the football team and the farcical marriage . . .

For Gallet's passion for sport, his funny stories and his amorous exploits were all that could be gleaned from the rambling tale of the inspector of indirect taxation.

A jolly companion . . . liked women even better than football . . .

'Will you be dining on the terrace, inspector?' asked Monsieur Tardivon.

Maigret had got there without noticing it. 'I don't mind one way or the other.'

'And how is your case getting on?'

'Let's say it's over.'

'What? Then the murderer is . . . ?'

However, the inspector passed him, shrugging his shoulders, went down the corridors full of cooking smells and went into the room where his files were still heaped on the table, the mantelpiece and the floor.

No one had touched the clothes representing the dead man. Maigret bent down, removed the knife from where it was stuck in the floor and began fingering it as he walked up and down.

The sky was covered with grey clouds, and by way of contrast the white wall opposite looked dazzling.

The inspector went from the window to the door, from the door to the window, sometimes glancing at the photograph on the mantelpiece.

'Come here a moment!' he suddenly said as he reached the window, perhaps for the thirtieth time.

The leaves shook above the wall, where Maigret had made out the poorly concealed face of Saint-Hilaire.

The owner of the chateau, whose first movement had been to shrink back, trying to make light of it but nevertheless sounding anxious, asked, 'You want me to jump?'

'No, come the long way round through the gate. It's easier.'

The key was on the table, and Maigret nonchalantly tossed it over the wall as he went on walking up and down the room. He heard the key fall on the other side among the collection of jumble. Then came the noise of the barrel being moved, and more sounds from the foliage and branches.

Saint-Hilaire's hand must have been shaking, for the key clicked against the lock for some time before Maigret heard the squealing hinges of the gate. However, when the owner of the little chateau reached the window he had his self-confidence back, and it was in a jovial voice that he said, 'Well, nothing escapes your eagle eye! I find this case of yours so fascinating that, when I saw you coming in, I had the idea of spying on you to get as good a view as yours, and then intrigue you at our next meeting . . . Shall I come round through the hotel?'

'No, no, come through the window!'

Saint-Hilaire did so easily, commenting as he looked round the room, 'How strange! The atmosphere in which you reconstruct what happened . . . those clothes. Did you arrange this spectacle?'

Maigret filled his pipe exaggeratedly slowly, tapping each pinch of tobacco down with his forefinger a dozen times. 'Do you have a match?'

'No, I use a lighter. I don't like matches.'

The inspector's eyes went to three pieces of greenish wood, burned at one end, lying beside the ashes of paper in the hearth.

'Yes, of course,' he said, not indicating what it was he approved of.

'You wanted to ask me something?'

'I'm not sure yet. I saw you . . . and as I am all at sea, I thought that an intelligent man might give me some ideas.'

He perched on the corner of the table and held out the bowl of his pipe to the lighter in his companion's hand.

'Well, so you're left-handed!'

'Me? Oh no, not at all. Just chance. I can't think why I'm offering you my lighter in my left hand.'

'Would you close the window? If you would be so kind.'

Maigret, never taking his eyes off the other man, noticed a hesitation in Saint-Hilaire's movements as, obviously paying great attention to what he was doing, he used his right hand to turn the window catch.

10

The Assistant

'Open the window.'

'But you've just asked me to . . . '

And Tiburce de Saint-Hilaire smiled, as if to say, 'Of course, whatever you say . . . I'm sorry if I expressed myself badly.'

Maigret himself was not smiling. If you had seen his face, you would probably have described the predominant impression as boredom. His gestures and tone of voice were gruff, he walked with a staccato step, and also in a staccato style he raised and lowered his head, picked up an object from one place to put it down in another, for no reason at all.

'Since the case fascinates you so much, I'll take you on as an assistant. So I won't wear kid gloves, and I shall treat you like one of my officers. Call Tardivon, will you?'

Saint-Hilaire did as he was told, opened the door and called, 'Tardivon! Hey there, Tardivon!'

When the hotelier came up Maigret, sitting on the ledge of the window-sill, was looking at the floor. 'A simple question, Monsieur Tardivon. Was Gallet left-handed? Try to remember.'

'Well, I never noticed. It's true that . . . Does a left-handed person shake another person's left hand?'

'Of course!'

'Then he wasn't. I mean, I'd be sure to have noticed. My guests here usually shake hands with me.'

'Go and ask the waitresses. They may have noticed that detail.'

While the hotelier was out of the room, Saint-Hilaire said, 'You seem to think this matter very important?'

But without replying the inspector went out into the corridor and called to Monsieur Tardivon, 'And while you're about it get someone on the line for me: Monsieur Padailhan, inspector of indirect taxation in Nevers. I think he has a telephone.'

He retraced his steps without so much as a glance for his companion, and spent a moment walking round the clothes spread out on the floor.

And now to work! Let's see — Émile Gallet was not left-handed. In a moment we'll find out if that detail is any use to us. Or rather . . . take that knife. It's the one used in the crime. No — give it to me. There you go, using your left hand again. There! Now suppose that, being attacked, I have to defend myself. And let's remember I'm not left-handed, so of course I hold the handle of the knife in my right hand. Come over here. It's you I'm lunging at. You're stronger than me, you grab my wrist . . . Go on, grab it! Good, so it's obvious that it's the hand holding the knife you want to immobilize. That'll do. Now, look at this photo of the body, it comes from Criminal Records. And what do we see? It's on the wrist of the *left hand* that Émile Gallet had ecchymosis.'

Maigret broke off. 'What is it, Tardivon? Nevers already? No? You say the waitresses all agree that Gallet wasn't left-handed. Thanks, you can go.'

'And now,' he went on, 'it's just the two of us, Monsieur de Saint-Hilaire. How would *you* explain that? Gallet was not left-handed, yet he held his knife in his left hand! And an examination of the scene shows that there was nothing in his right hand. I see only one solution to the problem. Watch this. I want to plunge that knife into my opponent's heart. What do I do? Follow my slightest gesture. I grab the sleeve over my left hand, because that hand is not going to be any use except to keep the knife pointing the way I want. My right hand is the stronger. It's the one I use to press the left one. Look! This movement . . . I hold my left wrist in the fingers of my right hand. I press very hard, because I'm feverish and it's a case of resisting the pain. I do it so well that I leave ecchymosis on myself.'

And he dropped the knife on the table with an offhand gesture.

'Of course, to accept that reconstruction of the facts we must also admit that Gallet killed himself. And he didn't have an arm long enough to fire at himself from a distance of seven metres from his face, did he? All in good time . . . let's try to find some other explanation!'

The same rather forced smile was still on Saint-Hilaire's lips. But the pupils of his eyes, looking larger than usual, were darting about with unusual mobility so as not to leave Maigret for a moment. Maigret himself was coming and going the whole time, making about fifty vague gestures for every useful one, picking up the pink file, opening it, closing it again, slipping it under a green file, then suddenly going to change the position of one of the dead man's shoes.

'Come with me . . . yes, over the window-sill. So here we are in the nettle lane. Let's suppose it is Saturday evening, it is dark, we can hear the sounds of the funfair and the rifle range. Perhaps we can even see the lights of the carousel with its wooden horses. Émile Gallet, having taken off his close-fitting jacket, hauls himself up to the top of this wall, not an easy thing for a man of his age to do, and he's also worn down by illness. Follow me.'

He made Saint-Hilaire go over to the barred gate, opened it and then closed it again.

'Give me the key. Right, this gate was locked, and as usual the key was in the gap you can see between two stones there. Your gardener himself told me about it. And now we're on your property. Don't forget, it's dark. And take note of this: we are only looking for the meaning of certain clues, or rather we are trying to reconcile contradictory clues. This way, please. Now, imagine someone in this park who is worried by what Émile Gallet is doing. There must be some people who feel like that about him. Gallet is a crook with God knows what else on his conscience. So on this side of the wall we have a man like you and me, a man who has noticed that in the course of the evening Gallet was nervous and who may know that he is in a desperate situation. Our man, whom we will call X, as if he were part of an algebraic equation, comes and goes along the wall and suddenly he sees the outline of Émile Gallet, alias Monsieur Clément, get up on top of the wall without his jacket on. Can this part of the wall round the property be seen from the villa?'

'No. I really don't understand what you're . . .'

'Getting at? Oh, nothing, we're pursuing our inquiries, ready to change track to a hundred different hypotheses if necessary — and wait! I'm switching to another track already. X isn't walking, he's caught sight of some empty barrels and, rather than climbing the wall to see what's happening on the other side of it, he's dragged over one of those barrels to give him a leg up. It's at this moment that the silhouette of Émile Gallet is outlined against the sky. The two men don't speak, because if they'd had anything to say to each other they'd have come closer. You have to raise your voice to be heard from ten metres away. And men meeting in such unusual circumstances, one of them on a barrel, the other balancing on a wall, wouldn't want to attract attention. Besides, X is in shadow. Émile Gallet doesn't see him. He comes down from his perch on the wall, goes back to his hotel room and . . . and here it gets more difficult. Unless we suppose that it was X who fired the shot.'

'What do you mean?'

Maigret, who had climbed up on the barrel, got off it again heavily.

'Give me a light, please. Ah, your left hand

again! Now, without wondering who fired the shot, we're going to follow the path taken by our friend X. Come along. He takes the key out of the gap in the wall. He opens the barred gate. But first he has gone somewhere to find a pair of rubber gloves. You'll have to ask your cook if she happens to wear rubber gloves for preparing vegetables, and if so whether they've disappeared. Is she vain?'

'I really don't see what that has to . . . '

Thunder rolled in the distance, but not a drop of rain fell.

'Let's go through. The gate is open now. X approaches the window and sees the corpse . . . because Émile Gallet is dead! The knife wound was inflicted *directly after* the gunshot; that's what the doctors say, and the bloodstains prove it. We saw just now that the knife wound looked just as if it had been inflicted by the victim himself. There are burned papers in the hearth of the room, still warm. And we find some of Gallet's matches there. However, friend X searches the case, and very likely Gallet's wallet as well. He puts it carefully back in Gallet's pocket and leaves the hotel room, but forgetting to lock the gate and to put the key back in its place.'

'And yet the key was found in the grass . . . '

Maigret, who for some time had not looked at the man who now spoke to him, noticed his downcast air.

'Come on . . . that's not all. I don't think I've ever known a case that was so complicated and so simple at the same time. We know, don't we, that the man known in these parts as Monsieur Clément was a crook? And now we see that he himself destroyed all traces of his criminal activities, as if he were expecting some important or indeed some major event . . . yes, this way! Here's the hotel courtyard, and on the left is the room that Émile Gallet said he wanted on the Saturday afternoon — the one he couldn't have because it wasn't vacant. Now, in the afternoon he was in the same situation as in the evening. At all costs he must have 20,000 francs on Monday morning, or whoever was blackmailing him would hand him over to the police. Just suppose he *had* managed to get that room. He couldn't have crossed the nettle lane and climbed the wall. So it was not a *necessity* for him to go along that wall. Or if you prefer, *it could be replaced by something else, something that the courtyard provided*. Now then,' Maigret continued, 'what do we see in that courtyard? A well! You will tell me, perhaps, that he felt like throwing himself into it. But in reply to that, I would tell you that if he left the room he was occupying he could go along the corridor and drown himself all the same. So he needed *the combination of a well and a room* . . . yes, what is it, Monsieur Tardivon?'

'Nevers on the telephone for you.'

'The inspector of indirect taxation?'

'That's right.'

'Come on, Monsieur de Saint-Hilaire. Since you want to help me, it's only fair that you are present at all stages of my inquiries. Take the receiver . . . Hello? Detective Chief Inspector

Maigret speaking! Don't worry, I only want to ask you a question that I didn't think of just now. Was your friend Gallet left-handed? You say he was? And he also preferred to use his left foot? He played outside left at football? You're certain of that, are you? No, that's all . . . oh, one detail. Did he know Latin? Why do you laugh? . . . A dunce? . . . As bad as that, was he? It's a strange thing, yes . . . Did you see the photo of the body? . . . You didn't? Well, of course he'd have changed since those days in Saigon . . . the only photo I have was taken when he was on a diet . . . but perhaps, one of these days, I'll show you someone who looks like him. Thank you . . . yes.'

Maigret hung up, uttered a laugh that was especially devoid of any humour and sighed.

'You see how easily one can get carried away! All we've been saying so far depends on one fact, which is that our Émile Gallet is not left-handed. Because if he is left-handed, he could turn the knife against his attacker. What it is to believe the word of a hotelier and the waitresses who work for him!'

Monsieur Tardivon, who had heard that, looked offended. 'Dinner is served,' he announced.

'I'll be with you soon. Might as well finish this . . . especially as I'm afraid of trying the patience of Monsieur de Saint-Hilaire. Let's go back to what they call the scene of the crime, shall we?'

★   ★   ★

Once there, he suddenly asked, 'You saw Émile Gallet in his lifetime. What I'm about to tell you may make you laugh . . . yes, by all means put the light on. With this gloomy sky, darkness seems to fall an hour earlier than usual. Well now, I never saw him alive, and since his murder I've been spending my time trying to imagine him. To that end I've come to where I could breathe the air he used to breathe, I've rubbed shoulders with those he used to know . . . Look at this portrait photograph, and I bet you'd say, as I do, that he looks a sorry sight. Especially when you know that his doctor gave him only three years to live. His liver was killing him! And he had a weak heart just waiting for an excuse to stop beating. I'd have liked to see Gallet in time as well as space. Unfortunately I can find out nothing about him until after the time of his marriage, because he was always unwilling to talk about his life before it, even to his wife.

'All she herself knows,' Maigret continued, 'is that he was born in Nantes and lived in Indochina for several years. Although he brought back no photograph, not so much as a souvenir — and he never talks about those days. He's a commercial traveller of no importance, a man with some 30,000 francs to his name. When he was thirty he was already clumsy, narrow-minded, melancholy. Then he meets Aurore Préjean and takes it into his head to marry her. The Préjeans have a high opinion of themselves. The girl's father is in dire straits: he can't find the funds to keep his journal going, but he was once private secretary to a claimant to the throne of France. He corresponds with princes and dukes. His youngest daughter is married to a master tanner. In that company our friend Gallet cuts a sorry figure, and if the family accepts him it is surely because he consents to invest his small capital in the journal, *Le Soleil*.'

Maigret went on with the tale of the family as he saw it.

'The Préjeans do not care for him. Having a son-in-law who sells silver-plated giftware is a step down in the world for them. They try to rouse higher ambitions in him. He resists that idea. He does not feel that he is made for a career that would bring him prestige. He already has liver trouble. He dreams of a peaceful life in the country with his wife, whom he deeply loves. But he cannot please her either. Don't her sisters have the audacity to treat her as a poor relation and pour scorn on her marriage?

'Then her father, old Préjean, dies. *Le Soleil* is done for. Émile Gallet goes on selling his shoddy gifts to the peasants of Normandy. And after his weeks of work he consoles himself by going fishing, inventing ingenious devices, and taking watches and alarm clocks apart. His son inherits his physique and his liver trouble, but he has the ambitions of the Préjeans. So much so that one fine day Émile Gallet decides to try something. He has the records of *Le Soleil*. He finds out that many people used to donate various amounts of money if you mentioned the legitimist cause of the rightful king to them. And he tries his hand. He doesn't tell anyone else about it. At first he probably carries on working as a commercial traveller, as a front for his still hesitant criminal activities. But they are what earns him more. Fairly soon he can even buy a plot on the Saint-Fargeau site and have a villa erected on it. He brings his good qualities of order and punctuality into his new way of life. As he is terrified of his wife's family, so as far as she and they are concerned he is still working in Normandy for the firm of Niel.

'He doesn't make a fortune. The legitimists don't have access to millions, and some of them are slow on the uptake. But at last he is living comfortably enough, and Gallet would be content with that if the family hadn't been blaming him, even under his own roof, for his unambitious ideas. He loves his wife, for all her faults. Perhaps he even loves his son.

'The years pass by. His liver trouble gets worse. Gallet has attacks that make him foresee a premature death. At that point he takes out life insurance for a large sum of money, so that after his death his nearest and dearest will be able to go on leading the same life. He goes to endless trouble . . . Monsieur Clément steps up his visits to the provincial manor houses, where he pesters the dowagers and gentlemen of the *ancien regime* . . . I hope you follow me?

'Three years ago, a certain Monsieur Jacob writes to him. This Monsieur Jacob knows the nature of his work and wants money every two months, a continuous flow of it, as the price of his silence. What can Gallet do? He has brought shame on the Préjean family, he is the poor relation to whom they send a New Year card, but none of his brothers-in-law, who are making their way in the world, want to meet him.

'On Saturday 25 June he is here, with the last letter from Monsieur Jacob in his pocket. It demands 20,000 francs on the following Monday. Obviously you don't come by 20,000 francs in a day by knocking on the doors of legitimists even on the most ingenious of pretexts. And anyway, he doesn't try to. He goes to see you. Twice! After his second conversation with you he asks for a room looking out on the courtyard. Did he have any hope of getting those twenty banknotes for 1,000 francs each out of you? If so, that evening all hope was gone.

'So tell me, what was he going to do in that room that he was unable to get, and then we shall know why he climbed up on the wall!'

Maigret did not raise his eyes to the other man, whose lips were trembling.

'An ingenious theory!' said Saint-Hilaire. 'But . . . especially where I am concerned, I really don't see what . . . '

'How old were you when your father died?'

'Twelve.'

'Was your mother still alive?'

'She died soon after my birth. However, I'd be interested to know what . . . '

'Were you brought up by other relations?'

'I have no other relations. I am the last of the Saint-Hilaires. When he died my father only just had the money to pay for my keep and my studies at a school in Bourges until I was nineteen. But for an unexpected legacy from a cousin whose existence everyone had forgotten . . . '

'And who lived in Indochina, I believe?'

'In Indochina, yes. A distant relation who didn't even bear our name. A Duranty de la Roche.'

'At what age did you get this legacy?'

'I was twenty-eight.'

'So that from the age of nineteen to twenty-eight . . .'

'I had a hard time, yes. I don't blush to say so, far from it. Inspector, it's getting late. Wouldn't it be better if we . . .'

'Just a moment. I haven't yet shown you what can be done with a well and a hotel bedroom. You don't have a revolver on you, I suppose? Never mind, I have mine. There must be some string around somewhere. Right, follow my movements. I tie this string to the butt of the weapon. Let's suppose it measures six or seven metres, or more, that's of no importance. Now, go and find me a large pebble in the road.'

Once again Saint-Hilaire was quick to obey and brought back the stone.

'Your left hand again,' Maigret commented. 'Never mind that. So I tie this pebble firmly to the other end of the string. We can have our demonstration here, if we suppose that the window-sill is the rim of the well. I let my stone down on the other side of it. Yes, that's right, into the well. I have the revolver in my hand. I aim at something, never mind what. Myself, for instance . . . Then I let go. And what happens? The stone, which is dangling above the water, goes down to the bottom of the well, taking with it the string and the revolver tied to the other end. The police arrive to find a dead body, but no trace of a weapon ... and what do they deduce from that?'

'A crime has been committed!'

'Very good,' said Maigret, and without asking for his companion's lighter he lit his pipe with matches taken from his pocket.

As he picked up Gallet's clothes, with the look of a man pleased with a long day's work, he said in the most natural voice imaginable, 'So now go and find me the revolver.'

'But ... but you didn't let go of it. You're holding it in your hand.'

'I mean go and find me the revolver that killed Émile Gallet. And hurry up about it.'

So saying, he hung the trousers and waistcoat on the hook in the room, beside the close-fitting jacket with its shiny elbows that was hanging there already.

11

A Commercial Affair

Now that Maigret's back was turned to him, Saint-Hilaire no longer kept firm control of the expression on his face, and a strange mixture of anxiety, hatred and, in spite of everything, a kind of self-assurance could be seen on it.

'What are you waiting for?'

He decided to go out through the window, walked over to the barred gate in the nettle road and disappeared into the grounds, all so slowly that the inspector, slightly worried, strained his ears to hear him.

It was the time of day when you could see, on the river-bank, the luminous halo of light from the terrace, where knives and forks clicked on plates, accompanied by the muted murmuring of the hotel guests' voices. Suddenly branches moved on the other side of the wall. The darkness was so complete that Maigret could hardly make out the figure of Saint-Hilaire on top of it. Another creaking of branches. A voice calling softly. 'Would you like to take it?'

The inspector shrugged his shoulders and did not move, so that his companion had to make the same journey in reverse. When he was in the hotel room again he firstly put a gun on the table. He had straightened his back, and he

340

touched Maigret's arm with an almost casual, albeit slightly gauche, gesture.

'What would you say to two hundred thousand?' He had to cough. He would have liked to act the *grand seigneur*, completely at ease, but at the same time he felt himself blushing, and there was an obstruction in his throat. 'Hmm . . . maybe three . . . ?'

Unfortunately, when Maigret looked at him without any emotion or anger, only a touch of irony between his thick eyelids, he lost his footing, stepped back and cast a glance all around him, as if to catch hold of something.

It was a swift transformation. The best he could manage was a coarse smile, which did not keep him from going purple in the face or the pupils of his eyes from shining with anxiety. He had not brought off his act as a *grand seigneur*, so he tried another, more cynical and down to earth.

'That's your bad luck! Anyway, I was being naive — what could you do about it? You have to obey the rules.'

That sounded just as false, and by way of contrast Maigret had probably never conveyed such an impression of quiet, confident power. He was enormous. When he was just below the ceiling light, he touched it with the top of his head, and his shoulders filled the rectangle of the window, in the same way as the lords of the Middle Ages with their huge sleeves fill the frames of old pictures. He was still slowly tidying up the room.

'Because you know I didn't kill anyone, don't you?' said Saint-Hilaire in a fevered tone. He took his handkerchief out of his pocket and blew his nose noisily.

'Sit down,' Maigret told him.

'I'd rather stand . . . '

'Sit down!'

He obeyed, like a frightened child, the moment when the inspector turned to face him. He had a shifty look in his eyes, and the defeated face of a man who does not feel up to his role, and is trying to swim upstream again.

'I imagine,' grunted Maigret, 'that it won't be necessary for me to get the inspector of indirect taxes for Nevers to come and identify his old comrade Émile Gallet? Oh, I'd have worked out the truth without him; it would have taken longer, that's all. I felt for too long anyway that there was something creaky about this story. You needn't try to understand, but when all the material clues manage to confuse matters rather than clarify them, it means they've been faked . . . and everything, without exception, *is* fake in this case. It all creaked. The gunshot and the knife wound. The room looking out on the court-yard and the wall. Severe bruising on the left wrist and the lost key . . . and even the three possible suspects. But most of all Gallet. He sounded as wrong dead as he did living. If the inspector of taxes hadn't spoken up, I was going to go to the school he attended, and I'd have found out the truth there. By the way, you can't have stayed very long at the school in Nantes.'

'Two years! They chucked me out.'

'Good heavens. You were playing football already — and no doubt chasing the girls! Can you hear how the story creaks? Look at this photograph — go on, look at it! At the age when you were climbing the school wall to go and meet your girlfriends, this poor fellow was worrying about his liver. I ought to have devoted some time to collecting the proofs, but I knew what mattered most: my man, who needed 20,000 francs in a hurry, was in Sancerre only to ask you for the money. And you talked to him *twice*! Then, in the evening, you were watching him over the wall! You were afraid he was going to kill himself, am I right? Perhaps he even told you he was?'

'No! But he seemed to me feverish. In the afternoon he was talking in an abrupt tone that made quite an impression on me.'

'And you refused him his 20,000 francs?'

'I couldn't do anything else . . . it was beginning all over again. In the end I think I'd have been broke.'

'It was at your notary's in Saigon that you learned he was going to inherit?'

'Yes . . . an odd sort of client had come to see my boss. An old maniac who'd been living in the sticks for over twenty years, didn't see another white man more than one year in every three. His health was undermined by fevers and opium abuse. I heard their conversation. I'm not long for this world, that's literally what he said, and I don't even know if I have any family somewhere. Could be there's a Saint-Hilaire left, but I doubt it because when I left France the last of them was in such a bad way I guess he's died of consumption. If there's a descendant, and if you

343

can track him down, then he'll be my sole heir.'

'So you already had the bright idea of getting rich at a stroke!' said Maigret thoughtfully. And behind the sweating, ill-at-ease fifty-year-old man before him he thought he could see the unscrupulous jolly companion who organized a grotesque ceremony to get his hands on a young Malay girl.

'Go on.'

'I had to go back to France anyway. It was about women . . . I went too far when I was out there. There were husbands and brothers and fathers who bore me a grudge. So I had the idea of looking for a Saint-Hilaire, and I can tell you it wasn't easy. I picked up the trail of Tiburce at the school in Bourges. They told me they had no idea what had become of him. I knew he was a gloomy young man, reserved, who never had a friend at school . . . '

'Good God!' Maigret laughed. 'He never had a penny in his pocket! There was just enough money to pay for his board until he'd finished his studies.'

'My idea at that moment was to share the inheritance by some means or other, I didn't yet know just how. But I realized it would be harder to share it than to take the lot. It took me three months to lay hands on him, in Le Havre, where he was trying to get taken on as a steward or inter-preter on a liner. He had ten or twelve francs left . . . I bought him a drink and then I had to get the information out of him word by word — he never replied except in monosyllables. He'd been a tutor at a chateau, a proof-reader, an assistant in a bookshop ... he already wore a ridiculous jacket and a strange straggly beard, reddish-brown ... So I staked everything on getting it all. I told him I wanted to go to America and make my fortune and I said that out there nothing helps a man more, particularly with women, than an aristocratic name, and I offered to buy his. I had a little money, because my father, a horse dealer in Nantes, had left me a small sum of money. I paid 30,000 francs for the right to call myself Tiburce de Saint-Hilaire.'

Maigret cast a brief glance at the portrait photograph, inspected the man he was talking to from head to toe and then looked straight into his eyes in such a way that he began talking at exaggerated speed of his own accord.

'It's what a financier does, isn't it? He buys up securities at 200 francs because he knows he can sell them for five times more a month later. But I had to wait four years to inherit! The old madman out there in his jungle couldn't make up his mind to die. I was the one who almost died of starvation now that I had no money.

'As for the real Saint-Hilaire, we were almost the same age. All we'd had to do was exchange our papers. The other man promised never to set foot in Nantes, where he might have met someone who knew me. As for me, I had to take hardly any precautions. The real Tiburce had never had any friends, and in his various jobs he often didn't use his real name, which didn't sound right for him ... I mean, how many bookshop assistants are called Tiburce de Saint-Hilaire? Well, at long last I read a little paragraph in the newspapers about the old man's estate and asking anyone with a claim to make himself known. Don't you think I earned the 1,200,000 francs that the old man in the backwoods left?'

He was recovering his self-confidence, encouraged by Maigret's silence, and looked as if he might almost have winked at him.

'Of course, Gallet, who had just got married at that point and wasn't rolling in money, turned up and blamed me for his plight — there was a moment when I thought he was going to kill me. I offered him 10,000 francs, and he finally took them. But he came back six months later . . . and then he came back again. He was threatening to tell the truth. I tried to show him that he'd be thought as culpable as me. What was more, he had a family — and he seemed afraid of that family. Gradually he calmed down . . . he was ageing fast. I really felt sorry for him with his close-fitting jacket, his beard, his yellow skin and the rings round his eyes. His manner was becoming more and more like a beggar's. He always began by asking me for 50,000 francs — just once and never again, he swore. Then I would fob him off with 1,000- or 2,000-franc notes. But add up those sums over eighteen years! I tell you again that if I hadn't stood firm I'd have been the loser. I was working hard, at that! I was looking for good investments. I planted all the land you see on the higher reaches of the property with vines. While he, on the other hand, was claiming to be a commercial traveller, but the truth was that he was nothing but a scrounger . . . and he got a taste for it. Under the name of Monsieur Clément, as you know, he went around looking for people . . . well, so tell me, what should I have done?'

His voice rose, and automatically he got to his feet.

'So on the Saturday in question he wanted 20,000 francs on the spot. I might have been inclined to give them to him, but I couldn't, because the bank was closed. And then again I'd paid enough, don't you think? I told him so. I told him he was degenerate. He returned to the attack that afternoon, taking such a humble tone that it disgusted me. A real man has no right to let himself sink to such a level as that! A man stakes his life, he wins or he loses, but he keeps more pride than that!'

'Did you tell him that as well?' Maigret interrupted, in a surprisingly gentle voice.

'Why not? I was hoping to stiffen his backbone. I offered him 500 francs.'

Elbows propped on the mantelpiece, the inspector had drawn the portrait photograph of the dead man towards him.

'Five hundred francs,' he repeated.

'I'll show you the notebook where I write down all my expenses. It will show you that at the end of the day he'd got more than 200,000 francs out of me. I was in the grounds that evening . . . '

'And not very much at your ease . . . '

'I was nervous, I can't say why. I heard a noise from beside the wall, and then I saw him fixing I don't know what in the tree. I thought at first he wanted to play some nasty trick on me, but he disappeared just as he had come. When I stood on a barrel for a better look he'd gone into his room, where he was standing upright beside the table, turned to me although he couldn't see me. I couldn't make it out. I swear to you that at that moment I was afraid. The gun went off ten metres from where I was standing, and Gallet hadn't moved . . . only his right cheek was all red, and blood was flowing. But he still stood there staring the same way, as if he was expecting something.'

Maigret took the revolver off the mantelpiece. A guitar string made of several strands of metal, like those you use when fishing for pike, was still tied to it. A small tin box was firmly fixed under the gun and attached to the trigger with a stiff thread.

Opening the box with his fingernail, Maigret found the sort of mechanism you can buy in shops these days allowing you to take a photograph of yourself. All you have to do is load a spring, which releases of its own accord after a certain number of seconds. But in this case the device had a triple movement and so should have set off three shots.

'The spring must have got stuck after the first bullet was fired,' he said slowly, in a rather muted voice. And the other man's last words echoed in his ears: *Only his right cheek was all red, and blood was flowing. But he still stood there staring the same way, as if he was expecting something.*

The other two bullets, for heaven's sake! He

hadn't entirely trusted the precision of the device for firing the gun. With three bullets, he was sure of getting at least one of them in his head. But the other two had never gone off! So he had taken his knife out of his pocket.

'He was unsteady on his feet when he pressed its blade against his chest . . . he was straight as he fell . . . dead, of course. The first thing to come into my head was that it was vengeance, that he'd been careful to leave papers revealing the truth, perhaps even accusing me of his murder.'

'You're certainly a prudent man! And talk about a cool head! You went to find rubber gloves in your kitchen . . . '

'You think I was going to leave my fingerprints in his hotel room? I went through the gate and put the key in my pocket. But my visit wasn't any use. He'd burned all his papers himself. I didn't like the look in his open eyes, so I got out of there in such a hurry that I forgot to lock the gate again. Well, what would you have done in my place? Seeing that he was certainly dead . . . I was even more frightened on the day when I was playing cards at the notary's and I learned that the revolver had been fired again. I went to take a look at it, close to, but I didn't dare to touch it, because if anyone got round to suspecting me it was the proof of my innocence. An automatic with six bullets in the chamber . . . I realized that the spring must have stuck after the gun went off, and then slackened again a week late . . . probably because of the atmospheric conditions. But there could still be three bullets

349

left, couldn't there? It's since then that I've spent so much time walking in the grounds, listening for them. Just now, when the two of us were here together, I avoided standing close to the table.'

'But you let me stand there! And it was you who threw the key into the nettle lane when I threatened you with a visit to your home.'

Some of the hotel guests who had finished their dinner were walking along the road. There was an intermittent noise of plates being moved about from the kitchen.

'It was a mistake for me to offer you money . . .'

Maigret almost burst out laughing, and if he had not controlled himself the sound of his laughter would probably have been terrifying. The other man was a head shorter than the inspector, with much narrower shoulders, and standing in front of him, Maigret looked at him with an expression that was both benevolent and fierce, swinging his hand as if to seize him suddenly by the throat or smash his head against the wall.

And yet there was something pitiable about this pseudo Tiburce de Saint-Hilaire, in his desire to justify himself, to regain his self-assurance.

A poor sort of villain, who didn't even have the courage of his villainy, perhaps was not even fully aware of it himself! And he was trying to show off! Every time it looked as if Maigret might move he flinched back. If the inspector had raised his hand he would probably have fallen flat on the floor!

'And by the way, if his wife needs anything I am prepared, discreetly and within my means, to help her.'

He knew he was on safe ground here, but all the same he was not easy in his mind. He'd have given much for a kind word from this police officer, who looked as if he were a cat playing with a mouse.

'He's provided for her himself.'

'Yes, I read that in the papers. Three hundred thousand francs' life insurance! That's extraordinary.'

Maigret could contain himself no longer.

'Extraordinary, isn't it? A man who spent his childhood without a penny to spend on his small pleasures. And you know what those schools are like. Among the former pupils of the school in Nantes are most of the great men of the centre of the country. He has a fine name. A name as old and lustrous as theirs, apart from that ridiculous first name, Tiburce. But as for him, he may eat and he has a right to have lessons, but he can't buy a chocolate bar or a whistle or marbles . . . At recreation time he's left alone in a corner. Perhaps the poor students paid to supervise the boys take pity on him, they're almost as wretched as he is.

'Well, he gets out of there. He sells books in a bookshop. He hopelessly goes around with his interminable name, his close-fitting jacket, his liver trouble. He has nothing to pawn . . . but he does have that name, and one fine day someone comes along and offers to buy it from him. Without the name, he's still in a miserable state, but with the name of Gallet he can at least attain a higher level: mediocrity. When he is hungry and thirsty, he can eat and drink. But his new family treat him like a mangy dog. He has a wife and a son. His wife and his son blame him for being unable to rise in society, earn money, become a departmental councillor like his brother-in-law. The name he sold for 30,000 francs is suddenly worth a million! The only thing he had possessed, and the one that had brought him most of his wretchedness and humiliation! The name he had got rid of.

'And the man who had really been Gallet, a jolly fellow, good company, gives him alms now and then . . . extraordinary, just as you said. He never succeeded in anything. He spent his life worrying himself sick. No one ever held out a hand to him. His son rebelled and left home as soon as he could to spread his own wings, leaving the old man in his mediocrity. Only his wife was resigned to her situation. I don't say she helped him. I don't say she comforted him. *She was resigned to her situation*, because she realized there was nothing to be done about it. A poor old man on a strict diet.

'And then he leaves her 300,000 francs! More than she ever had when she was married to him. Three hundred thousand francs, enough to make her sisters come running, to win her the smiles of the departmental councillor. He's been dragging himself around for five years, suffering attack after attack of his liver disease. The legitimists don't make him much more than begging would. In these parts he gets his hands on a 1,000-franc note now and then. But there's a Monsieur Jacob, who takes most of what he picks up in that way.

'Extraordinary, yes, Gallet-Saint-Hilaire. Because if he has to cut down on even his small expenses, he keeps up with payments on his life insurance, he spends 20,000 francs a year on it. He senses in advance that a time will come when he finally gives up the ghost, unless his heart is kind enough to stop of its own accord. A poor old man, all alone, coming and going, not at home anywhere unless perhaps when he's out fishing and doesn't see another human being.

'He's born inappropriately, into a family on its uppers that, moreover, has been stupid enough to spend the few thousand francs it has painfully managed to save on his education. He has sold his name inappropriately. And he has worked inappropriately for the cause of legitimism at the moment when legitimism was on its last legs. He married inappropriately — his own son is cut from the same cloth as his sisters- and brothers-in-law. People die every day when they don't want to, when they are happy and well. And he, inappropriately, doesn't die! Life insurance isn't paid if someone has committed suicide. He plays about with watches and springs . . . he knows that the moment when he can't go any further is not far away. And at last, Monsieur Jacob demands 20,000 francs!

'He hasn't got 20,000 francs, and no one will give them to him. He has his spring in his pocket. To put his mind at rest, he knocks on the door of the man who gained a million in his place. He has no hope — and yet he goes back again. But he has already asked for the room looking out on the courtyard, because he is not absolutely sure of his mechanism, and he prefers the simpler option of the well. All his life he has been a grotesque and unlucky figure. And now the room looking out on the courtyard is not available. That means he must climb a wall. And two of the bullets fail to go off. Just as you said: *His right cheek was red . . . blood was flowing. But he still stood there staring the same way, as if he was expecting something.* Hasn't he spent his life expecting something? A little luck? Not even that. One of those little everyday pleasures to be found in the street that people don't notice . . . He had to wait for his two last bullets, and they failed to go off. He had to finish the job for himself.'

The stem of the pipe between Maigret's teeth broke straight off because, as he stopped talking, he had suddenly clenched his jaws. The other man, looking past him, murmured with some difficulty, 'You're right, but all the same he was a crook . . . and for you there's a limitation clause, isn't there?'

'It seems to me that you know the law better than I do.'

'Oh yes, there's a limitation clause. And the law says that there has been no crime or offence when a son lays hands on his father's property by fraudulent means . . . so that Henry Gallet, according to you, has nothing to fear. So far he has only 100,000 francs. With his mistress's fifty, that comes to only 150 and he's going to need

500,000 to go and live in the country as the doctors advise.'

'Just as you said, Monsieur de Saint-Hilaire ... extraordinary! There's no crime, no murderer, no culprit. There's no one to be sentenced to prison. Or rather, there wouldn't be anyone except my dead man if he hadn't had the bright idea of sheltering from justice under a tombstone in the Saint-Fargeau cemetery ... made of stone that is *not too expensive, but in good taste and distinguished* ... Give me a light, will you? Oh, don't worry about using your left hand, *not now!* Come to think of it, there's no reason for you to deny yourself the pleasure of founding a football club in Sancerre any more. You'll be the honorary president ... '

Suddenly the expression on his face changed, and he said, 'Get out!'

'But I ... '

'Get out!'

Once again Saint-Hilaire was at a loss. It took him some seconds to regain his composure.

'I think you're exaggerating, inspector. And if ... '

'Not through the door, through the window. You know the way, don't you? Here ... you're forgetting your key.'

'When you've calmed down, I'll send you ... '

'Yes, do that. You can send me a case of the sparkling wine that you got me to taste.'

The other man didn't know whether to smile or be afraid, but seeing the heavy silhouette of Maigret advancing on him, he instinctively retreated towards the window.

'You haven't given me your address.'

'I'll send it to you on a postcard.'

He abruptly closed the window and was alone in the room, which was bathed in bright light from the electric bulb.

The bed was still just as it had been on the day when Émile Gallet entered this room. His suit of hard-wearing black fabric hung limply on the wall.

With a nervous gesture, Maigret picked up the portrait photo on the mantelpiece, slipped it into a yellow envelope with the letterhead of Criminal Records on it and addressed it to Madame Gallet.

The time was a little past ten. Some Parisian guests who had arrived by car were kicking up a great racket on the terrace, where they had started a portable gramophone playing. They were intent on dancing, while Monsieur Tardivon, torn between his admiration of their luxury car and the complaints of guests who had already gone to bed, was negotiating with the new arrivals, trying to get them into one of the hotel lounges. Maigret went along the corridors, through the café, where a driver was playing billiards with the local teacher, and arrived outside just as a couple dancing the foxtrot suddenly stopped.

'What's he saying?'

'He says his guests have already gone to bed. He wants us to make less noise.'

You could see the two lights of the suspension bridge, and the occasional reflection on the water of the Loire.

'Aren't people allowed to dance?'

'Only indoors.'

'How poetic that would be!'

Monsieur Tardivon, who was primly listening in on this discussion and admiring, with a sigh, the car that belonged to these difficult guests, caught sight of Maigret.

'I've had your place laid in the little salon, inspector. Well . . . is there any news?'

The gramophone was still playing. On the first floor, a woman in a camisole with a scalloped top was watching the newcomers and calling up to her husband, who must be in bed, 'Come down here and make them keep quiet! If we can't even sleep on holiday . . . '

By way of contrast a couple — they looked as if they might be a salesman in a big department store and a typist — were pleading the cause of the new arrivals in their de luxe car, in the hope of getting to know them and spending a more interesting evening than usual here.

'I won't be dining,' said Maigret. 'Would you have my baggage taken to the station, please?'

'For the 11.32 train? Are you leaving, then?'

'Yes, I'm leaving.'

'But all the same . . . you must have something to eat! Do you have our picture postcard of the house?'

Monsieur Tardivon took a postcard with a photo taken twelve years earlier, to judge by the poor reproduction and the women's fashions. It showed the Hôtel de la Loire with a flag hoisted outside the first floor, and the terrace crowded with guests. Monsieur Tardivon was standing in the doorway in morning dress, and the waitresses, holding platters, stood motionless in front of the lens.

'Thank you.'

Maigret put the card into one of his pockets and for a second turned towards the nettle lane.

In the little chateau, a light had just come on at one window, and Maigret could have sworn that Tiburce de Saint-Hilaire was getting undressed and recovering his composure by muttering things like, 'He had to listen to reason, anyway. First of all there's that clause of limitations . . . he could tell that I knew my Roman law as well as he does. And after all, Gallet was nothing but a crook. Come to think of it, what exactly did I do? Yes, what reason is there to blame me for anything?'

But might he not be looking with some alarm at the dark corners of the room?

In Saint-Fargeau, the light must be out in the bedroom where Madame Gallet, her hair pinned up, was divesting herself of anxiety about her dignity, was feeling the empty place between the sheets beside her and perhaps, before going to sleep, was sobbing quietly.

Didn't she have her sisters to console her, and her brothers-in-law, one of them a departmental councillor, all of whom would welcome her back into the comforting bosom of the family?

Maigret had gently pressed the hand of a distracted Monsieur Tardivon as his eyes followed the motorists, who had decided to dine and dance indoors. The suspension bridge, now deserted, echoed beneath his feet, and you could hardly hear the murmur of water running around the sandbanks. Maigret amused himself by imagining a Henry several years older, with an even sallower complexion, his mouth longer and thinner, in the company of Éléonore, her features hardening with advancing age and her figure becoming slightly ridiculous. And they would be arguing. About everything and nothing. But most of all about *their* 500,000 francs — because they would get their money.

'It's all very well for you to talk. Your father was a . . . '

'I won't have you talking about my father . . . and as for *you*, what were you when I first met you?'

'As if you didn't know perfectly well that . . . '

★   ★   ★

He slept heavily until the train reached Paris, and his sleep was populated by indistinct silhouettes and a nauseating sense of teeming crowds.

When he was about to pay for the coffee laced with something stronger that he drank in the buffet at Gare de Lyon, he took the postcard showing the Hôtel de la Loire out of his pocket. A young girl was sitting beside him eating a croissant and dipping it into a large cup of hot chocolate. He left the card on the zinc counter top. When he turned outside the door, he saw the girl dreamily looking at the end of the suspension bridge and the few trees that framed Monsieur Tardivon's hotel.

Maybe that girl will go there and sleep in the same room, he thought. And Saint-Hilaire, got up in his green hunting garb, will invite her to drink the sparkling wine produced by his estate!

'You look as if you are just back from a funeral,' remarked Madame Maigret, when he came into their apartment on Boulevard Richard-Lenoir. 'Have you at least had something to eat?'

'A funeral . . . yes, you're right,' he said, more to himself than her, looking with pleasure at his familiar surroundings. 'Since he was buried . . . ' And he added, although she could not understand, 'All the same I'd rather have a real murder victim and a real murderer . . . Wake me at eleven, will you? I must go and report to the boss.'

He did not confess that he had no intention of sleeping, but he was wondering just what to include in that report.

The truth pure and simple — the truth that would deprive Madame Gallet of those 300,000 francs of life insurance, would set her against her son, against Éléonore, against Tiburce de Saint-Hilaire, and would set her sisters and brothers-in-law against her again?

A tangled skein of clashing interests, of hatreds, of never-ending court cases . . . perhaps a conscientious judge might want to exhume Émile Gallet in order to question him again!

Maigret no longer had the dead man's picture, but he didn't need that faded image now.

His *right cheek was all red . . . blood was flowing. He was standing there staring at the same place, as if he was waiting for something.*

Peace, for heaven's sake, that's what he was

360

waiting for, growled Maigret, getting up well before the appointed time.

And a little later, shoulders squared, he was telling his superior officer, 'No luck. We can only write off that nasty little case.'

But at the same time he was thinking: the doctor claims he wouldn't have lived three years . . . let's suppose the insurance company loses 60,000 francs . . . it has capital of ninety million.

We do hope that you have enjoyed reading
this large print book.

Did you know that all of our titles
are available for purchase?

We publish a wide range of high quality
large print books including:
Romances, Mysteries, Classics
General Fiction
Non Fiction and Westerns

Special interest titles available in
large print are:
The Little Oxford Dictionary
Music Book
Song Book
Hymn Book
Service Book

Also available from us courtesy of
Oxford University Press:
Young Readers' Dictionary
(large print edition)
Young Readers' Thesaurus
(large print edition)

For further information or a free
brochure, please contact us at:
Ulverscroft Large Print Books Ltd.,
The Green, Bradgate Road, Anstey,
Leicester, LE7 7FU, England.
Tel: (00 44) 0116 236 4325
Fax: (00 44) 0116 234 0205

A CRIME IN HOLLAND & THE GRAND BANKS CAFÉ

Georges Simenon

When a French professor visiting the Dutch town of Delfzijl is accused of murder, Detective Chief Inspector Maigret is sent to investigate. The community seem happy to blame an unknown outsider, but there are culprits closer to home, including the dissatisfied daughter of a local farmer, the sister-in-law of the deceased, and a notorious crook. And in *The Grand Banks Café*, Maigret investigates the murder of a captain soon after his ship returns from three months of fishing off the Newfoundland coast. The ship's wireless operator has been arrested for the murder — but the sailors all blame the Evil Eye . . .

THE YELLOW DOG &
NIGHT AT THE CROSSROADS

Georges Simenon

In the windswept seaside town of Concarneau, a local wine dealer is shot. Someone is out to kill all the influential men, and the town is soon sent into a panic. For Inspector Maigret, the answers lie with the downtrodden waitress Emma, and a strange yellow dog lurking in the shadows . . . And in *Night at the Crossroads*, Maigret has been interrogating Carl Andersen for hours without a confession. Why was the body of a diamond merchant found at his mansion? Why is his sister always shut in her room? And why does everyone at Three Widows Crossroads have something to hide?